W9-BIR-527

JAN - - 2023

CITY OF
NIGHTMARES

ALSO BY REBECCA SCHAEFFER

The Market of Monsters series
Not Even Bones
Only Ashes Remain
When Villains Rise

REBECCA SCHAEFFER

CITY OF
NIGHTMARES

CLARION BOOKS
An Imprint of HarperCollins*Publishers*

Clarion Books is an imprint of HarperCollins Publishers.

City of Nightmares
Copyright © 2023 by Rebecca Schaeffer
All rights reserved. Printed in the United States of America. No part of this
book may be used or reproduced in any manner whatsoever without written
permission except in the case of brief quotations embodied in critical articles and
reviews. For information address HarperCollins Children's Books, a division of
HarperCollins Publishers, 195 Broadway, New York, NY 10007.
www.epicreads.com

Library of Congress Cataloging-in-Publication Data
Names: Schaeffer, Rebecca, author.
Title: City of nightmares / Rebecca Schaeffer.
Description: First edition. | New York, NY : Clarion Books, an imprint of
HarperCollins Publishers, [2023] | Audience: Ages 14 up. | Audience:
Grades 10–12. | Summary: "After a con goes wrong, nineteen-year-old Ness
finds herself at the center of a criminal syndicate conspiracy, in a
city where dreaming means waking up as your worst nightmare"—Provided
by publisher.
Identifiers: LCCN 2022020972 | ISBN 9780358647300 (hardcover)
Subjects: CYAC: Nightmares—Fiction. | Fear—Fiction. |
Conspiracies—Fiction. | Fantasy. | Fantasy fiction. | LCGFT: Novels.
Classification: LCC PZ7.1.S33557 Ci 2023 | DDC [Fic]—dc23
LC record available at https://lccn.loc.gov/2022020972

Typography by Molly Fehr
22 23 24 25 26 LBC 5 4 3 2 1

First Edition

To everyone who supported my first trilogy—
this book wouldn't exist without you.

1

My sister's worst nightmare was a giant, man-eating spider.

I know because that's what she turned into when she went to sleep for the last time.

So I understand something about what it's like to have a family member turn into a giant bug and try to eat you. It's not hard to find people in this city who've lost loved ones to Nightmares, whether they became one or were killed by one. But people who turned into homicidal giant bugs are actually surprisingly rare.

I suppose most people have much worse fears than bugs.

"And how did you know my husband?" Mrs. Sanden asks us.

She's in her forties, white, auburn hair just beginning to show signs of graying at the temples. She stands as stiffly as her starched, white button-up shirt and long, black skirt.

She's small and looks even smaller in her tiny apartment. Like most apartments in Newham, it's basically one room— double bed in one corner across from a tiny kitchenette against the wall and an attempt at a sitting room with one skinny sofa and table. Every available surface is covered in flowers.

A large wooden telephone watches me from the wall, the two brass bells on the front eerily resembling eyes and a long speaker dangling beneath like an elephant's nose.

"I'm afraid we never had the pleasure of meeting your husband," I say, stepping into the apartment. The door will be open for the next few hours, and people who knew the deceased will come and pay their respects. Priya leans against the wall in the hall—there isn't really room for both of us in the entryway.

Mrs. Sanden frowns a moment, taking in my distinctive powder-blue waistcoat and black trousers. Her expression shifts in understanding. "Oh. You're from that cult."

My mouth tightens. "It's not a cult."

"Put your flowers down and get out." Mrs. Sanden's lips thin. "I don't need you or whatever scam you have."

"Oof," Priya says with a grin, speaking for the first time since we've arrived. "Tough crowd."

I roll my eyes. "You could help."

"Me?" Priya widens her eyes innocently. "Are you sure?"

A wicked smile pulls at the corner of her lips, and she tips her head slightly, her short, black-and-turquoise ombre hair falling over her forehead. The hall lighting sharpens her already-sharp cheekbones and adds a reddish tint to her warm brown skin.

"No, actually," I admit. "I take that back. Don't help."

"Are you sure?" Priya's smile gets slyer. "I could—"

"Do you want to get kicked out?" I ask mildly. "Because after last time, the Director will definitely kick us both out."

Priya's mouth clamps shut and she frowns, casting me an annoyed look. I've won and she knows it. She may not like this gig, but she needs it.

Frankly, so do I.

"Are you going to leave the flowers?" Mrs. Sanden snaps, clearly irritated by our existence. This is common. Most people think of us like door-to-door salesman but for religious services. Which is only sort of accurate, but most people don't really stick around long enough for me to explain.

"Yeah." I take the flowers I brought and place them on top of the sideboard, on a pile of similar bouquets. Hanging on the wall above the flowers is a black-and-white picture of a white man with a large, bushy, black beard. He's smiling broadly. Even in the black-and-white photo, I can see the outline of the blue scales that covered his cheekbones.

Contagious Nightmare.

I tug at my gloves, ensuring they're secure. I know he's dead, and his body isn't even here because he turned into a Nightmare in his sleep, and even if it were, the blue scales weren't contagious by touch. But I still make sure my gloves are secure.

The blue scales were from the southern sea dragon, a Nightmare killed a decade ago. When it died, its blood spread in the water of Grand Lake, and anyone who drank that water grew scales, the severity of the scaling depending on how much blood they consumed. Given that most of the southern part of the country got its water from that lake, a lot of people have scales.

"There," Mrs. Sanden says. "You've put the flowers down. Now get out."

"Of course," I tell her, voice calm and measured. "If that's what you wish."

I take a pamphlet from my bag and place it on top of the flowers.

"Oh no," Mrs. Sanden says, marching forward. "You keep that. I'm not going to therapy or talking about my feelings or any of that nonsense. Especially not with *you*."

"You don't have to if you don't want to, Mrs. Sanden," I reassure her, pressing the pamphlet into her hand. She stares at it as though not sure how she managed to end up holding it.

The front reads **YOU ARE NOT ALONE. WE CAN HELP. PAY-WHAT-YOU-CAN-AFFORD NIGHTMARE TRAUMA THERAPY.**

"We're only here to tell you what's available," I tell her. "You're under no obligation to do anything you don't want to do."

Behind me, Priya is trying not to fidget, fiddling with something under her long, black coat. Probably a weapon. She's dressed like she hopes, part way through this meeting, a Nightmare will burst through the wall and she can single-handedly defeat it with her combat boots and her myriad of concealed weapons.

Mrs. Sanden crumples my leaflet into a ball. "I'm sure your little cult would like that, me going in so you can brainwash

4

me into believing my husband's death was a good thing."

"We're not a cult," I repeat automatically. "And no one's planning to brainwash you."

"You only say that because you're already brainwashed," she informs me, her expression haughty. "My husband was murdered in my own house, and I'm sure you're just planning to convince me not to file a complaint against those Nightmare killers."

I try to be patient. I signed up for this—a choice I am deeply and profoundly regretting.

Priya steps into the apartment, eyebrows angry slashes. "The Department of Nightmare Defense saved your life."

"They murdered my husband!"

Priya's eyes are shining with anger, or maybe reverence. They kind of look the same on Priya. "They took out a monster."

So not helping, Priya.

"This isn't another interview for Nightmare Defense," I hiss at her. "Don't make it worse."

Priya rolls her eyes. In Priya's world, everything is practice for an interview to join Nightmare Defense.

"Mrs. Sanden." My voice is gentle and patient, experienced at this. "I'm so sorry for your loss. I know exactly how it feels to lose someone you love to a Nightmare."

"I didn't lose him to a Nightmare! I lost him to those murderers!"

"No," I repeat gently. "Your husband was dead the moment he turned into a giant cockroach in his sleep."

"No, he wasn't!" Mrs. Sanden is waving her arm in anger.

"He was still my husband. We just couldn't communicate anymore because I don't speak giant cockroach!"

I stare at her, incredulous. Look, I, of all people, understand how desperately you can wish for the person you love back after the Nightmare changed them into something monstrous. I do. I wish every day that I had my sister back.

But the difference is, I know that she wasn't my sister anymore once she became a Nightmare.

"Ma'am," I tell her. "Your husband was trying to eat you."

"A misunderstanding!" she insists, still waving the only arm she has left.

I press my fingers to the bridge of my nose. "He ripped off your arm."

"An accident."

"He *ate* it."

"He was hungry. It's a shame to let these things go to waste."

Beside me, Priya snorts and leans down to whisper in my ear, "And I thought *you* were a little on the irrational side about Nightmares. I take it all back. Your quirks are normal compared to this lady."

"Wow, thanks, what a grand compliment. Such a high bar I've passed," I deadpan.

"Call me the queen of compliments." Priya grins, wide and sharp.

Mrs. Sanden kicks over her coffee table, sending doilies and flowers flying.

"Get out!" she snaps. "I don't have to listen to you mocking me!"

Okay, we deserved that. The woman is clearly in denial and needs help, and we've probably made everything worse.

"I'll just leave this here in case you change your mind," I tell her, slipping a pamphlet onto the sideboard as I turn away.

Priya leaves a stack more. "In case you get angry and destroy the first one. Or two. Or ten."

"Priya," I hiss.

She ignores me, piling up all the pamphlets she has. A gust of wind chooses that moment to come in through the small, open window and whip the pamphlets around the room, making them soar like it's raining therapy advertisements.

This does not please Mrs. Sanden, not at all. She screams, swatting them out of the air in a rage. Then she picks up a vase and hurls it at us.

I dodge out of the way, and it shatters against the wall.

"Out!" she screams. Her eyes are wide and bulging a little.

"We're going!"

"Ou—"

Her eyes roll up.

Oh no.

Mrs. Sanden tips backward, keeling over onto the floor with a heavy thud.

Priya and I freeze, staring at her still form for several shocked heartbeats.

"Shit!" I run over, kneeling beside the fallen woman. "Is it a seizure?"

"How should I know?" Priya paces, biting her lip.

"Your sister's a doctor!"

"But I'm not!" She frowns down at the woman, then shakes her head. "Actually, I think she's just fainted."

My skin prickles. "She's unconscious?"

Priya casts a sidelong glance at me, fully aware of why I'm uncomfortable. "Ness, we're in the city. The water has Helomine in it. As long as she's been drinking tap water, she's got the drugs in her. She won't dream."

I shift uncomfortably, wiping my gloved hands on my neatly pressed trousers. I forget that I can't wipe the sweat off my palms through the cloth.

My eyes never leave the sleeping woman. "But what if she hasn't?"

Priya sighs. "Ness—"

"No, listen. Her husband turned into a Nightmare, didn't he?" I look around the room, searching for something that would confirm my suspicion. "That's not supposed to happen if you're drinking the tap water."

I pace into the tiny kitchen area, eyes darting past the sink. I open the top cupboards and see glass jars of flour and rice and pasta, along with kitchen utensils. I close the wooden cupboard door and kneel in front of the small doors under the sink.

A large jug of brown liquid, unmarked.

Moonshine.

Priya's eyes widen. "Ah, fuck."

Prohibition bans alcohol across the country for the simple reason that alcohol nullifies the Helomine and most other Nightmare-prevention drugs.

Of course, it hasn't stopped people bootlegging and making

their own liquor. Because some people are stupid enough to take the risk—after all, you don't dream *every* time you sleep. And people always seem to think that Nightmares are a thing that happen to other people, not themselves.

Until they do.

"The bottle is half-empty," I whisper, my voice layered with the fear growing like a Nightmare in my chest. I reach out and touch it. "And it's damp. It's been opened recently."

Like, say, by a depressed woman whose husband just died and wanted to numb the pain.

Priya's eyes widen in understanding, and her head whips around to Mrs. Sanden.

Except she's not Mrs. Sanden anymore.

Her skin is morphing, stretching, melding, like there's some sort of living creature inside her and it's trying to burst its way out. With a horrible crackle of bone, her body lengthens, elongating into something stretched and contorted. Her skin darkens to the same stormy blue of the uniform of the Nightmare Defense teams, and her eyes stretch and bulge, changing shape into a parody of the goggles they wear.

"Oh no," I whisper.

Priya's eyes gleam. "Oh, hell *yes!*"

The Nightmare has risen, and it opens its massive mouth to reveal an empty void, a path to nothing, a sucking darkness.

It screams, and the air is pulled toward it like a vacuum. I scrabble for the cupboard doors, holding tight to them as the air whips around me, yanking me toward the Nightmare like a tornado.

Enraged, the Nightmare lunges for me.

I scream, loud and sharp, diving away from the monstrosity, smashing into the hardwood floor. I scramble across it on my hands and knees. A broken piece of the vase caught in the rug cuts my glove, slicing my skin beneath. I leave drops of blood behind as I scuttle away.

Behind me, Priya is practically dancing with excitement as she rips off her coat to reveal all the weapons underneath. She has a utility belt with so many different implements of murder it can't possibly be legal, but that's never stopped anyone from doing anything in Newham.

Priya dives for the Nightmare, gun out, firing, *rat-a-tat-tat*. The bullets go right through it.

It's made of smoke, formless and intangible, and it's like cutting through air.

Undeterred, still grinning, Priya whips out a spray can from her belt and starts spraying something in the air at the Nightmare. Pressurized salt, maybe. A lot of the ethereal Nightmares come from people's fears of old ghost stories, which means they can often be stopped with salt because that's what the legends say stop them.

Every single Nightmare is different, because every person's idea of what would stop their own personal monster is different.

The Nightmare shrieks, rearing back, and I take the opportunity to wriggle my way under the couch, covering my face like a small child. Maybe if it can't see me, it'll forget about me and go away.

I'm blind underneath the couch, but I don't need sight to figure out what's happening. It's perfectly clear from the crash of breaking pottery, the crunch of wood as Priya destroys the table, the angry and murderous wails of the Nightmare.

I know I need to get out. I need to call for help. Or assist Priya. I need to do *something*.

But my body is frozen, seized under the couch, completely trapped by my terror. My mind has snapped back to the me of eight years ago, the me who listened from my hiding spot as my father was ripped apart piece by piece, the bones crunching as my sister—no, as the Nightmare—slowly ate him alive.

2

"*What were you thinking?*" *the* Director of the Newham branch of the Friends of the Restful Soul asks me, with a look so pained I mentally up the level of shit I think I'm in.

I'm standing in his office, a tiny room with brick walls. On the wall behind him, a large Jesus on the cross judges me, and on either side of his bloody form, framed portraits of the four founding saints of the Friends of the Restful Soul look down at me in shame.

The one on the far left, Magdalena, looks particularly unimpressed. Supposedly, a hundred years ago, she killed an unstoppable demon traipsing through the countryside slaughtering people. Well, they call it a demon, but we all know it was a Nightmare—it was in the early days when Nightmares were just starting, and no one knew what they were yet.

No matter what you call it, doctrine claims she killed it when she was only eleven. When I was eleven, I cowered in the cupboard under the kitchen sink and prayed that the Nightmare crunching on my father's bones wouldn't consume me too.

I can feel the painting's eyes judging me.

Beside me is a wide window that's just big enough to crawl out. The rusting metal fire escape is visible through the warped glass, and a not-small part of me is sorely tempted to make a run for it.

I don't, of course. That would only make all of this worse. And it's already enough of a mess.

I smooth a gloved hand down my crisp waistcoat. I changed after I got back, knowing this was coming and that I needed to make the best impression possible. My long-sleeved, white shirt practically glows against my tight, black, button-up waistcoat, and the creases on my trousers are so sharp you could cut with them.

"I'm sorry, sir." I fold my hands in front of me. "But if I'm being honest, this isn't my fault."

"How do you figure that?" the Director asks, raising one eyebrow into the spiny folds of his lizard crest. His features are still human enough to discern expression—though I suspect a lot of that is due to reconstructive surgery—but there's no mistaking that the Director is a Nightmare.

Lots of people are—just because you become your worst nightmare, it doesn't always mean *you* change. Like that actress whose worst fear was to be ugly and so that's what she became. She never turned into a cannibal or melted people's flesh off or ate live children. She's just . . . no longer a famed beauty.

I don't know what the Director's fear was—something about lizards, based on his appearance—but I know it happened when he was young. They were able to do reconstructive surgery early, and he grew into his features. His mouth can reproduce human language, which is better than some Nightmares, who end up stuck in the form of something terrifying and then have to tap out messages in Morse code and shit.

But not all Nightmares come back sane.

I think of my sister, Ruby. My overprotective sister, who beat up kids at school who dared try to bully me. Who held me when I cried and would have given me the world if she could have.

My sister, who ate our father alive and nearly devoured me too.

The Nightmare didn't just twist her body into something monstrous—it twisted her mind too.

It always seemed viciously unfair to me that so many people came through their Nightmares twisted in body but not in mind but the one person who meant the most to me had become the thing I feared the most.

Why couldn't Ruby have come through the Nightmare sane?

"I don't see how it's my fault Mrs. Sanden turned into a Nightmare," I tell him. "She and her husband were drinking bootlegged alcohol. That's against the law."

He sighs heavily, his vibrant green scales dimming, a sure sign he's disappointed. "I'm not saying *that's* your fault. I'd never hold you responsible for something out of your control."

"Oh." I shift from foot to foot. If he's not mad about that, then . . .

"Ness, you've had basic training to handle people in distress," his voice is gentle. "And I know you've had basic Nightmare-containment training."

Of course I had. No one *planned* to have to face dangerous Nightmares when going door-to-door handing out pamphlets, but you had to be prepared just in case. That was just practical.

"I've had the training," I admit.

"What's the first rule?"

I hesitate. "Pull the fire alarm to warn everyone."

"Right. Was there a fire alarm in the room?"

He knows there was. There's a fire alarm in every apartment in the city. In Mrs. Sanden's apartment, it had been right beside the wall phone. I'd clocked it the moment we entered.

I look away.

"What's the second rule?" he asks me.

"Call for help. Find a phone and dial 666 for Nightmare Defense."

"And did you do that?"

"No."

"Was there a phone in the room?"

"Yes." I lower my eyes.

"Why do we do those things?" he asks me patiently.

"To minimize casualties in case the Nightmare is violent."

"That's right." He leans forward, eyes sad. "And instead of calling for help and warning the other residents who might have been in danger, what did you do?"

I clear my throat, not meeting his eyes. "Hid under the couch."

"And when Priya had the Nightmare contained and asked you to call for the police, what did you do?"

I rub my arm awkwardly. "Jumped out the window and down the fire escape."

"And while Priya was singlehandedly containing a violent Nightmare *and* calling for help *and* pulling the alarm, where were you?"

I lick my lips. "I get the point."

"Answer the question, Ness."

I sigh heavily, shoulders slumping. "I was running back here, where I went to my room and barricaded myself inside, then hid under the bed."

The words hang between us, heavy and awkward.

He's clearly waiting for me to say something, but I don't know what else there is to say. I screwed up. I saw the Nightmare, and I reverted into a scared child who couldn't do anything and then hid and ran, leaving my best friend to fight for her life alone.

Priya, of course, enjoyed the whole thing. I've never heard such sounds of delight from her before. She's been itching for a chance to fight a Nightmare and show the world—and Nightmare Defense—what she's made of.

But I didn't hide so Priya could shine.

I hid because I'm a coward.

I'm trying to look anywhere but at the Director. My eyes land on a newspaper open on his table. The splashy head-line across the front reads **MAYOR SENTENCED TO SIX**

16

MONTHS IN PRISON ON CORRUPTION CHARGES, SAYS IT WILL BE "GOOD NETWORKING OPPORTUNITY."

"Ness," the Director says, pulling my attention back to him and away from the newspaper.

"Yes, Director?" My voice is hoarse.

He examines me with the slitted lizard eyes, and his voice, when he speaks, is gentle. "Why are you here, Ness?"

I feign ignorance. "You called me into a meeting, sir."

"No." He sighs heavily, folding his long, green talons over the desk. "Why are you here? Why did you become an initiate at the Friends of the Restful Soul?"

My smile is sickly. "To help people, of course."

He gives me a skeptical look, like he can smell my bullshit a mile away. Who knows, maybe he can. I don't know how lizard noses work.

"Really," he says slowly.

"Really."

"I understand," the Director says. "But I wonder if this is really the best place for you to do that."

My head snaps up. "What?"

No. He can't be saying what I think he is.

"Please," I whisper. "Don't kick me out."

"I'm not kicking you out, child." His smile is gentle. "I'm suggesting you rethink your life path. Our organization is built on reaching out to people in need. And sometimes people in need lash out. It's not their fault they're going through terrible things. But you need to be able to handle that in a safe and professional way."

I swallow, fear making my chest ache. I can't lose this. "I can do it."

"But you don't *have* to," he insists. "I see how devoted you are to this organization. And that's wonderful. But maybe this path isn't the right fit for you. There's no shame in that."

"Please," I whisper, voice choked. "I have nowhere else to go."

I have to make this work. I *have* to.

If the Friends of the Restful Soul kick me out, I'll be homeless. I have pretty much no money, except the little bit of pocket change I sometimes have after running errands for Shenwei, who runs the kitchen.

I live here, in this building, with all the other disciples. I have my own tiny little cube room. Where else in this over-crowded, overpriced mess of a city can you get a place of your own? If I left, I'd be broke, sleeping on the streets. Even if I *did* get a job and manage to scrape up enough for rent, anywhere I stayed would inevitably have multiple people in a room. I'd seen the apartment ads for bunks stacked three high, eighteen people to a room, all sharing one toilet. I couldn't live like that.

I couldn't even sleep when *one* other person was sleeping in the room—you never knew what they might become while asleep.

I'd never sleep again.

"I—I know you know my history, sir," I stutter, scrambling to find the one thing that will make him reconsider sending me away. "My sister."

It's his turn to look away. There we go. I know how to lay this on thick.

"I just . . . After everything I went through, the Friends were so helpful at getting my life together." This is actually true. I'd been even more of a coward before I went through their free group therapy.

"I want to pay it forward," I tell him, using one of his favorite phrases. This part, of course, is nonsense. "I want to help people. No one should have to go through that alone."

The Director sighs heavily again, and I know I've got him. Pull out the dead-sister-trauma card and he can't help but pity me.

I don't mind being pitied. As long as it gets me what I want, people can think whatever they want about me.

"Give me another chance," I beg, leaning forward. "Maybe you're right, maybe going out and spreading the word isn't my calling. But there's so much else I can do here."

I need this place. I can't leave.

"Give me time to reflect, to . . ." What were they always saying in the sermons? "To see the error of my ways and find a path to enlightenment and self-improvement."

There we go. The Director always likes it when I spout doctrine at him.

He looks at me with clear eyes, and I know he sees right through my sad little attempts to manipulate him. Finally, he heaves a breath and presses his fingers to the side of his spiny ridge and massages the base of his horns.

He purses his lips. "And where do you think you'd fit

better? I can't in good conscience send you back to managing group therapy sessions. That was . . ."

A disaster. An absolute disaster.

I'd had a full-blown meltdown when someone with giant hairy legs that reminded me of my sister's Nightmare came in and nearly burnt down the building when I climbed up the curtain and hung on the candelabra, trying to reach the upper window to get away.

The Director shuffles some papers. "Maybe we could get you transferred to New Bristol. It's calmer there, less opportunity for . . ."

For me to screw up.

Which sounds great except for the fact that I don't want to go to New Bristol. It's built on the bones of an older city that was completely wiped out by a fire-breathing-dragon Nightmare forty years ago, and the survivors just never really recovered. It doesn't have the nicest reputation. They still don't even have the pipes working after forty years.

Which means no Helomine in the water.

And they're known for their drinking problems.

All of which is to say that I am absolutely *not* going to New Bristol.

"Please, before we think of transfers, let me try one more time," I tell him decisively. "Let me work mail delivery here, just for a week, while I reflect. And next week, I'll come to you with a long-term plan."

"Cindy's on mail this week," the Director points out. "We don't need two people doing it."

"Cindy hurt her ankle today."

"I hadn't heard that." He frowns. "Are you sure?"

"Absolutely," I tell him, and it's only sort of a lie because she hasn't hurt her ankle *yet*, but about ten minutes after I leave here, she's going to find herself with a sprained ankle.

Amazing how that's going to work.

The Director frowns. "Well. I suppose she can't do mail tonight if she's hurt herself. We'll need a replacement anyway." He rubs his scaly nose bridge. "Fine. I'll put you on mail. You can go grab the boat ticket from her and let her know you'll be taking over."

I let out a whoosh of air. "Thank you, sir. I won't disappoint."

He shakes his head mournfully. "I know you'll try your hardest."

Ouch.

The worst part is, he's right. I will try my hardest, and I'll somehow manage to screw it up anyway. Because the truth is, no matter where they put me, nothing will change. It's not about the job—it's about me.

I turn around, leaving the Director's office, heart heavy with the truth that I can't escape—that I've never been able to change since that horrible night eight years ago.

I'm a coward.

3

The first thing I do when I leave the Director's office is find Cindy.

The Friends of the Restful Soul own a massive, old brick high-rise in the heart of the city. From the outside, it's a carefully maintained facade of scrubbed stone and cheery mahogany doors that are always open to those in need. We always have someone standing just outside, passing out informational pamphlets to passersby.

I'd only managed three days on that job before a nearby alarm went off and I thought there was a Nightmare attack. It took them six hours to find me tucked between the boilers in the basement, and it turned out to be a false alarm anyway.

The inside of the building is more modern than the outside. The main central lobby has polished white tiles on the floor and a bank of ultra-modern phones on the wall—made of Bakelite, about the size of a human head, they're smooth and kind of slick to the touch in a way that creeps me out—and free for public use. The basement has a massive kitchen with a walk-in fridge (not a good place to hide, too cold) and two boilers (which I'm banned from going near now). The upper floors retain their older design: narrow halls with bare brick walls, warping wooden floors, and cracked window frames that have seen better centuries. A rusting metal fire escape is bolted to the side of the building, and it hasn't been up to code since the turn of the century at least. Not that anyone will do anything about it. The Friends of the Restful Soul don't approve of bribes, and that's the only way to get anything done in this city.

I find Cindy exactly where I expect her.

She's where she always is at this time of day, sitting in one of the empty therapy rooms taking her lunch break alone, instead of in the cafeteria with everyone else. As per usual, she's hunched over her notebook, her eyes focused and her lips pursed as she writes.

I stop in front of her, my shadow falling over her book so she has to look up at me. Her writing, as always, is in a mix of Korean and English, both so messy that I doubt either is legible to anyone but her. I catch what I think might be "waterfall" but could also be "rat tail" or "vest loft."

I know that she writes poetry, but that's about it. I've never really cared, to be honest. About either her or poetry.

She frowns up at me. Her bobbed black hair is a little mussed, like she's been running her hands through it a lot, and she's got a distracted look on her face, like her mind is still half on whatever she was writing.

"Ness." Her voice is cautious.

Cindy and I haven't liked each other from the first moment

we met. Or well, more accurately, her first week here she set up a therapy group time for a bunch of Nightmares in the room I was cleaning and didn't warn me, leading to me nearly burning the building down in a mad panic to escape.

She never apologized and I never forgave her.

"Cindy." I smile at her, all teeth.

Her shoulders tighten, her voice going cold. "Shouldn't you be in the therapy room now? I heard about the mess at the wake you were at. Doesn't doctrine say you're supposed to see one of the therapists after any traumatic experience?"

I wave her away, annoyed. Cindy's always harping on doctrine and seems particularly set on pointing out how I constantly and blatantly ignore it. I think she's just jealous of how good I am at getting away with sidestepping the rules.

"I'm not traumatized," I lie. "And besides"—I smile brilliantly—"doesn't doctrine also say you're supposed to seek the comfort of other disciples in times of trouble?" I spread my hands. "Well, here I am, with our most devout of disciples."

Cindy doesn't look impressed.

Fair enough. I laid it on a little thick.

"What do you want?" she asks, voice hard.

"Not much." My smile is too thin to be friendly, but I keep my voice chipper. "Just your boat ticket. The Director has swapped us. I'll be making the mail run tonight."

Cindy frowns. "What? I haven't heard anything about this. Why the sudden change?"

"Well, he thought it prudent, given how you hurt your ankle."

Cindy blinks. "I haven't hurt my ankle."

Before she can react, I press my boot against her ankle, tipping it to the side and pushing it to the ground. She jerks on her seat but doesn't fall because I'm holding the back of her chair, pinning her into a contorted position where she's stuck sitting in the chair, but her ankle and foot are against the ground.

If I press hard, her ankle will certainly be sprained, if not snapped.

I learned this from Priya, though I'm supposed to be using these moves against Nightmares, not other disciples.

"Are you sure about that?" I ask, my implication clear.

Cindy grits her teeth. Her eyes flick to me, her hands twitching where they're braced against the table, as though wondering if she could land a hit before I snap her ankle. I see the moment she realizes it won't work, that I've practiced this move and thought this through.

"You wouldn't," she grates.

I press my foot down a bit, applying pressure on the ankle I've twisted beneath it. "Wouldn't I, though?"

Sweat beads on her brow, and she makes a small sound. "Fine!" She rummages in her pocket and pulls out a ticket, which I pluck from her hand.

"Thanks, Cindy." I press down with my foot one more time, a sharp, jerking motion that makes her gasp in pain, and then step away from her. "Don't forget to milk that ankle for sympathy!"

Cindy leans over, hands reaching down to clutch her

injured ankle. She glares at my retreating back so hard I can practically feel it.

I whistle as I walk away, ticket tucked safely away in my pocket.

I wind my way up the stairwell, past ancient and modern paintings of the four saints of the Friends of the Restful Soul. They look down at me with judgment, as if they know I'm a fraud, know that I believe none of the teachings I've learned here, that I'm nothing but a scam artist using this place to hide away from the Nightmares that lurk outside.

I flip Magdalena off as I pass, because her expression is always the judgiest. Suen always looks a little sly, and I imagine he'd not have minded my lack of faith, and Irving always looks down kindly from his paintings. Alaina just looks like she's forgotten she's being painted and is busy staring at something out of frame.

I reach the top floor and walk over to the cracked window to look out over the city.

I used to sit on the roof and watch the city go by, but then I locked myself out there one day and panicked so badly I completely destroyed the door trying to get back in.

Now they lock the door to the roof so no one can go out.

But the view from the top-floor window is still good, and the city vista stretches out before me—tall brick buildings as far as the eye can see, and even taller, newer buildings made of steel and concrete cluster in the center of the city. Always building upward, higher and higher, until we reach the sky, the people at the top touching the clouds, while the shadows cast by the buildings block out the sun from those below.

Smoke from the factories across the river make the sky gray all the time, adding to the oppressive aura of the city. It's easy to get sick from the mold and smog, especially in the poorer parts of the city.

What am I going to do if the Director kicks me out?

No. No, I'll think of something. I've bought myself some time. It's going to be fine.

I take a deep breath and scrub my hand over my face. The worst part of all this is that this mess is all my fault. I know I'm sabotaging myself. Every time this happens, I know it's going to have consequences. But in those moments, I don't care. It's like my mind goes blank, and there's only the fear. It's not even rational half the time. Why couldn't I have rung the fire alarm before diving under the couch? Or called for help after jumping out the window?

My shoulders slump.

I'm such a mess.

"Did you break Cindy's ankle?"

I turn around to find Priya standing there, one brow arched, hand on her hip, faint smile playing across her face.

"It's not broken," I inform her, waving her concern away. "She's just being dramatic."

"So you did break it."

"I never said that."

"Uh-huh." Priya's expression says exactly how much she's buying this.

I allow myself a smile. "But hypothetically, I might have

27

suggested to her that she could either give me the boat ticket and tell everyone it was sprained or I'd sprain it for her."

Priya does this half snort, half laugh. "Only hypothetically though."

"Naturally."

She leans against the window beside me, peering through the dirty glass at the sprawling city. She's got a smudge of dead Nightmare dust on her cheek, and her hands are chapped and a little scratched up, probably from one of her salt weapons. She's visibly unarmed now—she doesn't dare walk around the Friends of the Restful Soul building armed—the Director would kick her out in a second—but I'm sure she's got a few things tucked into her combat boots or her loose military-style trousers.

"Anything interesting out here?" she asks, eyes outside.

I shrug. "Nah, I just like to look out at it."

Priya gives me a sly grin. "Oh? At what? The film poster across the road?"

Sure enough, when I look, there is a film poster on the exposed-brick side of a building below us. I like to look at the skyline, the strange spines of spiky buildings. I hadn't been paying attention to what was below.

"Ugh," I say when I see it. "Really?"

The film poster depicts a lurid scene where a blond woman is melting sexily into the arms of a deathly white man wearing a black cape, baring exaggerated fake fangs. Her neck is exposed, and he looks like he's planning to murder her, and she looks like he's about to give her . . . well. Something decidedly inappropriate for a film not shown in an adult-only shop.

"I hate those films," I mutter. "They just glorify monsters."

Priya laughs. "You know, not all Nightmares are monsters, even if the Director can be harsh."

"I know that," I snap, though I honestly have trouble with the Director some days too. "But it's different when the Nightmares actually, you know, hurt people."

Vampirism is one of the most confusing types of contagious Nightmare because there are so many strains of it. Different people had different Nightmares about becoming vampires, and because it's all folktales and fiction, everyone had different ideas of what a vampire *was*. So some strains are weak against garlic and some infect people when they bite them and some can even walk around in daylight.

But the thing they all have in common is they drink human blood.

"I don't think it's okay to romanticize vampires," I tell Priya, "because they're actually hurting people. How many dead bodies show up in the Newham morgue every year with bite marks? And there was that awful case where that vampire had a bunch of women kidnapped and trapped in his basement."

Priya rolls her eyes. "Yeah, okay, those guys are creeps. But like, they can't all be bad." She winks at me. "And I mean, real vampires aside, those movie ones are hella sexy. They can get it, you know."

I raise an eyebrow. "Oh? So if you were out dancing and a

hot vampire showed up, you'd go home with them?"

"In real life?" She snorts. "Hell no. I'm not an idiot. Way too big a risk." She shrugs. "But in the movies? It's sexy."

I sigh heavily. "Why is that? That people find things sexy in fiction that would creep them the hell out in real life?"

Priya shrugs. "I don't know, man. People are weird." She grins, winking at me. "Myself included."

I roll my eyes.

We look out over the city together for a moment in a companionable silence. Outside, a pterodactyl soars through the sky. It's almost majestic, iridescent scales glittering in the light.

Then it snags a man off the roof a few buildings away with its jagged maw. It carries him away, while he screams and struggles to escape.

Maybe it's a good thing I can't get on the roof anymore.

"*Soooo,*" Priya says, turning away from the scene outside. "How'd it go with ol' Spiny?"

I allow myself to be distracted. "He hates it when you call him that."

"I know, that's why I do it."

"You're incorrigible."

Priya's gaze slants to me. "And you're avoiding the question. How'd it go?" She frowns. "He didn't kick you out, did he?"

"No, no." I run my hand through my hair. It's slippery, a little longer than the more fashionable bob. Not that I could ever make it fall in a nice bob without an entire tub of pomade. "I wouldn't have bothered with Cindy if he had."

Priya perks up. "Ah, mail duty, then. You taking the boat to Palton Island tonight?"

"Yeah. Overnight one." It's a six-hour trip by boat, so most are overnight. I don't want to think about how many people will be sleeping on this trip.

"Don't worry," Priya says, like she can read my thoughts. "Those boats are all-night parties. No one's gonna be sleeping."

"Then what are the beds for?"

Priya gives me a look like I'm an idiot. "Do I really have to explain that?"

A blush creeps into my cheeks. "Please don't."

She laughs. "Seriously, I envy you. I always wanted a turn at the mail run. I bet I'd have a lot of fun on those boats."

"You would," I say, no judgment in my tone. Priya likes her fun. She likes to live life fast and joyful, living every day to its fullest. I don't think she's afraid of anything except slowing down.

I envy her. I wish I were as fearless as her.

"Are you going to be back in time for the weekly dinner?" Priya asks, her frown returning.

Priya's sister, Adhya, makes her come over for dinner once a week. Supposedly it's to keep in touch. Priya mostly sees it as Adhya's excuse to lecture her about life choices. Priya's not exactly wrong, which is how I ended up coming along every week too, because it's awkward for Adhya to question Priya's choice to join the Friends of the Restful Soul without also

31

questioning me, and Adhya is far too polite to ever question a guest's life choices.

"I think so," I tell her. "I'm overnight with the mail tonight, and then I'm supposed to stay at the branch there in a guest room for a day and then overnight back. So I should be back in time."

"Good." Priya makes a face. "She called the other day."

"Nagging about how dangerous Nightmare Defense is and how you should give it up for a safer career again?"

"As always." Priya rolls her eyes. "Second only to how I should get out of this cult."

I sigh. "Of course."

Priya raises her hands as if asking the sky for answers. "I just don't get why she has to disapprove of every choice I make!"

"Hey." I try to level a joke. "At least she hasn't turned into a giant spider and tried to eat you."

Priya stares me dead in the eye. "I'd honestly find that easier to handle."

Yeah, she probably would.

Even so, I would trade anything for my sister back. Even if we'd ended up with a complicated, messy relationship like Priya and Adhya's. Any relationship would be better than none.

And no matter how often they argue, Priya and Adhya love each other fiercely. It's hard not to be jealous of that. I wish I had someone who cared about me that way.

"So," I say, trying to pull my mind away from that pain.

"Did you get back here and then immediately call the Department of Nightmare Defense to tell them how amazing you were today?"

Her eyes instantly brighten. "You know it! I was on the phone to my recruiter before that Nightmare's blood was cold!"

"It was a shadow Nightmare," I point out. "It didn't have blood."

Priya ignores this. "He says that my bravery and competence in the face of danger are really standout. My application is being bumped forward." She bites her lower lip and looks at me, eyes full of hope. "I really might have a chance, Ness."

I don't want to get Priya's hopes up. She's been trying to get a job fighting Nightmares since she was able to stand and hold a gun, but she's been rejected for age, inexperience, quotas, all sorts of things. She only joined the Friends of the Restful Soul because she heard it would look good on her next wave of applications.

"I really hope so, Priya," I tell her, and I mean it. I want her dream to come true. She deserves it. She's sure worked hard enough for it.

I look down, examining the cracked brick at the edge of the window. Priya hadn't said anything about what I did today, and I know she's waiting for me to bring it up.

I don't want to bring it up.

But I know I have to. And at least with words, I'm a little less of a coward. Not much less, but a little less.

"I'm sorry," I finally tell her.

She's silent beside me.

I clear my throat. "I should have helped. Or at least rang the alarm or called Nightmare Defense. I shouldn't have left it all up to you."

"Ness, I'm not mad at you." Her lips quirk in a smile. "I can handle myself. You'd have only been in the way."

I really would have.

She looks at me, expression serious. "But, Ness. You *need* to do something about this. You can't keep running whenever something frightens you."

I look away. "I—I'm doing fine."

"You're not." She runs a hand through her hair. "Ness, you wear gloves on the off chance you'll meet someone with a contagious Nightmare that transmits by touch."

"And?"

"And there are only two of those in *existence*. And neither of them are even that dangerous. One of them gives you red irises and the other gives you diarrhea for a week."

"There might be others," I point out, fiddling with the hem of my glove. "Ones we don't know about."

"Ness." Priya sighs. "You won't drink water that hasn't gone through a purifier."

"Well, I don't want to end up with blue scales," I point out.

"There's no sea dragon blood in our water."

"But—"

"Ness. Stop." Priya massages her temples. "You have a problem. You know it."

I look down, shoulders slumping.

"I know," I finally say, voice barely a whisper. "But I don't know how to fix it."

"Have you considered going to therapy?" Priya asks. "It's free. You're a member of the Friends, this is literally what they do."

I grimace. "I did. This is the me *after* years of work. You should have seen the me before."

Priya winces. "Oh."

I stare out the window, at the picture of the sexualized monster, not really seeing it.

"After my family . . . died, I came to the city to live with my aunt. She was my only relative." I swallow. I hate talking about this. "She's the one who brought me to the Friends. She was poor as shit, and she saw I needed help. So I came here every week."

Priya blinks. "I had no idea you had an aunt at all."

I shrug. "She died. A few years ago."

"Oh." Priya swallows. "I'm sorry. Was it . . ."

"A Nightmare? No. Howling cough. She'd been a factory worker too long." I shrug. "After she passed, I signed up with the Friends."

Priya is silent, absorbing this. I press my forehead against the glass, staring outside, though I'm not really seeing anything. Priya's right, I do need help. I know it. I do. I've known it for a while. But I've hit the limit of what the Friends can do for me, and I just don't know where to go from here.

It's hard to stop being afraid when the whole world is literally full of monsters.

And anyone could become another one whenever they go to sleep.

A bell chimes somewhere else in the building, the tinny echo reminding me that it's midafternoon.

I step away from the window. "I've got to go get some sleep. I'm going to be up all night on that boat, so I need to rest now."

"All right." A knowing grin crosses Priya's face, all trace of the earlier solemnity gone. "I'm gonna be up all night too, celebrating."

The way she says that tells me *exactly* the kind of fun she's going to have celebrating.

I roll my eyes, but I'm smiling as I walk away.

My room is in the dormitory wing on the other side of the building and down two floors. It's one of the only single rooms in the building—it used to be a janitor's closet. There are no windows, just a bare bulb in the ceiling and brick walls all around. There's barely enough room for a bed, and I keep my clothes in a trunk I tuck underneath it.

I love it.

I love every part of it, from the cracking caulking on the brick to the stain on the ceiling. Other people might find it claustrophobic or ugly or just sad, but I never have.

To me, this room has always felt *safe.*

I step inside and close the door behind me, flopping back onto the hard mattress, finally letting my tense muscles loosen, my whole body relaxing in a way it simply never can in the outside world. All those physical manifestations of my fear—my tense shoulders, my clenched jaw—all of it rolls away.

This room is the only place in the world I ever feel safe. The only place I can let go of my terror and just *be*.

It's just me here. No one else. If someone else turns into a Nightmare in the building, I can hide here and be confident that even if they found me, they couldn't get through the multiple layers of brick wall.

The walls protect me from the world. They keep me safe inside, keep the monsters out.

And if the Director kicks me out, I'll lose it—this space. This precious sense of safety.

I can't afford that.

I'll do anything to keep this room.

I just wish I knew how to make the Director understand how much I need this place. How much it means to me. How completely destroyed I'd be if I lost it.

I close my eyes. If only I were good at literally anything, this wouldn't be a problem. He'd want me to stay.

I press my forehead to the cool wall, my fingers scraping possessively along the rough surface of the brick, and let myself be comforted by the solidity of it.

I'll figure something out.

I have to.

Finally I sit up and take a pill from my stash. I gulp it down, chasing it with some water from my thermos. Then I take a different one and gulp that down too. There are eight different medicines on the market to keep Nightmares away, not including the Helomine that's in the water supply. I have all of them with me at all times, and every time I sleep, I always take at least two different types. Just to be sure.

I won't end up like my sister.

I curl up in the bed, safe and protected, and when I fall asleep, I don't dream.

4

I wait in line for the boat with hundreds of other people.

I've got three massive leather-and-metal suitcases with wheels secured to the bottom, and I'm not the only one. At least half of the people here have multiple oversized suitcases, expressions bored as they wait in line to have their tickets checked before loading up the gangplank.

Like me, most of these people are carrying mail. The problem is the post. Sending letters, that's usually fine. They'll get where they're going. But if you want to send a package, then someone—probably multiple someones—is going to open it up and see what's inside. Naturally, if they find anything of value, it disappears and your mail just never arrives. Or sometimes it arrives missing pieces.

Which is why most big companies that do a lot of trade with other cities often have employees drag all the packages over personally. It's cheaper to pay for a round-trip boat ticket for one person than mail forty packages anyway.

Today, I'm getting on the boat heading to Palton Island, a resort island that's also its own state, which means it makes its own laws. And it's made those laws in such a way that every business in Newham has a branch in Palton for tax reasons. Also, the island is probably fifty percent casinos. The other fifty percent is burlesque shows, brothels, and booze.

Palton is a very rich island.

I shift from foot to foot as I wait in line to board. Police swarm the docks, writing tickets for people—loitering or disturbing the peace or whatever else they can make up in the moment—and then waiting for their victims to bribe their way out of the fine. Everyone is stuck waiting in line, so it's a good time for fake tickets. Of course, some of the police are fake, just people in stolen uniforms. Their tickets aren't real, but you can't tell. You risk a much bigger fine if they are real or a smaller bribe to make it go away.

Kids run around the dock, selling today's paper, penny novels, and pamphlets explaining how much to bribe an officer of the law depending on the situation.

Since the Friends of the Restful Soul refuses to pay bribes, I'll be stuck with a ticket.

But one of the nice things about wearing the Friends of the Restful Soul powder-blue vest with its logo—two hands linked—prominently displayed and lugging suitcases with the same logo on them is that most of the police and fake police leave me alone. They want bribes, and they know the Friends won't pay them.

I'm not the only person they avoid. A man in a tailored, very expensive-looking tuxedo is getting on the boat with no less than five bodyguards. He's got the smirk and the swaggering air that makes me peg him as either a gang lord or a politician.

A tall, lithe white woman with bobbed hair and wearing a black evening gown that belongs in a film waltzes up the gangplank, bypassing the police and the line. Diamonds glitter thick and heavy around her throat, and the man escorting her is flushed and flustered.

I wonder if she's an actress. I don't recognize her from anything, but that doesn't mean much. I don't watch a lot of films.

"Chestnuts, get your roasted chestnuts!"

My stomach grumbles hopefully, but I wasn't given any pocket money for the trip, so I'll have to abstain.

"Caramel corn! Get your caramel corn!"

Ugh. This is going to be a long night.

I'm one away from the counter, but it's still taking forever. The ticket taker is flirting with the girl ahead of me, a flapper with glow-in-the-dark radium-painted nails and even more bags than I have.

I tap my foot on the ground, trying not to look as impatient as I feel. I want to get on the boat, stow my packages in one of the locked safes, and then . . .

Well, actually I'm not sure what I'll do on the boat. I've never actually been on a party boat before. Or any boat, really. I have to admit, there's a small part of me that's a little excited. Will it be bouncy, the boat tossed recklessly by the waves, or will it be smooth, the boat so big the waves can't rock it?

What happens if someone becomes a Nightmare?

My skin prickles, and I force myself to push the thought away. I'm sure there are lots of places to hide on the boat. I'll be fine.

Probably.

Finally the girl moves up the gangplank and I step forward, hauling my luggage. It's all ridiculously heavy, and the auto that the Director hired to drive me here had nearly flipped when we tried to haul it all into the trunk.

The driver and I had barely gotten it out at the docks. I'm not looking forward to figuring out how to cram it into a storage locker all by myself.

"Name?" the ticketer asks. He's around my age, nineteen or twenty, Black, with his official hat jauntily perched sideways on his head.

"Vanessa Near," I tell him, handing over my identification papers and my ticket.

"Purpose of travel?"

"Mail delivery."

He glances at my suitcases and snorts. "If they fixed the mail system, this boat company would go broke the next day."

I laugh. "Good thing no one in power cares about corruption."

He snorts. "You heard the latest on the Mayor?"

"How she's been running a sweatshop using kidnapped children?"

"No, no, that was last week."

I rack my brain. "The jail time?"

"No, no." He leans forward. "Apparently she keeps a violent Nightmare! On a leash! Like an evil attack dog but with more teeth. It's a pterodactyl or something."

I cringe, remembering the man who'd been carried away by a pterodactyl-like monster earlier today. Maybe it was the Mayor's pet. That's probably why no one shot it down.

The worst part is, I'm not even surprised. Of course the Mayor has a pet pterodactyl that randomly eats citizens. At this point, I don't even consider this an odd thing to happen in Newham.

"Let me guess," I say. "Nightmare Defense just looks the other way because she's good for their budget."

He gives a full-body shrug, as if to say *What are you gonna do?* "Doesn't most of the money for Nightmare Defense end up in the pockets of the higher-ups anyway?"

"True." Tax dollars earmarked for any public service tended to get "lost" along the way. Kind of like people's mail. "Election coming up soon, though."

"Yeah. Not impressed by any of the candidates."

I wave my hand. "Wait until we're closer. At least half of them will be assassinated before elections. I never even look until a day or two before."

The ticketer nods sagely. "Wouldn't be Newham without a bit of friendly political assassination."

He pronounces Newham like *Noom*, a sure sign he was born and raised here. Unlike me, who pronounces it the country way, *New-ahm*.

The ticket salesman punches my ticket. "Have a safe trip."

"Thanks."

Corruption, assassination, fraud—none of that surprises the people of Newham. I think we'd be more surprised if we had an honest politician. Now those are scary. What are they planning? Why are they even running if they don't want to use the office for personal gain?

I wheel my suitcases up the gangplank with effort. The wood of the plank is pitted and the wheels don't want to go over it.

Finally, I get them all up on the top of the deck and pause to wipe the sweat from my brow. The sun has almost completely set, and the smooth, polished wood of the top deck gleams red in the final dying light. I couldn't see the whole boat from shore—too many buildings in the way.

But here, on the top deck, I can see it's even bigger than I thought, stretching multiple blocks in each direction. It's massive, practically an island in itself. I'd always known it was big—it had to be, to transport so many people across and all their luggage and have room for a restaurant and beds and private rooms—but this is another level. It's like the whole Friends of the Restful Soul building has been tipped on its side and is floating.

The last hints of sun fade, and the only natural light comes from the moon rising over the water. I heave a breath, steeling myself.

Then I wrestle the suitcases toward the lockers.

The second level, just below the main deck, is completely full of lockers, end to end. The entire floor. I suppose it makes

44

sense, since half the people who take this boat are transporting mail or other packages.

Naturally, all the floor-level lockers are taken. I'm standing there, wondering how I'm going to lift three cases I can barely drag into the second level of lockers, when someone interrupts me.

"Need some help?"

He's my age, white, a few inches taller than me. He's wearing a black button-up shirt with the top button undone, showing a hint of collarbone, and black slacks. He has a couple of leather bracelets around each wrist and a silver ring on his left hand. His thick black hair has been slicked back, and his eyes are heavily lined with black eyeliner, which makes the green of his eyes striking in contrast.

He's definitely here for the party aspect of this boat.

"Sure do," I reply. "I can't lift these into the locker."

He grins, a charming, flirty smile. "Let me help."

I don't dissuade the flirting because frankly I need the help, and if I tell him I'm not interested, he might be a dick and walk away. He might not, but why take the risk?

Together we haul the suitcases into the locker. He's stronger than he looks because I'm pretty sure he's taking most of the weight and he hasn't even broken a sweat. He doesn't look that muscular at a glance, which shows how much I know.

I close the locker and lock it with the double-key lock that the Director gave me. It's a heavy-duty thing. Emphasis on the heavy. It's a relief to get it out of my pocket.

The boy leans over and touches my shoulder. "Hey, so—"

45

I jerk away, and his hands hover over empty air.

My heart races in my chest, and for a moment, the fear rises up, threatening to swallow me. It insists that he was attacking me, that I can't get too close to anyone, you never know who's already a Nightmare—or who will turn into one.

I force out a long, calming breath. This is something the Friends were good at. Helping me recognize when a reaction is overblown, when my instincts are working too hard to keep me safe.

"Sorry." I force myself to stand still and not lean away. "I don't like it when people touch me."

"No, that's my bad." He raises his hands, palms outward. "I shouldn't have assumed."

Well, at least he's not being a dick about it.

"Thanks for helping me with the suitcases," I say.

"It was no problem." He smiles again, but it's more guarded now. "I'm going to head up to top deck. Maybe I'll see you there?"

I shrug. "Maybe."

He'll probably see me, but I likely won't be talking to him. I'm not looking for that kind of a good time, and he definitely is. He has the aura.

He seems to sense it too because he gives me one last smile and heads away without a backward glance.

I head the opposite direction, into the depths of the boat.

As I walk past the portholes, I realize we've already cast off. I hadn't even noticed.

The waves lap at the side of the boat, and the cityscape looms in the distance, large and towering, a jagged forest of brick and iron glowing against the black night sky. But it gets smaller the farther away we go, the streetlights and neon-lit buildings breaking apart in the mist, the light scattering until everything is just a blur of color in the distance, like an auto taillight as it drives away.

I rest my chin in my hands as I look through the porthole and it gets farther and farther away until it's nothing but a faint, eerie glow on the horizon. Then, it finally disappears.

I swallow heavily. I haven't left the city since I moved there after what happened to Ruby. There's something about leaving, about watching it disappear on the horizon, that makes it seem so small when, in my head, it's so very big, so all-encompassing. I already miss the narrow maze of alleys and the tall brick facades. The atmosphere as I walk down the streets, that feeling of security. The knowledge that I know what I'm doing, I'm in familiar territory. I'm in my element.

Out here, on the boat, everything is unfamiliar. It's a small adventure. It's not bad because I know I'll go back.

But what if I can't?

If I haven't figured out a more permanent solution to my fear, I don't think the Director will let me stay.

I need to either conquer my fears or find something I can do at the Friends that doesn't trigger them. And I've already tried every job they have.

Which means I have to actually deal with my fears.

The problem is, I *know* my reactions are overblown. I *know* not all my fears are justified. And even the ones that *are* don't change the fact that we live in a world full of Nightmares. I have to be able to stay calm enough to call for help when I need to. I have to be able to pull the fire alarm. People's lives could depend on it.

I know all this. I do.

But it doesn't seem to matter in the heat of the moment. My brain short-circuits, the panic takes over.

I'm a liability.

I'll be a liability at any job I take.

Unless I can find a way to cope, I'm going to lose my home, my safe space, and be left to fend for myself. I have to figure out a way to fix this. I have to overcome these fears.

Yeah. If only it were that easy.

I sigh, leaving the porthole behind to explore the rest of the boat.

The lower decks are full of private rooms and one large floor full of beds you can rent by the hour, which I steer clear of. I make a hasty retreat to the deck above. The halls are plastered with Nightmare Defense recruitment posters featuring Charlie Chambers, the golden-haired hero who killed the Great Sea Dragon. He's winking at people while strangling a snake that's probably supposed to be a dragon, the slogan beneath reading: "Anyone can become a hero! Even you!"

The next floor has a theater—naturally, it's overpriced. I don't think I have enough pocket change, but I ask the attendant if I can duck my head in to see what they're playing in case I want to scrape around and see if I have the coins. He just shrugs, which I take as a yes, and slip my head behind the curtain.

They're showing that vampire film I saw the poster for.

On the large screen, in black-and-white, a tall corpse-white man with slicked-back black hair and a wide, toothy smile with prominent fangs is grasping the arms of a slim blond girl with pouty lips and huge eyes. The man playing the vampire must be in his forties at least, but the girl he's grasping in his arms looks younger than me.

Based on the swelling music and the steamy looks the actors are giving each other, this is supposed to be romantic. The age contrast just makes it feel predatory.

"Oh, Dracuvlad!" the girl moans, her throat bared.

"I want you so much. I *need* you," Dracuvlad says, leaning into her, fangs gleaming. "I can't stop myself."

My skin crawls at his words. He *can* stop. He's in control of his own actions. It's not that he can't.

It's that he *won't*.

Because he cares about his own satisfaction more than he cares about this girl's right to her own body. He only cares about what *he* wants.

It's revolting that's portrayed as romantic.

I slip away from the theater before I have to see any more, rubbing my arms as though I can scrub away the slimy sensation those few seconds of movie have left on my skin.

Eventually I end up back on the deck, where the party is just getting started.

The music is loud, thrumming through my bones. There's a massive horn attachment to the boat's record player, and the sound blares across the boat so loud it can probably be heard back in the city. They're playing a fast song, something about a man diving out a window to escape his lover's wrath. Or maybe to escape his lover who turned into a Nightmare? It's hard to tell.

People are crowding around, laughing and dancing and singing. A lot of them are holding radium-covered glow sticks that light up the night, and the massive on-deck bar has a line that looks more like a swarm.

I head to the railing, as far from the partiers as I can, and look out over the water. It's surprisingly windy out, and the air smells like salt and dead fish. It's a strangely pleasant smell. I kind of like it.

I turn back to the boat to watch the people dancing. A part of me wants to go dancing with them too, to let my body free, to move with the flow of the music.

But I'm afraid.

What if there are contagious Nightmares in the crowd and I end the night with fish scales?

What if there are predatory Nightmares in the crowd, and they spike my drink and I end up unconscious, to be dragged away and devoured?

I swallow, looking down at my gloved hands. I ball them into fists.

I'm being stupid again. I can't let fear dictate my whole life. Priya is right—I need to face this.

I take a deep breath. A dance seems like a good, easy first step. I'm afraid. But the risk is, statistically speaking, low. I can just go in, dance for five minutes, and leave.

Exposure therapy, they'd call that in the Friends.

I can do this.

I take a step, then hesitate.

Maybe . . . maybe I'll watch for a moment first. Just until the end of the song.

Yeah. That's fine.

The partiers are drinking what are supposed to be nonalcoholic drinks—because, you know, prohibition, Nightmares, et cetera—but I would bet money are actually spiked. The people certainly dance like they've lost their inhibitions.

At the edge of the dance floor, the boy with the green eyes and slicked-back black hair is flirting with a redheaded girl wearing a crown of fake flowers in her hair. She's tipped her head back to laugh, and he's watching her with bedroom eyes.

Yep, I was right. He's definitely out for *that* kind of a good time tonight. And the girl he's dancing with seems to be very interested in the same thing, running her hand over his chest and giving him bedroom eyes right back.

The girl turns her head just as a server comes by with a silver tray. The boy doesn't notice until the silver is almost touching him, and then his eyes widen and he flinches away so violently, he knocks down the person behind him.

I freeze.

He's apologizing to the person he bumped into, and waiter and the tray are gone. No one else noticed.

He was afraid of the silver.

Humans aren't afraid of silver.

My breathing comes shallow and fast. My eyes flick up, to the full moon high above us. He's not any of the were-wolf Nightmare varieties, because they're all wolves right now. There's a particularly pernicious strain of contagious Nightmare worms that burrow into humans like a cocoon and burst from them, and they hate silver too. But they also hate salt water, and we're on a boat on an entire ocean of salt water, so that seems unlikely too.

I flip through my extensive catalogue of knowledge on contagious Nightmares, but silver is a common deterrent for a lot of Nightmares that were inspired by fear of folk-legend monsters.

That's of course assuming he is a strain of contagious Nightmare and not an original one, dreamed up just by him. Impossible to predict what he is then.

He's smiling at the girl, whispering something to her. She grins back at him, expression coy, and tugs him away from the crowd, toward the deck below, and the privacy of the now-deserted locker rooms.

He takes her hand and follows, his skin glowing in the night.

As they walk, they pass a brown girl wearing a mirrored dress. The mirrors on the dress reflect the people around her in a swirl of distorted color.

But they don't reflect the boy.

They reflect the girl he's with—her red hair and flowers are broken up into a thousand scattered shards on the bright mirrors.

But there's no sign of the black-clad boy in the reflections. My breath catches. I know exactly what he is.

There's only one kind of Nightmare that is averse to silver and doesn't show up in mirrors.

He's a vampire.

And he's going to lure that girl away and kill her.

5

There are twelve different known strains of Nightmares based on vampires.

People have a *lot* of different myths with vampires, and they've shifted and changed over the years too. It doesn't help that people make up new shit all the time.

Which means that every time someone's worst nightmare is becoming a bloodsucking monster, the vampire they become is different.

Of the strains, the only one people care about wholesale eradicating is strain eleven, which turns other people into vampires with a bite. Which means that if they're not contained, you end up with a mess like the outbreak on Creekwood Island ten years ago, and Nightmare Defense bombed that island right back into the ocean.

This boy isn't strain eleven—they don't have an aversion to silver.

The rest of the strains are subject to the same policy that applies to all other Nightmares—it's taken on an individual basis. It's not illegal to be a Nightmare. It's not even illegal to be a dangerous Nightmare. It's only when you commit a crime—say, drinking someone's blood and dumping their dead body over the side of the boat—that Nightmare Defense gets involved.

The problem is, vampires are notorious for murdering people and then bribing their way out of the consequences.

Some strains of vampirism tend to more violence than others, but by and large, they're all monsters. It's one of the things they have in common with each other, along with fangs, speed, and incredible healing.

And of course, they all drink human blood to survive.

After that, it gets complicated. Strains seven, eight, and twelve are weakened by garlic. Strains one, three, and seven melt when sprinkled with holy water. Strains six, nine, and twelve need to ask for an invitation for entering the house, but public places don't count, except for with strain nine.

So yeah, complicated.

But only one strain has both an aversion to silver and doesn't have a reflection.

Strain four.

It appeared about seventy years ago. We even know who the originator was, which isn't always the case. It began with man named Hugh Billings. Before his Nightmare, he'd been a "manly man," the kind who had a collection of firearms and used them to shoot men who didn't conform to his sweaty ideas of masculinity.

After he'd become his worst nightmare, he'd renamed himself Valentine Valence, exclusively worn lace and courtly foppish clothes, and gone on a debauched sex-and-blood spree across the country, where he'd turned every beautiful person he could find into a "child of the night" before getting staked by a sex shop owner for trying to avoid payment.

He's been the subject of dozens of plays, films, penny novels, and adult toys. But among the lurid details, people overlook that he killed dozens, and so did most of those he turned.

My hands grip the railing behind me so hard I'll probably find bruises tomorrow.

The vampire boy is twirling the girl now, and they're laughing and spinning toward the door to below decks.

A place where no one will see them. Where no one will stop him.

Strain four is known for luring their victims in with lust, and once they've eaten their fill, they leave the bodies to bleed out in the dark.

They're also supernaturally strong. No wonder he found it so easy to lift my heavy suitcases into the locker.

A chill slides up my spine.

Was I supposed to be tonight's victim?

My breathing starts to speed up, short and sharp and too fast and oh God, I was nearly that girl, it could have been me, I—

Stop.

I force myself to take a long deep breath. I'm okay. He doesn't have me. He isn't going to hurt me.

But he's probably going to hurt that girl.

My eyes rove over the party, looking for someone, anyone, to help. But there are no phones on a boat. No fire alarms

56

either, and nowhere to go if there were.

Every ship is supposed to have a security crew, but I can't see them anywhere, and the clock is ticking. That girl doesn't have long before he kills her. I need to do something, and I need to do it *now*.

I stay frozen by the edge of the boat.

I stare at the empty doorway where they disappeared. My hands are shaking and my breath is coming in uneven gasps. I know I need to do something, anything, but the fear has slithered into my heart and it's keeping me still.

I wish I were Priya. Priya wouldn't hesitate—she'd just charge in there, weapons out, excited grin on her face.

But I'm not Priya.

I'm a coward.

My jaw tightens, and for a moment, I'm back in my childhood home, hiding in the cupboard as I listen to my father's bones crunch and crack, the slurping sound as the giant spider that was once my sister sucks the marrow out.

No.

I can't keep living like this, always hiding when the monster comes out. I left Priya to fend for herself against that Nightmare, and it turned out all right, because she's Priya and she's unstoppable.

But this girl doesn't even know she's with a monster.

If I don't go warn her, I'm condemning her to death.

There's no time to get help, and I don't see anyone around except partiers, and most don't look like they can stand straight, never mind fight off a vampire.

Either I do something or that girl dies.

This is it.

The moment of truth.

I can tell myself whatever I want to get out of dancing. It doesn't matter at the end of the day if I danced for five minutes. No one cares except me.

But this is different. I can't let the fear rule me this time.

I take a deep breath and force myself to take a step forward. I don't want to be the kind of person who's so busy cowering in the cupboard she can't even be bothered warning everyone else about the monster. I don't want to be so paralyzed by my fear that I can't act to save someone's life.

So I force myself forward, breathing shallow, muscles tight. I scramble at my belt for the pepper spray I keep there. It works well on pretty much anything with eyes.

I can't take a vampire down, but maybe I can get that girl out of there.

Then we can both run.

I walk stiffly through the door, my whole body tense, ready to run at any moment. Electric lights line the halls as I descend from the main deck to the lower level, and every step I take rings too loud, too ominous, like I'm descending into a horror movie.

I should run. I want to run.

I stop on the stairs, jaw clenched, my mind telling me desperately to flee.

I keep going.

The soft whisper of voices, a man's slow and languorous,

a woman's high and fluttering with laughter.

She's still alive. I can do this. I just need to warn her. That's it. Warn her and run.

At the bottom of the stairs, the lockers loom large on either side of me. One corridor heads toward the front of the ship, under the partiers. It's well lit, and I can see all the way to the end.

No one's there.

I turn the other way, down toward the back of the ship. My steps are too loud for comfort, and I try not to breathe too heavily as I pace away from the thrumming music above me, along the long hallway of lockers.

I walk and walk until I feel like I must have walked halfway back to the city, when I reach a massive steel door.

I hesitate, taking one final deep breath, and open it.

It leads outside. A long, skinny strip of ship sticking out in front of us like a spike or some sort of strange ship tail. We're far away from everyone else. It's the perfect place for privacy because no matter how loud you screamed, no one would hear you.

The two of them are there.

She's got her back pressed against some sort of beam—a support? Tall thing I can't really see in the dark that looks like part of the boat—and he's kissing her, his body molding to her form. She's running her hands through his hair and making appreciative noises while his hands have settled around her hips.

I step outside.

The girl sees me first and she pulls away from the boy. "Um. Oh. Uh, did you need something?"

The vampire pulls back to look at me too, his carefully slicked hair all mussed and mouth smeared with her lipstick. "Oh, it's you. Did you need help getting something out of your locker?"

My mouth is dry, and they're both staring at me expectantly. I didn't anticipate how incredibly awkward this would be.

The fear is sliding its fingers over my chest, stealing the breath from my lungs, so it takes me a few uncomfortable heartbeats to get the words out.

"Nightmare," I croak.

The boy stiffens and his eyes widen, the light from the hallway reflecting on them and making them seem to glow.

The girl freezes. Her eyes are on mine as I slowly shift my gaze to the boy she's with.

She gets it immediately.

"Where's the Nightmare?" the boy asks, his voice a little high as he looks around, trying to feign misunderstanding. "On deck?"

The girl has slid away from him in that moment, and she makes like she's stumbling in shock, but it takes her several steps away from him.

Our eyes meet.

She makes a run for it, darting toward me as fast as she can go, fear in her eyes.

The vampire, realizing he's been caught, stiffens. He turns to run, but there's nowhere to go except off the side of the boat. His head whips around, as though looking for another ship to leap onto.

The girl races past me, back inside the ship. She doesn't even stop to thank me.

I try to follow her. But the fear has frozen me again, and I'm stuck, my heart racing, the panic filling me. He's right there—he's going to turn around and he's going to realize the only way he survives this is if he gets rid of the witnesses. He's going to kill me and I need to move, to run, but I'm stuck, my feet rooted to the floor, my muscles completely locked.

It figures. Now that I'm at the stage where I *can* actually run, my stupid body decides it's time to freeze up.

The door bangs closed behind the girl with a heavy thud, and the noise is enough to startle me forward, loosening my frozen muscles. The spell is broken, and I propel myself backward, to the door, scrabbling for the handle.

I twist it. It doesn't open.

I scream, tugging it, again and again, trying to rip the door open with the sheer power of my terror, rattling the handle like I can tear it off and crawl through the hole it leaves behind.

The door doesn't budge.

I'm trapped outside with the Nightmare.

6

I'm trapped.

My mind can't process it, won't accept it. I scrabble like a wild animal at the door, no thoughts, only panic. I can't be here. I can't die like this. The one time I try and get over my own fears to help someone else and I end up locked out with the Nightmare I was trying to rescue her from?

It's not *fair*.

One of my nails rips as I claw at the door seam. Blood runs down my hand, sparking an even worse panic, because now he can probably smell my blood, which will make him hungrier and even more likely to kill me.

I'm crying now, but I don't care. All I know is the desperate rattling of my heart and the scratching in my mind, like a rat in a cage, desperate to escape.

"Hey."

His voice is close—too close. Oh God, why is he so close? I scramble away, jerking from the door and scuttling backward across the deck like a crab. He's staring at me, his brows drawn.

I hit the edge of the ship and try to continue backward,

as though if I push hard enough against the side of the ship, I can warp the fabric of the universe and make more space between me and the boy.

But I can't. There's nowhere left for me to go.

My throat is choked, and I can't seem to get enough breath even though my chest is heaving as I suck in air.

"I was going to ask if you were a Nightmare hunter," he says slowly. "But I think you've already answered that question for me."

I stare at him, eyes wide and wild. He's toying with me. He's one of those sadistic ones, playing with his food. I don't know if it's better that I have more time or worse because now I have to suffer my terror longer.

I make a small choked sound.

No. I'm not dying here. I can't run. I have to fight back.

"I—I am a Nightmare hunter!" I snap, fumbling at my belt for my pepper spray. "And you better not come any closer or you'll regret it!"

He stares at me blankly for a moment.

"Okay," he finally says, his voice slow and patient. He raises his hands so I can see them. "I'll stay over here. It's all right."

I have the worst feeling that he's humoring me. That he can see exactly how terrified I am, and he's just letting me have my delusions of power. I feel small and weak and utterly pathetic.

"I'm not going to hurt you," he says slowly, like he's talking to a skittish alley cat.

I keep my pepper spray up. "Forgive me if I don't believe

that, given that you lured that girl out here."

He sighs heavily and rubs one temple. "I wasn't going to hurt her either."

"Oh yeah, then what were you doing out here?"

He gives me a look like I should have figured that out already. "We were just going to have some fun."

"Fun for you," I point out. "I doubt it would be fun for her having her blood sucked out."

He rolls his eyes, the motion so dramatic it's clear even in the semidark. "I wasn't going to *eat* her." He pauses. "Well. Not *that* way."

It takes way too long to figure out what he means.

When I do, my face flames scarlet.

"You're just trying to throw me off by saying dirty things," I snap.

He snorts. "If I were going to do that, I'd have said the part of my anatomy I was hoping to be using tonight wasn't my teeth."

I choke.

"See?" He nods as I reel in awkward horror. "Much more effective at throwing people off."

I'm pretty sure my face is so hot you could roast a kebab on it. Priya wouldn't be thrown off by this. She'd probably have a dirty joke to sling right back at him.

But I'm not Priya. As much as I wish I were.

"Look." The boy leans against the door. "I just want to get to Palton, same as everyone else on this boat."

"And maybe eat someone on the way."

He runs a hand over his face and looks up at the sky as

though asking it for patience.

"You know what? Think what you want. I don't care." He turns to the door. "I'm going to rip this stupid door open, and then I'm going to go back inside and hide out until the boat arrives. You can stay out here or hide in the security room, being afraid for no reason, I don't care."

That hits closer to home than I want to admit. Am I being irrational? Am I letting my fear cloud my judgment again?

Or is he just gaslighting me?

I can't even tell anymore.

He grabs the door handle and wrenches.

It doesn't open.

He stares at it as though he's never encountered a door that wouldn't open for him. Who knows? He's pretty and monstrously strong, so maybe he hasn't.

He tugs the door handle again. It doesn't budge.

Swearing, he braces his legs on either side of the door and then yanks, muscles straining, jaw clenched.

The door stays firmly closed.

"Oh, come on!" he yells, kicking it. "What is this made out of? Super steel? Why do you need a door like this on your boat? This is a damn safety hazard!"

My breathing has evened out. It's going to be okay. Enough time has passed—that girl should be bringing security. They'll arrive any minute now, open the door, capture the vampire, and I'll be okay. As long as he stays occupied with the door, I just need to wait this out.

But it's odd—security really should be here by now.

What's taking them so long?

A slow chill slides up my spine. That girl went to security, right? She wouldn't just run off back to the party and not tell anyone about the dangerous Nightmare, would she? No one would be that callous.

Except me.

Fuck.

The vampire boy seems to be thinking along the same lines. He runs a hand through his hair, messing up his carefully gelled spikes even further. "Well. We might be stuck out here until the boat gets close enough to jump off and swim to shore."

What? No. That's hours away.

I can't stay here for hours, terrified that at any moment he's going to decide he wants a snack. And there's no one here to stop him, and as tightly as I cling to my pepper spray, I'm not actually sure it'll do more than buy me a few minutes.

A few minutes to do what, though? Jump off the damn boat?

Real helpful.

He sighs heavily. "Would you please stop looking at me like that? I've *told* you, I'm not going to hurt you."

My smile is sickly. "Sure, sure. But you don't mind if we just, ah, stay separate, you know? I'm over here. You're over there . . ."

He pinches the bridge of his nose. "Fine. But you don't have to crouch there with your can of pepper spray like a cornered feral animal."

"I'm good."

"It's a long ride to shore, and your arm's going to get sore soon."

"I'll be fine," I say, even though my wimpy arm is already sore.

He looks at me like he doubts it but clearly isn't planning on fighting a pointless fight on this. He turns back to the door, examining it like it's a puzzle and he only needs to figure out the single clue that will make it open. He pokes at the smooth exterior, the hinges inside and unreachable.

I look around, my eyes skittering nervously. Maybe I can find a better weapon. Some other way out of here. This can't be the only way back into the main part of the boat. It's just not practical.

Then I see it. A ladder.

There's a ladder on the side of the boat.

Maybe it leads to something. Another entrance?

My heart rate slows, a tiny piece of calm coming over me. This could be my way out. I don't have to stay here with a ticking time bomb just waiting for me to let my guard down so he can attack.

Of course, he doesn't need to wait for me to let my guard down, not really. Even with my guard up, I'm probably not much of a fight.

But that's not the point.

The point is that I've found a way out.

I'm just leaning over, getting ready to crawl onto the ladder—

—when the boat blows up.

7

I've never been in an explosion before, and for the first few minutes, I have no idea what's happening.

What I piece together after is that I survived because I was pressed against the side of the ship. When it blew apart, the force of the explosion hit the wall and then shot it out into the ocean. I went with it because I was standing against it. So nothing slammed into me, which would have probably killed me, or at least broken my body badly. And the wall shielded me from the worst of the heat until I hit the water.

But in that first moment of the explosion, I don't know any of that.

One moment, I'm wedged in where the wall meets the side of the boat, eyeing the ladder to escape while the vampire curses out whoever designed the door to lock us outside.

The next, I'm in the air.

The wind is whipping past me, or I suppose I'm whipping past it.

The wall is smashed against my body, like I'm tied to the front of an out of control train, and all I can do is scream.

I can't even hear the scream. I can't hear anything at all except the roar. A deep, thundering sound that blocks out all other sounds. It's a combination of a gunshot, though a thousand times louder, and the sound of splintering wood and metal whistling through the air as it torpedoes into the sky.

It's hot.

Everything is so bright I have to close my eyes. Even closed, everything still glows so painfully I'm afraid I'll never be able to see again.

It's getting hotter.

Then, suddenly, I'm in the water.

Cold shocks my system, but instead of giving me sudden clarity or sharpening my mind like in the penny novels, it makes me even more disoriented.

The piece of metal is pressing down on me, pushing me into the depth with its weight, and even though I don't understand what's happening—my mind is foggy with panic and confusion and sheer shock—I know enough to know I need to get out from beneath this piece of metal before I'm propelled all the way to the bottom of the ocean.

My arms flail, and I find the edge of the scrap of metal and grip it to pull myself out from beneath the heavy rubble.

I bend and twist in the water, freeing myself as it sinks deeper, into the darkest depths that light will never reach.

Above me, the water is lit by a blazing inferno, a beacon calling me upward, giving me direction even though, beneath the water, shocked by the cold and lack of air, I've lost all sense of up and down.

The problem is, if I surface, I'll die in the flames.

If I stay under, I'll drown in the depths.

I'm in pain, I think, but I'm not sure, the world is ringing, and underwater, the silence sounds like noise and I can only tell up because of how bright and deadly it is, a swirling mural of red and orange.

I'm going to die here.

The certainty settles like a chain around my chest, choking the air out of me.

No, wait, that's the drowning. I'm drowning.

I choke, but that only lets more water in, and I scramble for the surface, flames be damned, but my clothes are heavy and wet, and my arms are weak, and I don't seem to be getting any closer.

Black spots dart through my vision, and my hands are reaching for the surface, but I'll never make it. Even without the metal wall weighing me down, I'm still sinking.

Something grabs the back of my shirt.

I try to scream, but only bubbles come out and I'm choking on water, gasping for air but only liquid comes in and then—

I surface.

Water pours from my mouth. My chest heaves, spasming like I'm both hiccupping and vomiting at the same time, a horrid, painful feeling as I expel water. I'm trying to breathe in but there's still too much water in me, and I choke it out, along with some spit and maybe some stomach acid.

It is possibly the most horrible feeling I've ever experienced.

I keep making choked sounds as I gasp in air, even though

my lungs are finally empty of water, and I realize I might be sobbing too.

I'm alive.

Water trickles down my cheeks and I can't even tell if it's because I'm crying or it's just my wet hair. I heave another half breath, half sob and let the tears of relief fall. I survived. I'm not dead. I don't know how, but I'm not dead.

The inferno is still going, rising high into the air, taller than the boat ever was. The flames lick upward and outward, nothing of the boat left except the ball of scorching light, so hot that even this far away, I can feel it baking my skin, hot enough that I might have a sunburn tomorrow.

I'm far enough from the blaze that I'm safe. Something has towed me away from certain death.

Or someone.

"What the fuck."

A soft whisper of a voice behind me, and I turn around to see who saved me from the brink of death.

It's the vampire.

He's staring at the inferno with massive, horrified eyes, the flames reflecting on his pupils like he's drinking the fire in, like it's burning its way right into his soul.

His hair is plastered to his scalp, all its styling gone, his eyeliner streaking down his cheeks now like black tears.

I scramble away, paddling in the water, trying to keep myself afloat while getting away from him. "You!"

"Me," he agrees, his eyes finally leaving the fire to look at me. "You're welcome. You know. For saving you from drowning."

My eyes narrow. "Hardly. I bet you only saved me to eat me later."

He gives me a flat, drowned-rat look. "Does it look like I'm eating you?"

It doesn't, but I'm not willing to concede this point, so I don't respond.

His eyes shift back to the boat, which has begun sinking into the water. It wasn't clear before, because the flames were so high and bright, but now the boat is halfway sunk because the flames are slowly lowering into the water and being snuffed out.

For a moment, I wonder if others survived, but the thought dies as fast as it comes. The flames have completely consumed everything that's still above the water. There's no chance anyone is left alive on that.

"I can't believe someone blew up the boat," he whispers. "Who blows up a *whole boat*?"

"It could have been an accident," I say, paddling in the lapping waves, trying to keep my head above the water. I'm lucky it's fall and the water isn't killing cold. "Maybe a gas tank rupture."

"Maybe," he replies, but it doesn't sound like he believes it.

If I'm being honest, I don't either. This is Newham, after all.

We watch the fire together in silence. The tongues of flame flick the air, desperate to find a safe place to land as the ship cracks and groans, slipping into the water and into the dark. When those flames reach the water, they're snuffed out, destroyed by their own greedy hunger.

As the flames dim and slow, sinking beneath the ocean, darkness returns to the world. I blink a few times, trying to adjust to the dimming light, but it doesn't work. I feel like my eyes have been burned by the brightness and they'll never be able to perceive light the same way again.

The last flame flickers out, and the only light left is the moon high above.

The vampire slips away into the water, silent and lithe as a shark.

"Where are you going?" I call, and I hate myself for the fear in my voice. I need to make up my mind whether I'm more afraid of him or of being alone.

But the problem is, I'm afraid of everything, so that's just a lost cause.

A few moments later, he returns with a chest-size piece of wooden rubble and a piece of twine that must have been thrown from the ship in the initial explosion.

"No other survivors." He shakes his head. "Not that I expected much . . ."

"Yeah." I don't question if he ate any survivors he found. Mostly because I saw that inferno and I don't believe there could be other survivors. "How the hell are we alive?"

He considers. "We were at the very far tip of the boat."

"And?"

"Maybe the explosion was on the other end. You know. Where all the people were." He shudders. "We were blown out onto the water by the force of the blast before the fire got us."

Goose bumps rise on my cold, damp skin. If I hadn't chased him down, if we hadn't been trapped outside, I'd also be—

No. Don't think about it.

"Here." He gives me the rope he's brought.

I blink. "What's this for?"

He rolls his eyes. "So I can tow you."

I just stare at him.

He sighs heavily, paddling forward on a piece of floating wood. There's no telling what it originally came from. He hands it to me.

"Get that under your chest so you're floating, and then hold on to the rope." He gestures to himself. "I tied the other end around my chest, so I'll tug you along as I swim."

My shocked mind finally catches up with reality. "Where are we going?"

He looks at me like I'm an idiot. "Shore?"

Yeah. I am an idiot.

I swallow. "But . . . won't there be rescue boats coming . . ."

He shakes his head. "It'll take them hours to get out here. Assuming they even know what happened."

"The boat exploded—they'll have seen it for miles!"

"Sure, but we're far enough from the city—from any land—that means they won't know what the light is. No one's going to assume the boat exploded."

I hate to admit it, but he's right. If rescue is coming, it'll be a while.

"Look, if you want to stay in the wreckage, I'll see if I can find you a bigger piece of debris to lie on," he says. "But I'm going to swim to shore. I can pull you along or not."

I can't swim to shore myself. No human could, not from this distance, unless they were a professional swimmer. He's right, I could be waiting a long time for rescue, and these waters aren't empty. There are sea Nightmares. And sharks. And Nightmare sharks.

But is going with a different Nightmare any safer?

He stares at me, waiting for my answer, his expression tired and his face streaked with black. He's probably planning to eat me when we get to shore, a snack to replenish his energy after a hard swim. I don't even have my pepper spray to fight him anymore.

But it's still better than being a sitting duck for sea monsters here.

"Okay," I say. "Take me with you."

"You sure?" he asks, brows raised. "I'm sure the sharks would be happy for you to stay."

I glare at him.

He smiles, a hint of tired amusement. "What's your name?"

"Ness."

"I'm Cy."

"Your name is *Sigh*?" My voice is incredulous, like this, of all things, is the strangest part of the day.

He sighs heavily, and suddenly the name really seems to suit him.

"It's short for Cyril."

"I'm sorry, did you say your full name was *Squirrel*?"

"*Sir*-rell. No Q!"

"How on earth do you get Sigh from Squirrel?"

"Well, what other nicknames do you see? Sir?"

He has a point. "What about Rill?"

"Like the penile dysfunction drug?"

Right. That.

"So where did Sigh come from, then?"

"My mother." He looks away. "She was from New England. So when she said my name, it sounded like Sigh-rill."

"That sounds like a better name than Squirrel."

"*Sir*rell."

"Who even picked your name?"

"My father." His expression shutters suddenly. "I'm named after him."

Ah. Hence the need for a nickname. No one wants to have the exact same name as their parent, whether they're on good terms or not. It's just weird. And parents who name their kid their own name are almost always pretentious assholes.

"Cy it is, then," I say. "It's nice to meet you."

He snorts. "You sure didn't think so earlier."

"Well, earlier the boat hadn't exploded and you hadn't generously decided to rescue me and tug me to shore."

And probably eat me when we get there. But I don't say that part. I'm not sure what I'm going to do about that yet.

He looks up at the moon, frowning. "Speaking of, we better get started. We have a long way to go."

He turns away and starts swimming. I grip the rope tightly, the piece of wood positioned just under my chest. He tugs me along behind him, pulling me away from the shattered remains of the boat.

My heart is loud with fear, but I force myself to breathe deeply.

It's okay. I don't have a plan now, but I have the whole trip to shore to figure one out.

8

I don't figure out a plan on the trip to shore.

I barely manage to hold on to the rope. My arms ache, and my body is sore all over, in places I'd never been sore before and had no idea how they'd gotten sore. Had I hit something as I was flying through the air? Had the blast broken some bones? Who knows? Definitely not me.

It's all I can do to cling to the rope and let myself be dragged to shore.

I don't even have the energy to be scared anymore. I'm too exhausted to care. If Cy turned around and ate me, I'd probably just lie there because I don't have the strength to put up a fight.

But he doesn't stop and eat me—he just keeps tugging me along, even though he must be even more exhausted than me.

My skin is clammy and pruning by the time we wash up on some random rocky beach. Pine trees line the shore, towering high and proud, as far as the eye can see. We're west of Newham, probably somewhere in the Timberwolf Forest, if I had to guess.

The shore isn't like the pictures in the films or papers. No sandy beaches we can slowly and majestically walk up on. No, the coast is all massive boulders, jagged and slippery with water and a green moss that feels like the slime that forms on milk when you forget it for a few weeks after it's gone bad.

My numb hands scrabble at the stone, trying to find purchase, but I keep sliding back down and banging my knees on more rocks as I try to get out of the surf.

Cy has to scramble to the top of the boulders and then reach down and haul me up. It makes me feel even more weak and useless, but I don't reject the help because, frankly, I'm not getting out of the water without his assistance.

When we finally make it over the boulders, we're crunching on the fallen pine needles at the edge of the forest. The trees loom above us, dark and unforgiving, with no sign of civilization anywhere near.

Cy looks as dead on his feet as I feel, his wet hair hanging limp and his shoulders slumped in exhaustion. He rubs his eyes, smearing the last traces of his eyeliner so he looks bruised, like someone's given him two black eyes.

I need a plan of action before he remembers he's supposed to eat me. But my brain is mush, all washed up and worn out from the explosion and journey. If you asked me to count to ten, I'm not really sure I could do it. I'd probably get to five and forget what a number was.

Cy flops against a tree, just breathing, staring vacantly ahead. He looks on the verge of complete collapse, as though he'll just fall asleep against that tree for a thousand years, like in a fairy tale.

I stumble away from him, scanning the forest floor, looking for a weapon. I need to get ahead of him. I need to get my weapon before he strikes.

There.

I rustle in the undergrowth and haul out a massive branch that I can use as a club. It's so heavy I nearly fall over.

I should have lifted more weights. Priya is always working out in her spare time, and she's invited me dozens of times to join her. If I survive this, I'm going to take her up on it next time.

"What are you *doing*?" Cy asks, his voice layered with utter exhaustion.

I spin around, branch raised in case he's attacking. But he's still lying against that tree, looking at me with the most defeated, bone-tired expression. As if the exhaustion has leeched into his soul.

"I'm defending myself," I mumble, equally exhausted.

This branch is so heavy, I sway on my feet and then straighten myself.

He raises his head to the night sky and whispers, "For the last time, I'm not going to eat you!"

I stare at him and he stares back, and I don't know that I believe him, but this branch really is too heavy to hold for long and I'm really damn tired, so I put it down.

He lets out a huff and rises slowly, leaning against the tree for support. He runs a hand through his dripping hair, pushing it out of his face, and turns away from me. He putters along the edge of the forest, his feet crunching against the twigs and acorns on the ground.

I stumble after him. "Where are you going?"

"I'm looking for animal trails. Or human trails. Or any trails."

"How the hell can you see anything in this?"

He turns back to me, eyebrows raised. "Really?"

I flush. Right. Vampire. Good eyesight. "Yeah, okay, look, I got blown up and dragged through the ocean. It's not really all pistons firing in my head right now."

He stares at me dead-on. "I can tell."

I glare at him. "You're an asshole."

He turns away. "Someone's sure grateful about their life being saved."

"I'm still not convinced you did that for me."

He sighs again. Dramatically.

Yes, I decide. It really is a very appropriate name.

I'm not sure how long we walk the shore before we find a trail. I don't know how to tell time in the dark, and every moment feels like an eternity because I'm so tired. But I also often zone out and find that we've been walking for ages and I haven't even noticed. Time does weird shit when you're this exhausted.

But we do eventually find a trail. It's packed down in a way that implies it's a human trail, not a deer one. But it's also old and overgrown and hasn't been used in a very long time.

We follow it anyway.

It's almost dawn and Cy is getting visibly concerned about the impending sunlight when we finally reach the end of the trail.

And the cabin.

It's a small but fancy cabin. The patio has a once-magnificent, now-stooped-and-rotting trellis and a firepit with decomposing wooden chairs around it. Vines have grown up the side wall of the house, and the ground around it is being reclaimed by the forest.

It looks like, at one point, it was a vacation cabin. They were popular for a long time after the Nightmares first started a century ago, especially before Helomine was put in the water supply in Newham. Rich people would escape the city and the Nightmares there for the relative peace and safety of the forest.

This one probably hasn't been used in at *least* a decade, if not longer. Which means that there's no one here to help us.

But also no one to stop us breaking in.

I stumble toward it, my wet clothes sloshing, with the eagerness of a puppy looking for treats.

We walk around to the front of the cabin, where a rusting auto sits on the road. For a moment, my heart lifts when I see it, thinking we can drive back to civilization, but the hope vanishes as fast as it comes.

The auto is destroyed.

Time has corroded it beyond use, and the front metal is warped and bent. A sapling has twisted through one of the tires and is coming out the window, and a bird's nest is wedged in the cracked driver's door. If we tried to start that auto, best case, nothing happens, worst case, the expired gas blows up.

And the last thing we need is another explosion.

I walk up to it anyway, peering inside, hoping that something useful will appear. But everything has long degraded, and all I find is a metal talisman hanging over the mirror, a prayer against demons that was popular in that first decade when people thought that the Nightmares were people making deals with the devil or demons that had escaped hell.

No one thinks that anymore—mostly because all the groups that had, primarily fundamentalist Christians and the like, believed their faith would keep them safe and didn't take medicine to prevent dreams. So of course, they all eventually turned into Nightmares.

Nightmares didn't care how religious you were. They only cared that you dreamed.

Cy steps up onto the porch and rattles the cabin door. It doesn't open. He gives it a disgusted look and then rips the door handle right off the rotting wood.

"Now, that's how doors are supposed to work," he mutters, clearly still irritated by the door on the ship, even though it locking probably saved our lives.

The door swings inward, and we step inside.

It takes my eyes a moment to adjust to the dark, but when they do, I draw a sharp breath.

Bones litter the inside of the cabin.

Human bones.

"Are those . . ."

I can't finish my sentence.

"Bite marks," Cy says. "Something ate these people." He nods to the other side of the room. "Probably that."

Sprawled across a moldering couch, the skeleton of a monster is draped casually, as though it lay down for a nap and never woke up. Spines rise out of its back, massive and sharp, and its long, viciously clawed talons lie in a puddle on the floor.

But its skull is all too human.

"It looks like a family," Cy says, stepping deeper inside, making the fine layer of dust rise up from the floor and into the air like a cloud. "Someone became a Nightmare and then . . ."

He doesn't need to finish.

My hands are clenched into fists by my side, and I'm trying my best not to think of how similar this little cabin looks to the small house I grew up in. Trying not to think of how this awful scene mirrors so closely what happened when I was a child.

Trying not to remember the feeling of powerless terror that first moment I realized the monster rending my father apart piece by piece had once been my sister.

"Did no one ever find them?" I whisper, my voice hoarse.

What would have happened if no one had come for me?

I'd have starved, probably, tucked away in my hiding spot. My sister hadn't seen me. She'd killed our father and left the house, and then she'd gone out and murdered two more people before she'd been shot down by the local volunteer Nightmare Defense. They hadn't known who she was until the next day, when neither of us showed up for school and someone was sent to check on us.

I'd still been hiding under the cupboard, trembling and crying.

If no one had come and pulled me out of that cupboard . . . well, I suppose I'd still be there. Just like these people were still here. Maybe someone would have stumbled into our house and found my bones.

"I guess no one looked for them." Cy shrugs, unbothered. It's not like this is uncommon. "If the whole family came out here, maybe there was no one left to look. Or maybe no one knew where their cabin was."

I shift my feet and something crunches beneath my boot. Bones. Small bones.

A child's bones.

I shudder, a full-body thing. Those could have been my bones. If things had gone a little differently, they would have.

I step back, out onto the porch.

"I'm not going in there," I say. My voice is raspy but steady.

He looks up at me, exhaustion in his eyes. He doesn't seem to notice me acting any different than normal. "It's almost dawn—I'm not going anywhere else today. And you're dead on your feet. We need to rest."

"I'll rest on the patio."

He shrugs, too exhausted to care. "All right."

I'm so thirsty that I'm amazed I can still talk, but I can't bring myself to go inside, not even to see if there's water. After this long, I doubt it's safe to drink anyway. There are probably things living in it.

Cy searches the cabin, ducking into rooms and opening closets, and I try not to look at the bodies on the ground, the crime scene we've inadvertently walked into. I can't look at them and see anything but my own body.

I wrap my arms around myself and try not to shake.

"There's nothing here," Cy finally says. "No blankets, no food, no water. Everything's rotted."

My shoulders slump. Of course there isn't. I should have expected that.

Outside, the sun is starting to rise, painting the world behind me in orange and red. Cy narrows his eyes and then crawls into the closet.

"I'm going to sleep now," he tells me. "Please don't murder me while I'm asleep."

"That's my line."

"We all know who's been threatening people here and it's not me."

I give him a disgusted look but don't dignify him with a reply.

He closes the closet door firmly, blocking out the light and sealing himself away from me.

I turn around, away from the horrors of the cabin and toward the rotting auto in front of the house and the road beyond it. It's a wide gravel road, obviously where this family drove in from. I bet it leads to a real road. And from there to somewhere with a phone or a train or a car or some way back home.

If only I had enough energy to follow it.

Instead I crawl onto the porch, into the sunlight, where I know I'm safe in case Cy decides he wants a midday snack. A spot where I can't see the bodies of the Nightmare and its victim, can't be reminded of the horrible fate that befell the inhabitants of this house.

I curl up and glance worriedly back into the cabin, where Cy is sleeping. What will I do if he becomes a different Nightmare in his sleep?

People can only ever have one Nightmare, and then they're done. Which is a blessing and a curse—it means that once you've had your dream and become your worst nightmare, even if your worst nightmare changes, you can't be changed again. You're safe.

But that only applies to people who *had* a nightmare.

You don't need to have a nightmare to catch a contagious Nightmare, like vampirism. There's no limit to how many contagious Nightmares you can get either. You could be turned into a vampire *and* a werewolf *and* a zombie *and* have blue scales and any number of other things.

And then you could still have a nightmare and change into something much worse.

Since vampirism is a form of contagious Nightmare, Cy is as vulnerable in his sleep as I am to becoming something else.

Maybe I should offer him some of my pills. I reach into my pockets, but they're empty.

I have no pills.

They must have washed away in the water.

I swallow heavily, my heart beating a nervous rhythm. I should still be okay. It takes at least a day for the Helomine in the city water to go through your system, and that keeps the nightmares away just fine. I don't really need the other pills. They're just backup.

But fear slides through me all the same, clutching at my chest. I think of the Nightmare corpse, so close to me. Of my sister and her long, hairy spider legs, of blood on the floor.

I should stay awake. I shouldn't risk it.

But before the thought can finish, my eyes are closing, as if the effort of even keeping them open is more than my body can handle right now.

And I sleep.

This time, I dream.

9

The nightmare begins where everything always begins and
ends for me.

The night my sister became a monster.

It doesn't start with the night itself. It starts in another
memory, one from a few weeks before she died.

My sister, Ruby, and I are sitting out on the patio in the
summer heat. The air is muggy and ripples like a mirage,
making the long driveway up to our small wooden house
shift and change, becoming strange and windy, like another
realm.

Ruby is feeding the birds. She has a row of carefully
tended birdhouses hanging on the porch, and all the local
birds come and roost there, pecking for seeds and cawing
so loud. They're always causing a ruckus—our father hates
them. They poop on everything, and he's constantly making
Ruby scrub it off the entryway.

Our mother had started the birdhouses, so Ruby tells me,
but I don't remember. I don't have a lot of memories of our
mother. She died when I was little. Nightmare attack—one

of the children a few towns over had turned into a giant ten-story-tall lizard he'd seen on television. He smashed through dozens of towns before Nightmare Defense contained him.

Ruby smiles at me in the memory, her expression soft and gentle. Her long, dark brown hair is braided down one side of her face, and she wears a white summer dress.

I take some birdseed and fill up one of the birdfeeders. A small blue bird lands on my hand and pecks seeds from it.

"Ness," the memory of Ruby says to me, but I've forgotten what she sounded like, and so even though I hear her words, I don't hear her voice.

I wish I could. I'd give anything to hear her voice again.

"Yeah?" My own voice I remember, small and childish.

Ruby strokes my hair lovingly. "Are you going to miss me?"

My lower lip trembles in the dream memory, but the pain I feel is all too real. How much more those words hurt now that she's gone forever.

"No," I tell her, but it's a lie. Ruby was my whole world. Of course I was going to miss her.

"I'll be back every summer," she tells me, still stroking my hair. "I know the idea of boarding school is scary, but this scholarship is a big opportunity for me."

I hated that scholarship, hated that it was going to take her away from me at the end of the summer. I'd even snuck into her room once to get rid of the scholarship letter, burn it into nothing and prevent Ruby from leaving me alone. I'd stared at that Newham Academy logo, an eagle with wings spread over a cityscape, for what felt like hours, trying to get the courage up to destroy it.

Eventually, I'd admitted defeat. I couldn't hurt my sister that way, even if it meant I'd be hurt.

Of course, it hadn't ended up mattering. She became a Nightmare before she ever got to go anywhere. It makes me a little ashamed, how much trouble I gave her over something she wanted so badly. Especially given that she never got the chance to actually live out her dream.

Ruby hugs me tight. "I'm going to miss you so much, my little Loch Ness monster."

I grip her back, sniffling into her shirt. "No you won't. I'm going to get a scholarship too, for next year! Just you wait!"

I don't know where this misplaced confidence came from. I was a terrible student even then.

Ruby laughs, stroking my hair. She kisses the top of my head.

"Of course you will," she says softly. "Nothing can tear us apart."

The scene cuts, jagged and sharp, like I'm watching a film and there's been a scene change, but the film roll is stuck for a moment on that in-between space, and the screen is black and white, white and black.

Suddenly, I'm inside our house. I haven't been there since Ruby died, and it's eerie to see how well I remember it. The small kitchen, with the square, wood table that tipped to one side. My and Ruby's jackets hanging on the coat racks. The oil lamp in the corner of the room, because no one had bothered extending the electricity this far out of the city.

I'm eleven years old, sitting at the table, humming to myself, small legs swinging. I'm also floating above the scene, watching it, as my current age. My view shifts and changes moment to moment, but it's not disorienting—it seems to make perfect sense in the dream.

My father is sitting across from child-me, an abacus on one side and stacks of paper spread across the rest of the table, doing whatever it is that adults do. I know better than to disturb him—he'll just go into one of his long-suffering lectures about how he has work to do, he has to make the month's budget or he's applying for a second job or some other adult thing. It's hard, raising two kids by yourself, and our father is absent even when he's here.

Ruby is the one who raised me, really. Maybe it's wrong, but even though the sound of my father being eaten alive has stuck with me my whole life, his death itself impacted me less than the fact that Ruby was the one who killed him.

That Ruby, my protector, my big sister, became a monster.

The dream shifts focus a little, darkening, focusing on the tableau of me and my father sitting at the kitchen table. Ruby is standing, talking to my father. This is the last conversation they'll ever have.

"You're still driving me to the school next week, right?" Ruby asks. She's been fussing over the scholarship plans all week, as though, as the date to leave for school approaches, she gets more and more obsessed with it. I caught her the other day letting the potatoes burn because she was so busy going through her scholarship paperwork for the billionth time.

"Of course!" Our father looks up from his abacus. "I wouldn't let you go alone."

"I could take the train," Ruby says with that tone that says she's an adult and can do things herself and doesn't need a parent hovering over her.

He gives her a stern look. "Ruby, you're thirteen. You're not taking the train to *Newham* alone."

He says the word *Newham* like one would say "Nightmare-infested den."

"Nick is loaning us his auto," our father continues. "Maybe we'll even have time for some sightseeing before I drop you off!"

"Sightseeing!" Ruby grins, her smile huge and bright. "Can we go to the top of the famous clock tower?"

Our father smiles back. "Of course!"

Ruby's eyes are alight, as though dreaming of all the wonderful things she'll get to see.

Things she never got to see.

The dream jerks and shifts, like the reels of memory have been sped up. Ruby is gone now. She always goes to bed first—she's one of those "early to bed, early to rise" people.

A small stack of pills sits by the kitchen sink in a bucket. Unlike in the city, we don't have Helomine in our water. The towns and villages that pepper the countryside need to use pills, and we've all been trained since birth to never forget to take medicine to prevent Nightmares.

Neither I nor my father even bothered to check the bucket of pills or ask Ruby if she'd taken her meds. Why wouldn't she? She'd never forgotten before.

But all it takes is once.

The first tap is soft, almost tentative, like the person tapping is unsure how much weight to put behind it. It's so soft I don't even notice it.

The second tap is heavier, more confident. More of a thud.

My father and I both raise our heads at the third tap, which is much louder, much heavier. Much angrier.

By the fourth thud, we're both on our feet because whatever is making those sounds is far too heavy. That's not a bird hitting the birdhouse or a tree branch knocking against the house.

It's something much bigger—and it's getting closer.

The fifth thud reveals a leg as it comes around the corner. Massive and hairy, almost as tall as my father and nearly as broad, the spider limb slides into the room, the rest of its body still concealed in the hall.

The hall where Ruby was supposed to be sleeping.

My father knows what has happened instantly, no pause, no moment of shock. I stand there stupidly wondering where Ruby is, why she isn't screaming or running or if she's actually sleeping through a giant spider invasion.

I don't really remember my father's voice either—it's been so long. But in this memory, for the first time in years, I hear him speak, the last word he ever spoke to me.

"Hide."

But I'm frozen, my eyes glued to that leg, held hostage by the terror, the knowledge of what lies on the other side and just how massive that body must be.

I don't remember how I got into the cupboard under the sink. I suppose I must have ripped everything out and crawled in, but I have no memory of this, and the nightmare doesn't provide it. It just glitches forward, to the point where I'm hiding under the sink, my knees tucked against my chest, my arms wrapped around my body, my teeth biting down on the fabric of my shirt to prevent myself making any sound that could give me away.

Crunch. Rip. Slurp.

The sounds of screaming have stopped. They stopped a while ago—sometime after the sound of shotgun fire cut out. My father kept a shotgun handy just in case we had a Nightmare attack, but I'd never heard him fire it before.

It hadn't seemed to do much.

Now all I hear are the sounds of eating.

The wet ripping as my father's limbs are torn off one by one. The crunch of his bones in the teeth that shouldn't exist in a spider. The smacking, sucking sound as it slurps down his juices.

I know how this ends. I know that the spider never sees me, that it crawls out the window and onto the porch and scuttles away. I know that it kills two more people before it's taken down.

But in this nightmare, I don't know that anymore. All I know is that I'm here, beneath the sink, and my father is being eaten just on the other side of the cupboard.

"It's no fun when you hide," a male voice whispers, and my head whips around, but there's no one here.

This isn't part of the memory.

Suddenly I'm not in the cupboard anymore. It's another cutaway, and now I'm in a blank void, completely alone. I'm not small and weak anymore—I'm my own age, my own self, wearing the same filthy clothes I am while awake.

The world around me coalesces, taking shape again. I'm standing in my childhood kitchen again.

It's empty.

My breathing is ragged, the memory of what happened fresh in my mind.

"Ness? Ness, help!"

My head whips around, toward the hall where the spider came from. It's been so long, and I don't recognize the voice anymore, but I know, deep in my bones, in a way I can't explain, that it's Ruby calling me.

My feet seem to move on their own, like I'm not in control of my body. I want to run, to escape before the horror begins again, but instead I walk to where she's calling for help, down that terrible hall the spider emerged from. The bedroom door is closed, and I press my hand flat to it. It slowly creaks open.

My sister lies trapped on the bed.

White mist roils around her like a swarm of flies. It's fractured and sharp looking, like it's not made of air but a swirling cloud of jagged, ground-up bones. It coils and shifts, and I catch a glimpse of her terrified face before it covers her again, writhing around her like something alive.

The bone mist buzzes as it coalesces around her left arm, densifying and hardening, focusing on that one place until it's a slick, beetle-like shell. Like it's built a bone carapace over her. My sister screams, back arching in agony, as her limbs crunch and bend.

And then she doesn't have an arm anymore—she has a spider leg.

She's still screaming.

My chest tightens like I'm being choked. I can't move. I can't scream. I can't even breathe.

"Is that supposed to be me?"

It's the voice from before. I turn my head slowly. I don't know what I expect—the voice is smooth and pleasant, but this is a nightmare, and anything is possible.

It's a boy.

He appears about my age, around nineteen, maybe a little older. He's taller than me, which isn't shocking—everyone is taller than me. He's shorter than Priya and Cy, so I suppose he's in the middle of the height spectrum. At first glance, he seems . . . normal.

But he's not.

His straight, white hair falls unnaturally smoothly, like it's spun spiderweb instead of hair. His skin is white, but it's not a natural white. White people are actually kind of pink, from pigment and blood flow and all sorts of things, but he's not. He has no color at all, no change in shade or tone where the skin gets thin over the top of the hand, and his nail beds are black, like he's put on nail polish, but I don't think he has. I think the blood beneath his skin isn't red at all—it's black.

He turns to me and I gasp.

His eyes are black. Pupil, iris, whites, everything is a formless black hole that seems to want to suck me in. His mouth, when he smiles, is full of sharp, pointed teeth.

"It's not a very good likeness," he comments idly. His breath is like ice, like he's breathing frost when he speaks. He gestures to the bone mist morphing my sister into a monster. "That's supposed to be me, right?"

"It's supposed to be the Nightmare," I whisper, my voice barely audible.

He nods. "Yes. A terrible likeness."

The Nightmare boy stands before me, head tipped to one side, watching my sister.

If I thought I'd been afraid before, it's nothing like now. The Nightmare is here. I didn't even know the Nightmare was a person—being? Sentient thing?—which makes me suspect that the people who see him don't retain the ability to speak about it afterward.

He's going to change me. He's going to take my body, break my bones, and reform me into a monster. I don't know what kind, but it doesn't matter. Whatever I become, it won't be me. My identity, my humanity, my soul, the thing that makes me myself—that will be gone.

And something hungry and hideous will be left in its place.

My breathing comes in panicked sounds almost like sobs. I want to beg, I want to plead, I want to tell him not to change me, but I can't seem to find the breath. My lungs have seized, and I can't even get the air to cry for mercy.

Did Ruby plead? I wonder. *Did she beg him to spare her?*

The Nightmare boy is still watching my sister change, limb by limb, each horrific, crunchy transformation bringing her closer to the giant, man-eating spider.

"It's rare, you know," he says, turning to me.

"What is?"

"Lucid dreams."

"I don't know what that is."

"This." He gestures between us. "You're controlling the dream, shaping what you want to see. Most people, it's a distortion of images and confusing nonsense their subconscious creates, but your mind is pulling up memories, and you're aware and controlling how you view them."

"Oh." This is my first dream, so it's not like I know what's normal. "This isn't what most dreams are like?"

"Not really. Most people aren't self-aware enough in the dream to converse with me."

I'd also rather not be conversing with him.

I'd rather not be dreaming at all, in fact.

He sighs dramatically as he continues to observe my sister's brutal transformation. "People used to train themselves to have lucid dreams, but not anymore."

Yeah, because no one dreams if they can help it.

My eyes skitter around, looking for an escape, because this conversation can't last forever, and then . . . well. I know what happens next.

His expression is nonplussed as he watches me, like he's looking at a particularly ugly housewarming gift.

"Why are you so afraid of me?" he asks, tipping his head to one side and examining me with his black void eyes. "I'm only trying to help."

"Help?" I choke out. "Help? You turn people into *monsters*."

He laughs. "Is that what you think?"

"It's what I know."

He shakes his head. "You've got it all wrong. I help people."

I stare at him, stunned. "You *what*?"

"I help them conquer their fear." He gives me a wide, sharp-toothed smile. "We fear things because they are more powerful than us. I simply equalize the playing field."

"You . . . turn people into their worst nightmare so they can *face* that nightmare?"

"And win!" His smile is brilliant, as though he's terribly proud of himself.

I stare at him, confounded. "What the *fuck* kind of logic is that?"

He just laughs. "Don't worry. You won't be afraid for long."

He raises his hand and opens his mouth. I stumble back and—

I jerk awake.

I gasp, heaving in great, heavy breaths, like I've run a marathon or swum all the way to shore myself. My eyes are watering, my hands shaking.

But I'm me.

I sit up quickly, patting myself all over with my hands. But my face still seems like mine, and I can't see any talons or feel any new teeth.

I'm okay.

I survived.

I woke up in time.

My shoulder throbs, and I touch my stiff, salty clothes, gently brushing my hand over my shoulder. I wince in pain.

"Sorry about that."

I look up, and Cy is sitting at the edge of the doorway to the cabin, hidden from the dying sunlight. He nods to a rock on the ground beside me. "It looked like you were having a nightmare. I thought it best to wake you."

I swallow heavily. What would have happened if he'd waited even a moment later to wake me? I'd almost been— I could have—

But I wasn't.

I'm okay.

I wrap my arms around myself, trying to stop the shaking. My chest heaves, and my eyes burn, and I think I might cry, but I don't. I just sit there, shaking and half sobbing, my mind flashing back to the memory of the nightmare over and over, on that last second, that moment I almost lost myself forever.

What would have happened if I hadn't woken up?

What would the Nightmare boy have turned me into?

I can't stop shaking, a full-body shake, teeth rattling, muscles spasming, and for a moment I wonder if I'm having some sort of panic attack–induced seizure because I can't stop—I'm shaking so bad it's physically painful, and then I'm crying, the tears coming fat and hard, making my chest seize and heave.

I was seconds from the worst death I could imagine.

A few words away from my own body being turned into a weapon.

"Ness?"

Cy's voice is concerned, and I scrub my eyes with the back of my hand, trying to hide my fear, but it doesn't work. It just makes my hand wet.

"Hey, Ness." Cy's voice is soft. "Ness, it's all right. You woke up in time."

No, I didn't wake up. Cy woke me up.

He saved my life.

Again.

I take a deep, shuddering breath. I'm okay. I'm alive. I'm still me. The tears slow, and my eyes are sore and puffy and sting when I wipe them. I'm so thirsty I feel like I'm going to die of dehydration before I ever get a chance to sleep again, and it's a weirdly comforting thought.

I'm such a mess.

But I take another deep breath, because it's over and Cy is looking at me with that worried expression and I need to pull myself together. We still have a long journey back to the city.

I wipe my face, and force myself to shift the topic, to move it to something else so I can push it out of my mind. "Why didn't you have a nightmare?"

He raises an eyebrow and then gestures to himself. "I mean, I already am one. Isn't that why you don't like me?"

"No, I mean . . ." I gesture vaguely at him. "You're a contagious Nightmare. You can still have one yourself, right?"

"Ah, no." He shifts, looking away. "I'm not a contagious Nightmare."

I blink, genuinely surprised. "What? You—you actually had a Nightmare? Your worst fear was becoming a vampire?"

His mouth presses into a thin, angry line. "No," he corrects, voice hard. "My worst fear was becoming my father."

Then he rises and turns sharply away, disappearing back into the darkness of the cabin.

10

We leave the cabin at sunset.

Before we leave, we find a well where the family must have gotten their water from. The lid is rusted shut, but Cy rips it off and we pull up bucketful after bucketful of water. I drink until I feel sick, and then I pour it over myself when I can't drink anymore, as though I can absorb it through my skin.

I still haven't found food, and my stomach cramps and groans. I don't want to mention it though, because Cy hasn't eaten either, and I don't want him to be thinking about eating since the only food he has available is me, and I'm not keen on being dinner.

But I can't stop my stomach grumbling loudly. Cy presses his lips together tightly every time he hears me, which means he must be hungry, but he doesn't say anything about it. He doesn't try to emotionally manipulate me into feeding him because he saved my life, which I was fully prepared for and not looking forward to. I'm pleasantly surprised to find he's not, in fact, going to be a manipulative asshole.

So maybe he isn't going to eat me.

And maybe he wasn't going to eat that girl on the boat.

But how was I supposed to know that? Vampires don't have a good track record, no matter what films like to portray. I've seen the stats. Almost every vampire has killed someone, and honestly, better safe than dead.

We start down the gravel road in the dark. It's wider than the crumbling path we arrived at the cabin on, and since we know that an auto drove that dead family here on this road, chances are it leads back to civilization. Eventually.

I just hope it doesn't take us weeks of hiking to get there.

"How do you think they got the bomb on the boat?" Cy asks, breaking the silence of our steady hike.

I plod forward with the diligence of the desperate, one exhausted foot after another. "We don't know it was a bomb."

He gives me a look. I don't even need to see him that well to know what that look says.

"Okay," I concede. "It was probably a bomb. But it's not like I'm a bomb expert. I can't tell a gas leak explosion from a bomb. They both go boom."

He frowns. "Bombs are . . . more deadly?"

It's my turn to give him a look.

He shrugs. "Look, if it were an accident, wouldn't there have been more survivors?"

"Pretty sure that's not how this works."

We carry on, trudging along in silence before he continues.

"So for argument's sake though, how would someone have gotten a bomb on the boat?"

I sigh. It's not like we have anything better to do, so I'll play along. "I dunno. The luggage maybe? A lot of people brought a lot of luggage on board, and it's not like anyone checks it to see if there's a bomb in it."

"Yours *was* very heavy." He casts a side-eyed look at me. "Do you think your boss had you bring the bomb on board?"

"What? No!" I stumble, shocked at the mere idea of the Director hurting so much as a fly, never mind an entire boatload of people. "Are you kidding? You saw how many people transporting mail there were. Why would you single out mine?"

"Yeah, but most of them weren't assassins."

"I'm not an assassin."

"Isn't that what you told me you were on the boat?" he points out.

I know he knows I was bluffing.

"So you're part of a Nightmare assassin group," he continues on. "That feels like the kind of violent group that would plant a bomb."

"I'm not part of a Nightmare assassin group," I insist, even though I know he's just messing with me. "I'm part of the Friends of the Restful Soul."

His mouth drops open, and his eyes widen. He's genuinely surprised.

"The cult?" he asks.

"It's not a cult," I insist.

He gives me a disbelieving look. "It's called the *Friends of the Restful Soul*. It's *so* a cult."

I make an exasperated sound. "You can't judge things by their names!" I nearly trip on a rock but catch myself. "We're a charitable organization. We offer pay-what-you-can therapy to Nightmare attack survivors and host support groups. Not exactly blow-up-the-boat kind of people."

"It's always the nice ones." He shakes his head. "I mean, no one's that nice. They're definitely up to something."

I sigh heavily. "Trust me, whatever they're up to, I doubt it involves bombs."

He makes a small, disbelieving *hmm*, but I don't rise to the bait.

"So who do you think blew up the boat?" he finally asks.

"No idea." I tip my head to one side. "I still think it's just too weird to be a bomb."

"Weird? How?"

"Well." I shrug. "It's just—why blow up a whole boat? If you're trying to assassinate someone, an alley really is better. Blowing up a boat is just messy and a lot of extra dead people. It seems like a lot of effort."

"Could be a statement. Like a . . . I don't know, some evil group introducing themselves. And showing they're serious."

I shake my head. "You mean like the Chaos League a few years ago?" I consider this. "I don't think it makes sense. They took the Mayor hostage and then threatened to blow up the mayoral palace. It wouldn't have worked if they'd blown up a boat. No one would even have realized what they'd done until like two days later."

I shrug. "It's just not practical. If they were trying to prove a point, they would have picked somewhere in Newham with a lot of people. The Newham City Library or the clock tower or something."

He considers this. "All right, you make a fair point. If this was some sort of show of force, they probably would have picked something more dramatic." He taps his finger against his lips. "But I still think it could be an assassination thing. You say it's messy because of all the extra dead people, but lots of people don't care about that."

"You really think someone blew up the boat to kill one person?" I ask, skeptical. "Would anyone really do that?"

He shrugs. "If my father knew I was on the boat, I bet he would have."

I stop and stare at him.

It takes him a few steps to realize I've stopped, and he pauses, looking back at me, a question in his eyes.

"Did your father know you were on the boat?" I ask.

His gaze shutters, and something painful crosses his expression. "Maybe."

I consider: Did it make sense to blow up a boat if you were trying to kill a vampire?

Vampires are notoriously difficult to kill—most Nightmares are. A regular gun or knife doesn't usually work. You need larger weapons or to hit specific places. Fire is generally pretty reliable though, and explosions sure have enough of that.

So, if you were trying to assassinate a Nightmare, would blowing up a boat make sense?

Maybe.

If you were a raving psychopath with no regard for human life. Which does, to be fair, describe a lot of people.

"Did you tell him?" I ask. "That you were on the boat?"

His eyes widened in terror. "No, god, no, never."

"Then why do you think he knew?"

Cy looks away and starts walking again. I trot to catch up with him.

"Cy." My voice is hard. "How do you think he knew?"

He looks away. "I got a message from a friend. Ex-friend. I dunno. He wanted to meet. I was going to see him."

I frown. This isn't the direction I expected this conversation to go. "Was he an ex-friend because he had a murderous grudge against you?"

Cy snorts. "No. No, if anything, I'm the one who should have a grudge against him. He has no reason to hate me. Or want me dead."

"So why do you think your father knew?"

He looks away. "Dunno. Maybe he was spying on my friend." He licks his lips. "Maybe he's the one who pushed my friend to reconnect with me, just so he could kill me."

And I thought *I* was paranoid. I have nothing on this.

"And maybe," I point out, "it's just a coincidence."

He doesn't look convinced.

I sigh. "Look, if he was setting you up to die and you were already being lured somewhere, doesn't it make more sense to actually lure you there and get rid of you quietly?"

Cy considers this, then lets out a soft breath. "I suppose so."

He still doesn't look like he believes it, but that's the paranoia. I know that well—when the fear has a hold of you, it's hard to see the truth because your mind warps and twists everything into a potential threat.

The trees thin and the gravel peters out, and suddenly we're out of the forest.

We've hit a road.

Pavement, smooth and flat, greets us, stretching off in either direction, a highway to freedom.

We exchange slightly manic grins, like we've both found winning lottery tickets and not just some small rural road.

It's not large, and no autos are currently driving on it. But it's paved, and honestly, that's all I care about. That means it leads somewhere.

And that somewhere will have autos.

And food.

And water.

And likely a small train station, because every tiny town in the country has a train station. Even the town where I was born, which was as rural as you got, had a train station.

And all trains lead to Newham.

Cy looks around before pointing. "Maybe that way? Toward the city."

I agree. "More chance things are developed closer to the city."

So decided, we start down the paved road. The moonlight shines down on us, illuminating our path. The air is crisp and clear, and I'm so hungry I could eat pretty much anything and so thirsty I would even drink that nasty bitter tea the Director likes. Without milk or sugar even. And cold.

I don't care at this point. Anything will do.

The road stretches ahead of us, and as time passes, I grow more and more aware of the blisters on the soles of my feet. They burn as I walk, each step sending a shooting pain up my leg.

"So what happened?" I ask, trying to distract myself. "Between you and the friend you were going to see. Ex-friend."

Cy shrugs. He runs a hand through his hair, and I wonder if he's going to answer or just change the subject.

"Not much," he finally says. "We were best friends growing up. We were really close, shared everything. You know the story."

"And?"

"And then he met a girl." Cy shrugs again, faking casualness, but I hear the bitterness in his voice.

"And you liked the girl too?"

"Huh? Beth? Oh, no, no." He shakes his head vigorously. "*Very* not my type."

I laugh. "That's quite the strong rejection."

He snorts. "She had that personality, you know the one, where they have to be in control? Not just in control of her own life, but in control of everything around her. Always planning, always thinking, always moving, trying to push people into the path she'd decided was best for them." He pauses. "Not in a malicious way—she really thought she was helping."

"Even if you didn't want that help," I finish for him. "And it was, in fact, not what you wanted to do at all with your life."

"Exactly."

I nod sagely. I do, in fact, know this personality. "She sounds like my friend's sister."

He smiles slightly. "How often does she tell you to leave the cult?"

"It's not a cult," I correct absently. "And all the time."

He grins. "Sounds right."

He's silent, and I prod him gently. "So your friend?"

"Yeah." His voice dims. "Well, Beth and my friend started dating. He's very kind but indecisive. They balanced each other well. I was happy for them." His smile falls. "But . . . she got jealous. She didn't like our friendship."

I frown, tipping my head to the side. "Why? Were you sleeping with your friend?"

"No." He laughs. "Alas, he's very straight."

"How unfortunate."

"Tragic, really. Can you imagine limiting your options that way?" He shakes his head.

I roll my eyes. He'd probably get on fabulously with Priya.

"So what was Beth jealous of then, if you weren't sleeping with him?" I ask.

"Our closeness," he whispers, voice soft. "That's what he said the day he told me we couldn't be friends anymore. She was jealous of how close we were. She said he was 'cheating emotionally' with me."

I'm quiet. His voice is full of pain—old pain—and I don't know what to say to that.

"I just don't understand," he says, looking up at the moon. "Why do people get so wrapped up in romance? Why does one person have to be your everything? They have to satisfy your sexual fantasies. They have to be your emotional support lodestone. They have to take on all your problems and all your desires and that's just so *much*." He looks at me, and his green eyes are wide and confused. "Why can't we have more than one person supporting us? Why do people feel like you have to give up or grow apart from your friends when you get into a relationship?"

I look away. I've never thought about it. I try and imagine what it would be like if Priya found someone, someone she was desperately in love with.

And just . . . left me.

Even the thought sends a wave of hurt through me, a deep-seated feeling of loss, like a piece of me is being torn away. Our friendship has been a rock that has kept me afloat in the storms of my fears. She's the best friend I've ever had.

If I lost her because her new partner didn't want to share her attention . . . I don't know what I'd do.

I swallow painfully.

"I miss him," Cy whispers. His voice turns bitter. "And now, of course, I'm never going to get another friendship like that because I'm a goddamn blood-drinking monster and any sane person runs away when they realize it."

I wince.

Well, at least he admits that my fear on meeting him was sane.

"I just wish that the world weren't so wrapped up in this type of toxic love," he whispers. "This fantasy that you have to be tangled up together in some sort of horrible, parasitic ball that you can't escape because you killed off all your friendships to get into it and now there's no one to help you out if you're not happy."

What a wonderful picture he paints.

I can't say I think he's wrong though. When I think of all the films I've seen, all the penny novels, I have to admit, I can see the issue. The complete obsession with one other person at the cost of everything else in your life is often portrayed as romantic.

But I just keep imagining Priya leaving me, abandoning me, for some random person she met and wants to live with forever and the pain that would cause. For both of us.

Cy is right—that kind of romance is *wrong*.

We're quiet for a long time.

The pavement crunches beneath my feet as I finally find the words. "Not everyone in the world is like Beth. Emotional cheating? Really? Sounds like a bunch of nonsense to me."

He blinks, turning to me. "Really?"

"Yeah." My mouth twists in distaste. "It just sounds like an excuse she made because she's jealous of anyone her boyfriend spends time with. She's just possessive. You and your friend both deserve better."

Cy's expression softens. "A little late now."

I sigh, voice gentle. "Not every romance is like that. Lots of people in healthy relationships still have friends outside it." I gaze at him seriously. "You'll make friends again. Better friends. Friends that won't leave you just because they find other kinds of relationships."

He looks at me out of the corner of his eyes, a glimmer of a smile pulling at his mouth. "Oh? You volunteering?"

I blink. "I—I hadn't thought about it."

He nods, smile falling away, hair hiding his face, and I realize too late what a callous thing that was to say.

"The thing about friendships," he says softly, "is you have to feel safe in them. The friend you mentioned earlier. Do you feel safe with her?"

"Yes." The answer is instant. "I've always felt safe with her. To be honest"—my voice lowers, something like guilt coiling through me—"that's actually why I tried to befriend her originally. She wanted to join Nightmare Defense. I have a crippling fear of Nightmares." I bow my head. "I wanted to be her friend because I thought . . ."

"You thought she could protect you."

I nod. "It sounds so selfish now. But I really love her. She's the best. And not just because she's an incredible fighter and saved me from a murderous Nightmare a few days ago."

"I don't think it's a selfish reason to start a friendship." He tips his head up to the sky. "We approach people for all sorts of reasons. Most of them aren't particularly deep. You sit next to a person in a classroom because you think she's pretty. Or because he's from the same church as you. Or because you like the vibe from the way they dress." He shrugs. "At the beginning, it's all shallow. It can't be anything else because you don't know each other yet."

"It's the stuff after that's important. If you click, you get closer, and things become less shallow." He smiles at me. "If it really were a one-sided relationship, where you used her for protection, she'd have ditched you a long time ago."

I blink. I hadn't thought about it like that before.

"I guess you're right," I admit.

My shoulders loosen, and I feel like a weight has lifted from me, a guilt I never realized I was carrying sliding away.

"Besides, of all the reasons to befriend someone, because they make you feel safe is a good one." His tone is musing. "I think . . . you can't be friends without trust. Without feeling safe with them. I think, honestly, that's critical to a real, healthy friendship."

He swallows and bows his head. "And that's why I won't ever get a real friend again. Because how can you trust someone who wants to eat you? You approached your friend because she made you feel safe. People approach me because I make them feel *scared*."

I hadn't thought of that, but he's not wrong.

He's so sad, and I want to tell him that I'll be his friend. That he won't be alone. But I can't. Because it would be a lie.

I've figured out at this point he's probably not going to hurt me. I've actually kind of enjoyed chatting with him and spending time with him. I don't think he's a bad person, even if he has been turned into a blood-drinking Nightmare.

But knowing that doesn't make my fears go away. It doesn't make me feel safe with him. My fears are entrenched deep, and no matter what he does, they aren't going anywhere. Because it's not him that's the problem—it's me.

I look at him, bathed in the moonlight, pacing forward, his green eyes sad, lost somewhere in the past, and I wish I could figure out how to make myself less afraid.

Because I think I'd actually like to be his friend.

11

We finally stumble into a town in the middle of the night.

We'd seen the lights from a distance, a beacon glowing through the dark. We'd stumbled forward, our legs rubbery and weak, our eyes desperate, the end finally in sight. We drew closer and closer, until the blurry glow formed into a row of lamplights in a tiny town, no more than a dozen buildings.

And a train station.

The station was tiny, a simple, whitewashed shack by the side of the tracks, but it was a real station. Back at the turn of the century, there'd been a big push to connect every community by railroad tracks. Mostly it had been funded by train companies, who'd been hoping to put the brand-new auto industry out of business. It had not put automakers out of business—Koval Enterprises, one of the first auto companies, is now so rich it owns half of Newham—but it had made the whole country extremely well connected.

We check the schedule, which looks like it's been updated in the last year. It would have been just our luck to end up in some disused and abandoned station.

The first train of the morning arrives at 4:15 a.m., getting into Newham at 5:58, well before sunrise.

Cy's shoulders slump in relief when he sees that.

"What would you have done if it was after sunrise?" I ask him.

He makes a face. "The main station is underground, so I probably would have gotten off and then sat on a public bench for however many hours until sunset."

"Fun."

"Not really."

We explore the train station, but everything is closed and shuttered. The ticket booth gate is locked and doesn't look like it's been opened in the last year, given all the rust on it. A big sign out front says that you can pay for your tickets on the train. Then it lists the price.

I don't have a single penny on me, but that seems like a problem for when I'm on the train.

We wander the station, looking for anything useful. Mostly I'm looking for food and water. I would murder for any kind of food. I haven't eaten in more than a day, and after all that walking, I'm thirsty again. Humans weren't meant to go this long without food and water, and my body feels like sandpaper scratched out all my insides, so they're rough and scraped and dried out and hollow.

We find a vending machine on the other side of the wall, a clunky, old thing. It's got postage stamps on the top row, dream-prevention pill packets on the second row.

But the third row has food. Dried and packaged nuts. Corn chips. Chocolate bars.

My dry mouth is already salivating.

Cy looks around, as though double-checking we're alone.

Then he puts his fist through the glass.

The crash is loud in the silence, as is the soft tinkle of glass falling on the pavement. Cy pulls his fist out of the machine and plucks out pieces of glass embedded in his skin. One removed, the small cuts close up, smoothing like they never existed at all.

This is why Nightmares are so hard to kill. Scary things always are, and when we imagine monsters, we imagine them unstoppable.

But right now, I want to do the exact opposite of killing Cy.

"One of us should eat." He pulls out a bag of chips and hands it to me.

I don't even pause to thank him before ripping it open and scarfing it down. The chips are old and extremely stale, but they're not poisonous and that's all I care about. Honestly, I'm so hungry I might not even care if they were poisonous.

I shovel them into my mouth like a wild animal, shredding the bag and licking the crumbs from the inside.

Cy kicks the side of the machine, and something inside crunches. He nods to himself, then feels around on the bottom before grabbing something tightly and *ripping*.

The sound of tearing metal, groaning and creaking, and then the final snap is so loud I'm sure the whole town will wake up and come find us. But the night remains empty and silent, the town as quiet as a grave.

Cy has torn out a large metal box from the machine, and

as he wrenches it open, I realize what it is.

The cashbox.

Glittering silver coins gleam up at me, and I grin widely. I guess we won't have to worry about the train fare after all.

I grab another bag of chips and devour it while Cy counts out the coins from the machine, pocketing enough for both our train fares, and then counting out enough for me to also carry my own fare. I appreciate that. I've always hated it when other people hold my tickets or documents—it feels like a power play because they're the ones holding something that I need.

I'm glad Cy doesn't try that nonsense.

He nods at my stack of coins beside me. "Be careful your pockets don't rip. Maybe divide the coins."

I grimace but do as he suggests. All the coins are small change but heavy, so they feel like rocks weighing me down.

"Won't they be suspicious?" I wave at the vending machine we've destroyed. "Especially since we're paying in pennies?"

He shakes his head. "Nah. We're buying the ticket on the train. By the time we pay anyone, we'll be well away from here."

I shove another handful of chips in my mouth. "A'ight."

His smile is tight and tired. His eyes go to my chip-dust-covered mouth for a moment, and then he turns quickly away, heading for the edge of the platform.

I wonder if it's hard for him, watching me eat and knowing he can't eat until he gets back to the city and . . . gets blood from wherever he gets it.

Where does he get it?

Ugh. I don't want to think about this.

But I am thinking about it, wondering if he murders people and drains their blood in the night. But I'm pretty sure he doesn't or I'd be dead too. So I'm left sitting there, munching on chips, with absolutely no idea how he eats, and my mind inventing more and more elaborate ideas.

(Currently, my mind is stuck on some sort of bite he disguises as sex play, which seems vaguely plausible, but also, I know nothing about sex, so maybe it's not plausible. But the more I think about it, the shadier this seems. If his partners don't consent and don't know he's biting them, is that some kind of assault? But maybe they do know. Those vampire movies are popular. Maybe it's considered sexy? What the hell do I know? Maybe it's a kink for certain people to be bitten?)

I really need to just shut off my brain because all this is putting some *really* weird images in my head that I'd definitely prefer weren't there.

The train comes three minutes late, pulling up with a screech of metal against metal, cars shuddering and shaking. It's an older model, the windows cracked and dirty, the doors broken so they're constantly partly open and have to be wrenched wide enough to get through and then wrenched closed. The smokestack looms like a thundercloud at the back and trails a line of smoke behind.

We step into an empty car. Long benches run on both sides of the car, and at each end, a large wooden luggage rack is bolted into the wall. The car is filthy, dirt collecting in every corner, and something I think might be a dead rat is tucked under a bench.

We're the only people in sight. Which makes sense—it's early, not a workday, and this is a rural train that stops at every station. It's also still dark out, and most people like to wait for dawn, out of a mistaken superstition that there are fewer Nightmares during the day.

They're wrong.

Most Nightmares don't care what time of day it is.

Someone has left a copy of yesterday's newspaper on the bench, and Cy paces over and picks it up as the train starts up, rattling down the track and speeding us away from the small town and back toward the city.

We sit beside each other, not quite touching, the paper spread between us so we can both read the headline.

BOAT EXPLOSION KILLS MORE THAN 600. FUEL TANK RUPTURE SUSPECTED CAUSE.

"There you go," I tell him. "Not a bomb."

He frowns. "Maybe."

We both lean over the paper, looking over the article. And the ones following it. The list of known victims is long, and some of them are pretty famous.

For example, one of the victims was a famous Nightmare professor. According to the paper, Dr. Abender claimed he'd discovered the cause of Nightmares. It's always been a mystery—why had Nightmares suddenly appeared a hundred years ago? They'd plunged the whole world into chaos when they'd appeared, vastly altering the course of history pretty much everywhere in the world.

And no one knew why.

Theories abounded, of course. People said that it was a curse, though they never agreed on what kind. Some said it was because archaeologists had disturbed magical graves and let something loose. Others said it was a powerful magic cast by the leaders one of the conquered empires of the last era, maybe Tawantinsuyu or Constantinople or Prussia.

Of course, no evidence had ever been discovered to support any of this.

I think of the young man I'd met in my nightmare. His spider-silk-white hair and black eyes and shark-teeth smile, and shiver. I don't know if he was real or just another part of the nightmare, a figment of my imagination that needed to give a solid form to the monster that haunted me.

I've never heard other people talk about having conversations in their nightmares. So it probably wasn't real.

Probably.

And this professor's theory probably also wasn't real, just a publicity stunt. But if it was real, if he'd really found the cause of Nightmares? That would change everything.

Too bad he was dead.

"He's a scammer," Cy says, noticing my expression. "Dr. Abender."

"How do you know?"

He shrugs. "I read all the articles on Nightmares since . . ." He looks away. "Anyway, his theory is that there's a demon trapped in our dreams, and we need to exorcise it."

I think again of the black-eyed boy with his sharp, sharp teeth. "A demon?"

Cy shrugs. "Dr. Abender went around telling people if they donated to him, then he'd put the money toward a dream exorcism."

"Ah." My concerns over demons vanish. "Definitely a scam artist, then."

Cy smiles crookedly. "Very definitely."

I skim the rest of the article. "Oh, look, some gang lord was on the boat. Gangs are always blowing each other up. I wonder if it was some gang war gone wrong." I go a little further. "Oh, and an ambassador from Sweden. Aren't we sort of at war with them? That sounds like a good motive."

"I don't think we're at war with them anymore."

"Are you sure?"

"Yes, I'm pretty sure we lost." He considers. "Also, I don't think it was a war. I think it was an attempted annexation."

"Right, we tried to conquer them and failed."

"Pretty much."

"Sounds like fodder for a lot of bitter people. And we know the military loves blowing people up."

He grimaces.

"Oh." I point to another part of the article. "Look, a mayoral candidate. It's about time for them to start assassinating each other about now."

Cy covers his face with one hand. "That's a joke, right?"

"No."

He groans. "Of course it's not. Why is Newham like this?"

I shrug. "Look on the bright side, huh?"

"What bright side?"

"Well," I tell him, "pretty much all of these people were more likely targets for assassination than you. So it probably wasn't your father and your ex-friend."

He snorts, but he's smiling a little. "I suppose there's that."

The train rattles along, and eventually a Black man in a blue-and-white National Rail uniform comes down the aisle. We buy tickets from him, and he looks entirely non-plussed that we pay him in loose change. It takes forever to count it out, and the train keeps jerking and we keep dropping coins, but eventually the money is counted and he gives us the tickets before making his slow, wobbling way to the next car.

A small spider crawls along the bench toward me, and I roll up the newspaper and crush it, absurdly satisfied with myself. I used to be afraid of spiders too, after what happened to Ruby, but that's one fear I *have* managed to conquer.

Now, if only I could conquer the rest of them.

We're rattling closer to Newham, the lights far in the distance coming closer every minute. I press my face against the window and wish I could make the train go faster through sheer force of will.

I'm almost back. Almost home.

I'm going to crawl back to the Friends and lock myself in

my room for the next year. I'll curl up on my perfect, tiny bed, the walls pressing in around me, comforting and protecting me, and I won't leave. I'll lie there, my body finally relaxing, and I'll finally feel safe again.

My fingers curl into claws, and my whole body is tight with a need that's almost desperation. I just need to hold on a little longer. I'm almost there.

Almost safe.

"Can I ask a favor?" Cy's voice is hesitant, breaking me from my thoughts.

I don't turn to him, still staring out at the fast-approaching lights of Newham. "I'm not feeding you."

He rolls his eyes. "Really? You're still on that?"

"Just making it clear."

He sighs heavily.

I snort, turning my head away from the window and settling back into the seat properly. "You're too easy to tease."

He glares at me.

I lean back. "So what's the favor?"

"You're going to go home after this, right? Back to your cult?"

"Still not a cult."

"Whatever. Back to your not-a-cult." He runs a hand through his messy, dark hair. "The media will figure out real fast that someone survived the explosion. It'll be all over the papers. Police will come question you."

I nod slowly. "I suppose they will."

"So I was hoping . . ." He hesitates, fiddling with a button on his shirt that's coming off. "Could you keep me out of it? Say you drifted to shore or swam there. You got back on your own. You're the only survivor."

I raise my eyebrows. "You don't want to be known as a hero?"

"Not really." He looks away, shoulders tight. "I don't want my father to know where I am. And if—if he was part of the explosion, I don't want him to know I survived."

I tip my head slightly. "Why are you so convinced he's trying to kill you?"

He shakes his head, lips pursed, eyes worried. "Look, just trust me, I have good reason to believe it." His eyes turn to me, and they're intense, the green in them practically glowing as he stares at me, the urgency in his voice reflected in his gaze. "So will you keep quiet?"

I hold his gaze a long moment, and he doesn't look away. He's genuinely terrified of his father.

I should have known as much, given that he told me his father was his worst nightmare.

"All right." I shrug, breaking eye contact. "It doesn't affect me much. I can keep you out of it."

His whole body slumps in relief. "Thank you."

"Nah. It's the least I can do."

I look out the window. The bright lights of the city are almost upon us. We're close enough I can see the shadowy outline of the jagged skyline, like the teeth of a giant monster. It's hideous and wonderfully familiar.

"Thanks, by the way," I say.

He blinks.

"I never said it before." I can't meet his eyes, so I keep my gaze on the cityscape. "But thanks for pulling me to shore."

He smiles then, a soft, gentle thing. He's already good-looking, but this expression makes me actually realize he's good-looking not just because he's physically handsome but because he, as a person, is pretty nice. It's amazing how a good personality makes people massively more attractive.

"It was no trouble," he says, which is a blatant lie. We both recall in excruciating detail exactly how much trouble it was.

The train is cast into sudden darkness as we plunge underground. We've reached the city, and now we'll make our way to the central station beneath it, through the extensive subway networks. The lights in the train itself are dim and flicker occasionally, casting everything in shadow.

It's not far now. This is all almost over. I'm almost back. Almost safe.

It feels like years ago that I first boarded that horrible boat, but it's only been two days. Two very long, very exhausting, very miserable days.

I'm surprised to realize a small part of me is actually sad it's over, not because I enjoyed it but because it was simple and concrete. We had a goal—get home. There was no room for anything else.

Now that I'm back in Newham, the rest of my life is going to take over. I still need to figure out how to convince the Director to let me stay with the Friends. I'm still at risk of being kicked out. Of losing my room, my home, the only place I feel safe.

My shoulders tighten, the familiar stresses settling over me.

"Hey, look," Cy says suddenly. "If you ever need to get ahold of me . . ."

"Yes?" I ask, grateful for the distraction.

"The Lantern Man's on Eighty-Sixth. Ask for Estelle." He looks away, awkward. "She knows how to reach me."

I memorize the information, though I can't think of any reason I'd need to be in touch. I'm surprised to find that disappoints me a little. I kind of like Cy, even if he is a bloodsucking Nightmare. I never thought that would happen.

For a moment, this makes me inordinately pleased. Maybe this means I'm getting less afraid. Maybe I can stop screwing my own life up.

"If you call the main number for the Friends of the Restful Soul and ask for me, they'll find me," I tell him, hoping this remains true and that the Director gives me another chance.

I don't want to contemplate what will happen if he doesn't.

The train pulls into the station with a screech of metal brakes. The car tilts wildly before settling into a stop, slightly crooked.

We both rise, peering hungrily out the window at the familiar crumbling pillars, filthy ceilings, and grimy walls of the central station. A homeless man pees in a corner while screaming at a girl walking by, who makes a rude hand gesture at him.

Ah, Newham. How I missed you.

"Well, it's been fun." Cy grins. "But next time, maybe we can skip the part where we get blown up."

I laugh, following him down the steps and onto the platform, breathing in the scent of urine and dust, barbecue and burnt coal.

I'm home.

12

I stumble through the doors of the Friends of the Restful Soul at the crack of dawn. The lobby is empty but open. We're staffed twenty-four hours a day in case people in need come to us in the middle of the night. That's when we get most of our runaway kids and teenagers, at that hour. They're fleeing abusive families or parents trying to sell them to organ harvesters, brothels, child-eating Nightmares—well, I could list places all day. Child trafficking is a *massive* business. Newham isn't a safe place to be a kid, that's for sure.

Or to be an adult, actually.

But the Friends of the Restful Soul has a reputation as a safe place to run if you're in trouble, and that's a pretty rare thing in a city like Newham.

The homeless shelter down the block had to close because it turned out they were kidnapping half the people who came there and selling them to some mad scientist for experiments. Someone burned the whole place down last month, and we're still not sure if it was the mad scientist, someone who worked at the "shelter," or one of the people staying there.

Cindy is staffing the desk, writing in her book like she always is. She's scowling at it, her expression pinched and hard, like she's contemplating murder, not poetry. Above her, the four saints look down on the lobby benevolently, the painting's eyes always seeming to track my movements.

I pause for a moment, watching her while she's unaware I'm there. I've never really understood why Cindy's running mail and doing menial chores at the Friends of the Restful Soul. She doesn't seem poor and desperate, like most of our staff, nor does she have a crippling trauma that needs regular therapy and her own tiny corner to hide in—like me.

Maybe this is what that elusive piety or religious feeling I'm supposed to be faking looks like.

I take a deliberate step forward, boots clicking on the tiles, and Cindy finally looks up from her book. Her eyes widen when she sees me.

"Ness!" Her mouth drops open in a little o of shock. "You're alive!"

I'm suddenly struck that she was supposed to be on the boat, not me. It seems unfair that I ended up with her rotten luck.

I make a shocked sound. "Am I? I hadn't noticed."

She scowls, lips pursed as though remembering that actually, she doesn't like me.

"Can you let me in?" I gesture at my bedraggled state. "I need to go tell the Director I survived and then go sleep for the next three years."

Cindy opens her mouth, her eyes flicking over me, but she

turns aside, whatever she was about to say tucked away. She simply rises and unlocks the door to the interior of the building.

I stumble toward it and she grabs my arm. "Ness."

I stare at her hand on my arm numbly. "What?"

She hesitates, eyes flicking over me, before shaking her head and letting me go. "Nothing. Congratulations on being alive."

"Uh, thanks."

Cindy's being weird again. Whatever, that's nothing new.

I walk past and up the narrow metal staircase, clanking my way upward, toward the Director's office. All I really want to do is go back to my room, take half a dozen pills to prevent myself from dreaming, and sleep all day. Unfortunately for me, I lost everything in the explosion and subsequent swim, so I don't even have the keys to get into my room anymore.

Which means the first stop is the Director.

It's early, but he's always up early. He's always been a rise-with-the-sun kind of person. Lizard. Whatever.

I don't even knock on the smooth mahogany door, just push my way in.

The Director is in the middle of closing the wall.

I stare at him.

He stares at me.

His mouth has dropped open in shock, revealing tiny little ridged teeth that don't even look like teeth. His green scales are flushed and his eyes bug out of his head.

"Ness?!" he gasps and clutches his chest with webbed hands like he might be having a heart attack.

"The one and only." I point at the crack in the wall that obviously contains a second room, hidden in the first one. "I didn't know we had a fake wall with a secret room."

He blinks, looking from me to the wall. "Oh. This is Newham. Every building has secret rooms. I use this one for filing cabinets."

He pushes open the wall and shows me a room much like the office we're in now. Brick walls, lamps on every corner, but no window. No way to see out or in. Wooden cabinets line the walls, and a couple of pieces of mail sit on a tray in the corner.

"What was the room originally for?" I ask.

"Oh, I think the original building owner kept his mistress locked up in here." He pushes his glasses up his long reptile nose. "We found a wide array of . . . interesting sexual instruments in here when we bought the building. And her corpse, of course. After the old owner died, I imagine she starved to death."

Charming.

"But more importantly." He closes the wall to the secret room and turns to me, eyes glistening. "You're alive."

"You said that already."

"But I—how?" He steps forward, hand reaching out, as if to confirm I'm not a mirage, and I flinch back.

I wince. I'm not actually afraid of the Director. He's perfectly sane and in control of himself, and he's not going to hurt me.

But sometimes my mind screams *Nightmare*, and normal, rational thought goes away.

The Director steps back, giving me space, and I look at the floor, feeling unreasonably ashamed.

"How are you alive, Ness?" He shakes his head in wonder. "I heard there were no survivors."

"I . . . swam. To shore. After the boat blew up."

"Saints save me." The Director puts a hand over his heart. "That's incredible."

I shrug and don't say anything. I'm not incredible, but Cy sure is for swimming all that way while tugging me behind him like dead weight.

"We have to call the police." The Director is still talking. "Tell them there's a survivor. The explosion has been all over the news. I'm sure they'll want to talk to you."

Ugh. I don't want to talk to them. I don't even have any money for bribes, and you should never talk to the police without bribe money. That's just good sense.

"Can I . . . sleep first?"

He blinks, and his expression melts. "Of course. Goodness, where are my manners. You must be exhausted, Ness. Rest, and I'll take care of everything."

My shoulders loosen in relief. It's so nice when someone else takes care of my problems for me.

"Okay." I clear my throat. "I'm sorry about the packages. You know. Not delivering them and instead watching them get blown up in a fiery explosion."

He gives me an absolutely baffled look. "Ness, who *cares* about the packages? You're *alive*. That's all that matters."

I let out a sigh of relief. I hadn't realized how worried I'd been that he'd kick me out, since I'd failed again. Even

136

though I knew that I hadn't been at fault, even though I knew I couldn't have done anything different. A part of me was still afraid that, somehow, I'd be blamed for it.

But it's fine. Maybe the explosion was even a good thing. He can't kick me out now, not right after I've gone through something like this. He's not that heartless. It would be against doctrine anyway, to turn away someone in distress. That explosion bought me time. Time I desperately need.

"Right." I clear my throat, trying not to smile. "Um. Thanks. I'm just going to wash up and go to bed now."

The Director hesitates. "About that . . ."

Oh no.

"We thought you were dead." The Director's voice is pleasant. Placating.

No, no, no.

"We gave your room to a new initiate."

I stare at him.

He gave my room away.

My room.

My sanctuary.

My safe place.

The only place I know no Nightmares will reach me.

My home for the last three years.

The place I'd been fighting so desperately hard to keep. The entire reason I'd conned my way into that stupid mail run.

"I was only gone two days!" My voice is high and panicked. "Two days!"

They can't have given away my room.

They can't kick me out.

Not now.

Please.

The Director winces. "We thought you were dead. And we have so many people on the waitlist for single rooms."

"Kick them out then!" I scream, reedy and scratched, aware that I'm way out of line but too panicked to care. "It's my room!"

"We can't do that." His voice is patient. "You know that, Ness."

I don't care. It's my room.

I open my mouth to tell him so, but the Director interrupts me.

"Look, just for now, stay with Priya," he says. "Her roommate is out visiting family all week. We'll figure out what to do after everyone has had time to sleep and calm down and think about things clearly."

He's never giving me back my room.

The realization hits me like a truck. I'm not getting it back.

He was always planning on kicking me out, he'd decided well before I went on that boat. The explosion hasn't delayed anything. It hasn't bought me time or pity.

It's sped things up.

"Ness." His voice is gentle. "Go see Priya. Get some rest. I'm sure she wants to see you."

I just stare at him, my mind spinning, whirling, spiraling downward as the panic sinks deep into my bones.

I'm a liability. I always have been. I've let my fear ruin

everything, and I knew it. I knew I'd be in trouble for letting Priya handle that Nightmare herself and I didn't care. I knew I'd be in trouble every time I hid, and it didn't matter.

Now it's too late.

Even if I somehow manage to make myself less afraid, prove to him that he can rely on me, it's too late. He's already made up his mind.

It's only a matter of time before it's not just my room that's gone.

He'll ask me to leave the building.

Then where will I go? What will I do?

My hands shake by my side, and my breathing is harsh and frightened.

How long do I have?

"Ness."

My head jerks up and my voice comes out stilted and wrong. "Yes?"

"You need to sleep." His voice is gentle. "I promise, we'll talk about this again after you've slept. Okay?"

He rises and walks over to me, hands reaching out to direct me to the door, and I move before he can touch me. His hands lower, but he's won. I'm out in the hall now, nowhere to go except where he told me to.

This conversation is over, and he's won.

Just like he'll win the next conversation, the one where he finally throws me out of the Friends.

What will I do?

I don't have money. I don't have anywhere to go. I don't

know what I'll do alone, on the streets of Newham. Probably get kidnapped and used in a terrible science experiment or eaten by a roving Nightmare.

I sink against the wall outside the Director's office, slowly sliding down until I'm crouched on the floor, hands wrapped around my knees. My whole body is trembling, and my fingers are clenched so tight around my legs, I'm going to leave bruises. My chest hiccups painfully, part sob, part gasp for air, like I'm drowning, I'm trapped back in the water after the boat explosion, a hair's breadth away from death.

But this time, I'm not drowning in water—I'm drowning in fear. Fear of what will happen to me out in the world, vulnerable and alone. Fear of losing the only place that has felt safe since my sister died.

And unlike drowning in water, I can't just expel it from my lungs, clear my airway, and breathe the fresh air again.

If only it were so easy.

I didn't cry after the boat blew up. I didn't cry on the long journey home. I held it together because I knew I had a place to go back to. I held tight to the image of my tiny little room, my safe space.

And now it's gone.

So finally, miserably, I cry.

13

I can't sit in the hall crying forever. I really do need sleep. And all the crying made my eyes hurt, so now I'm thirsty and kind of headachy and feeling even more miserable. I thought crying was supposed to be cathartic. What a load of horse shit. I feel even worse.

No, that's a lie. I don't think I can feel worse. My whole world is collapsing around me and I haven't showered or slept right in days. Being stabbed might actually be a nice distraction.

I stumble down the hall to Priya's room and knock on the door numbly.

Rustling on the other side, but it doesn't open.

I knock again.

Finally, a swear and then the thud of angry footsteps before the door swings open.

"Do you know what time—"

Priya freezes midsentence when she sees me. Her hair is a mess, and her eyes are red rimmed, like she's been crying. Her pajamas are wrinkled and stained with food, giving the impression she hasn't changed out of them in a day or two.

"Ness?" Her voice is small and sad.

I grin tiredly at her. "The one and only."

Priya bursts into tears.

I stare at her, frozen in the doorway. I don't think I've ever seen Priya cry. She's always been the tough one, the capable one. She always knows what to do, no matter what the situation, and she does it with a grin on her face, no matter how terrifying.

I guess I'd started to internalize the idea that nothing could faze her, nothing could stop her, nothing could bring her down. She'd taken on an almost-mythical feeling in my mind, like a god, not quite human. Someone to aspire to, someone nothing could shake.

Wow, have I been wrong.

I reach out, tentative, and gently touch her shoulder. She takes this as invitation to throw herself into my arms, nearly knocking me over with the strength of her hug. She's got a good foot on me, and she's probably twice as strong as me at least. I feel like a toy doll in her arms.

Usually, I feel safe, protected by her strength. Now I wrap my small, weak arms around her and try to give her the feeling that she's safe with me, the way I always feel with her.

"I really thought you were dead!" She chokes, her tears dripping off her face and into my hair. "I actually—I don't— what the hell would I do without you?"

My throat closes up. Isn't that my line? I'm the coward, the one who can't do anything without Priya there to protect me.

"What are you talking about?" I croak. "You'd be fine without me."

She pulls back to glare at me, wiping angrily at her tears, as though offended they're there. "Are you kidding? After a year of dealing with my family drama, you really think I'd be fine on my own?"

I've always hated myself a little for my friendship with Priya. I felt like I was using her. Priya is so strong and I'm such a coward—what value could she possibly be getting from our friendship?

But she's right—this has never been a one-sided friendship. I know how hard her issues with her sister have been, how much she's struggled to get into Nightmare Defense. Just as she's supported and kept me safe through my fear of Nightmares, I've supported and kept her sane through the trials of her life.

We've always had a good friendship. I've just felt so guilty over how scared and helpless I feel that I've twisted it in my mind, made myself into the monster of the narrative.

But the only monster here is my fear. The only one being toxic is this terror in my mind warping my perception of reality.

"Sorry," I tell Priya.

"What on earth are you sorry for?" Priya smiles at me, bright and wide. "You're alive!"

I smile slightly. "So I am."

"So what happened?" Priya asks, expression full of curiosity.

I shake my head. "An explosion."

She leans forward, clearly expecting more.

But I'm swaying on my feet, and the weight of the last few

days is so heavy on me I can barely stand. I want to tell Priya everything—about the explosion and Cy and our miserable march. But not right now.

Right now, I want to collapse.

I slump against the wall, eyes heavy. "Can I tell you after I sleep? I'm exhausted, and—" My voice chokes. "The Director gave away my room."

Priya purses her lips, and her eyes are angry. I wonder if she's going to go beat up the Director after I go to bed. I kind of like that image.

"Take Lettie's bed." She nods to a neatly made-up bed across from hers.

I stumble toward it, trying in vain to remove my boots as I walk. But they're leather, and they've gotten soaked and been dried, and they now form to my feet and ankles in a way that makes me wonder if I'll ever get them off again.

I finally succeed in wrenching one boot off. The stench is horrifying.

Priya pinches her nose and then goes to the small window and opens it. I take off my other boot and debate throwing them out the window, but I might need them if I'm kicked out. I don't have other shoes.

"When you get up, you have to tell me *everything*." Priya informs me. Her voice is stern.

"Yes, ma'am," I mumble, flopping into the bed.

I don't lie down yet though. I look up at Priya with tired eyes. "Pills?"

She hands me a small bag of them. I pop a few different ones. I'm not taking chances after my near miss. I don't ever want to dream again. I don't want to see Ruby or the spider she became. And I sure don't want to meet the Nightmare boy again.

I don't think I'll be lucky enough to wake up in time twice.

"I'll go." Priya puts on her boots. "I know you can't sleep with other people around, so just relax."

My body eases. Priya understands. I can't even find the words to express how grateful I am for this simple kindness. I don't have to explain anything, don't have to face the awkward conversation where I ask her to leave her own room.

"I'll come get you for tonight's dinner?" she says, but it's a question, like she's not quite sure.

I stare at her, blanking before remembering. "With your sister."

She winks. "You came back just in time to save me from her nagging."

I roll my eyes but smile. "All right, all right."

I strip the hideous, salty clothes from my body, but I don't have the energy to do more than crawl under the blankets.

I fall asleep the instant I hear the door click shut behind Priya.

My magical, dreamless sleep is interrupted by a knock on the door—the Director, telling me that the authorities are in the lobby and want to talk to me about what happened.

I groan and roll out of bed. I'd managed to shed the stiff, salty clothes I'd been wearing for the last however many days, but I still feel like a trail of slime in human form. Sticky like spilled soda, and like half the dirt in the forest stuck to me.

The human embodiment of the floor of a theater bathroom.

I can't stand it another second.

I decide the authorities can wait five minutes while I hose myself down in the communal showers. It's more than five minutes because I scrub myself all over, every nook and cranny, with a rough bar of soap, and practically rip half my hair out cleaning it. It's a good thing I keep it short.

I don't know where my things are, so I borrow some of Priya's clothes. They're all too long, and I have to roll up the sleeves and the pant legs, but at least it's clean, and it's better than showing up for a police interview naked.

I'm somewhat presentable when I show up in the boardroom, where the Director has put the police officer to wait. I'm also twenty minutes late. I hope that's not a crime because I don't have anything to bribe my way out of it.

The officer waiting for me is Black, older, with salt-and-pepper hair and round glasses. He doesn't seem bothered by my lateness as he rises and shakes my gloved hand.

"I'm Detective Timmons, from the Intercity Investigative Department of the Newham Police," he says, and I nod along, like I know what the hell that is. It sounds official, but he could be a con artist and I'd never know. I never bothered learning anything about the police except how to bribe them.

He sits down and gestures for me to do the same.

"So," he says, immediately down to business. "Tell me what happened."

I do, going over the explosion and how I swam to shore, alone, and my long trek back to civilization. I mention the cabin with the dead bodies in it, and he makes a note of its general location and tells me he'll get someone to look into it.

I sip water as I talk because I've been thirsty since I came back and I'm not sure I'll ever not be thirsty again anymore. Also, because it's full of Helomine, and I want to be absolutely sure I never dream again.

"So," he says when I'm done telling my story. "Let's go over the explosion again."

I shrug. "Okay?"

"You say you were at the back of the ship?"

"Yeah," I tell him. "I think I was far away from whatever the source was because I was blown off the boat before the fire hit me." I consider. "Or maybe the fire was in the ship, and the door protected me from the fire?"

I have no idea how fires work. Or explosions. Based on his expression, he can tell.

He makes a note. "Did you feel the pressure coming from below, from the side, or both?"

I stare at him. "Uh. I dunno. It was kinda. There. It was huge. I couldn't say."

He makes another note.

I realize as he continues questioning me that he's probably trying to figure out *where* the explosion originated, in case it's a clue that leads to what actually exploded. I feel like I'm not being very helpful though. All I remember is the boom and being thrown into the water.

He sighs, rubbing his temples. "When you were in the water, was it on fire too?"

I blink. "Pardon?"

"Was the water on fire?"

"It's water."

"I'll take that as a no?"

"It's water."

He sighs heavily. "Many flammable materials float. Gasoline. Oil. I'm trying to see if anything spilled across the water."

"Oh." I blink. "I didn't know that was a thing that could happen."

He gives me an expectant look, and I think back, to the flames above me, to how Cy had to drag me several feet away before we could safely surface.

"I'm not sure," I finally admit. "But maybe?"

"That's fine," he says with a heavy sigh, and then it's onto the next question.

After an hour, he leaves, and I slump back in my seat, exhausted. We went over every single detail of that night. Multiple times.

I got the sense I was profoundly useless at remembering a single important thing.

I sigh, massaging my temples. I do wish I could help, give them some key clue that would reveal what happened, but honestly, I saw pretty much nothing. And maybe that's for the best. If it *was* an assassination thing, it would probably be dangerous if I remembered anything useful.

No, in this case, it's better that I'm incompetent.

I rise and leave the meeting room, heading down to the lobby. The Director will be running a seminar around now, and I want to catch him and find out where my stuff is. I need clothes that fit, and they were all in the trunk under my bed.

A familiar pain blooms when I think of my bed, my tiny little room, my safe space, stolen from me. I press my hand against my heart as though that will help, but all it does is make me aware of just how deep that pain lies in my chest.

I push the feeling down, down, down. Ignore your emotions when you don't like them. Avoid the pain at all costs.

That's basically the opposite of what the Friends of the Restful Soul tell people to do, but whatever. I can't afford to crumble again, can't afford to just sit here, crying like a child over everything I've lost.

It's much easier to focus on finding a way to get it *back*.

I'm lurking in the main lobby, hoping to ambush the Director after his seminar to ask about my trunk—and plead my case for my room again—when I spot a familiar figure.

He's older, white, with a shock of thick, gray hair and a tweed jacket. He's just coming into the building, heading to the receptionist.

It takes me a few minutes to figure out where I know him from. When it finally clicks, my jaw nearly hits the floor.

I completely forget why I'm in the lobby in the first place and pace over to where he's distractedly talking to the receptionist.

"Mr. Columb?" I ask, coming up to him.

He turns to me, adjusting his glasses and frowning. "Do I know you?"

"It's Ness," I say. "Ness Near. Blue Creek Public School math class?"

My old math teacher's expression brightens in memory. "Yes, yes, I remember you! Ness Near, the one who yelled at me for recommending her sister for the scholarship!"

I flush and look away. What an awkward memory. Ruby had needed teachers to write reference letters to get the scholarship she wanted, and instead of telling Ruby I didn't want her to go to some faraway boarding school, didn't want her to leave me, I'd gone and yelled at all the teachers who'd helped her.

Not my best moment.

"Goodness, I should have recognized you." Mr. Columb is prattling on. "You look just like your sister."

His words are a knife in my chest. Ruby never lived long enough to be my age. She never got to grow up and become the kind of person that I could remind people of. She didn't even get to leave a beautiful corpse, like they talk about in bad poetry.

His expression falls when he sees my pain. "I'm so sorry. I wasn't thinking."

"It's fine," I insist, trying to smile. "It's just been a while since . . ."

He nods, his expression solemn. "Poor Ruby. What a tragedy. Such a bright future."

I can't count how many times I've heard those words. Ruby was destined for great things. Ruby was going to change the world. Ruby was brilliant, a genius, a once-in-a-lifetime prodigy.

I don't know if it's really true. She wasn't the smartest student, but she worked hard, hard enough to get a scholarship to her dream school. But in death, she became something more. Someone impossibly intelligent, savant-level gifted. Something bigger, something larger than she'd ever been in life.

Literally. That spider was fucking massive.

I swallow heavily. For a time, I was jealous of the way people talked about her, like she'd become someone I could never live up to no matter how hard I tried.

Over time, that jealousy disappeared. Ruby never got to have a life. She never got to graduate or come to Newham or fall in love with a dream or a person or a career. She never got to live out her life, to see all of it realized in color.

"She was amazing, wasn't she?" I smile slightly, the memory of her brilliant laugh echoing in my ears. The soft twitter of the birds she fed on the porch and the feeling of warm sunlight slips across me, a memory of the way she made me feel more than a memory of the girl herself.

"It was such a shame," he replies, his expression weathered and sad. "I always wondered if she did it on purpose."

I frown, pulled out of the warm memory with a sudden jerk. "Pardon?"

He seems startled to realize he's spoken aloud. He waves it away. "Ah, nothing. An old man's ramblings."

"No." I step toward him, my brows pulled together. "What do you mean, you wondered if she did it on purpose?"

"Nothing, nothing."

But I can't let this go. "You think, what, Ruby purposely didn't take her pills so she could become a Nightmare?"

"I—I'm sorry, I didn't mean—"

"Why would you think that? Why would you ever think she *wanted* that?" My voice has risen in anger, and I don't know why I'm so angry at even the thought of this, even the *idea* that Ruby had chosen to become a Nightmare.

That she'd chosen to destroy everything and everyone I loved in one single horrific night.

"I'm sorry." His eyes dart away. "I have to go."

He hurries off before I can ask anything else, moving fast for an old man. I don't follow, too stunned by his implication to move.

He's wrong.

He has to be wrong.

I think of the crunch of my father's bones in the spider's teeth, of child-me crouched under the sink, biting the fabric of her shirt to keep from screaming. Of the next day, when I was quietly told exactly how many people she'd killed, when they told me I'd have to leave town, move in with an aunt I'd never met.

Why would Ruby have wanted that?

The answer is simple: She wouldn't.

She wouldn't have wanted to become a Nightmare. She had everything going for her. She was leaving in a few days to take up a scholarship at her dream school. Our father had recently gotten a raise, so we'd been eating cheesecake—Ruby's favorite—every week.

And most important, Ruby had loved me. She'd have done anything to protect me, to make me happy. Turning into a monster, killing our father, and trying to eat me *really* wasn't the way to do that.

She'd never have wanted any of that.

But as I look at the empty space my old math teacher had stood a few minutes earlier, I wonder why he'd think she would have.

What does he know about my sister that I don't?

What could possibly make him believe she'd *want* to become a Nightmare?

14

I'm still obsessing over what Mr. Columb said when Priya drags me to her sister's place for dinner.

I located my trunk of clothes right before we had to leave and am now wearing a button-up white shirt, pressed gray trousers, and matching waistcoat and gloves, all of which actually fit. Priya had laughed when she'd seen me sloshing around in her clothes and pointed to my trunk under her bed.

We take the subway most of the way, rattling through the dark. I sit tightly, bunched into myself. I don't like the subways—there's nowhere to hide if a Nightmare appears. And sometimes people fall asleep to the rocking motion, which is even worse.

"So, spill," Priya says, leaning toward me. "What happened on the boat?"

I shake my head, looking meaningfully at the person across from us, who's reading a newspaper with the words **SURVIVOR OF BOAT MASSACRE FOUND**. The man reading the paper is pretending to read, but I can tell he's actually listening to us.

"Later, when we're alone," I tell Priya.

I still don't know if I should tell Priya about Cy or not. On the one hand, she's my best friend and I tell her everything. On the other hand, I promised Cy I'd keep him out of this, and he *did* save my life.

Priya is an amazing person, but she's also kind of obsessed with getting into an organization whose sole job is to kill dangerous Nightmares. I know she said vampires were kinda sexy in films, but I don't actually know how she'd react to one in real life.

I don't want to put Cy in danger. But I also don't want to lie to my best friend.

When did things become so confusing?

"Hey," I say, trying to distract Priya. "Have you ever heard of someone in dreams talking to you? Like the nightmare having a personality?"

"Oh, you mean the Phantom," Priya says, nodding.

"The Phantom?"

"Some people say they see someone in their nightmare that talks to them," Priya says. "But lots of people don't. Scientists say it's just the mind's way of coping with what's happening because it's easier to think of an individual doing something to you than to believe some creepy faceless force or whatever is changing you."

"Oh," I say, thinking of the Nightmare boy—the Nightmare Phantom. Was he really just a trick my mind had played on me? Or is it only those who lucid dream that see him? "Why don't they think the Phantom is real?"

She shrugs. "Probably because no one really describes it the same. There's no consistency in the reports—on gender or looks or personality. Sometimes it's friendly, sometimes cruel, sometimes manic. It appears as loved ones or as monsters or any number of other things."

"I see," I murmur, but I'm still not entirely convinced. He didn't feel like a figment of my subconscious, unless my subconscious is a lot more messed up than I thought.

Which, now that I think about it, is possible.

A woman walks into the subway car, her skin red, her eyes black. Twisted horns rise from her head, and her hoofs click as she walks.

I shift closer to Priya, my hands bunched into nervous fists in my lap as she seats herself and starts reading a penny novel.

Priya sighs heavily. "Ness . . ."

I squeeze my eyes closed tightly. I'm being absurd. Yes, she's a Nightmare. Yes, she's terrifying to look at. But she's reading a penny novel and ignoring me. I don't need to be this tense.

This isn't a reasonable fear; this is my brain playing tricks on me. I need to ignore it, recognize I'm overreacting, and that I have no cause to be afraid.

My mind is like rats scratching to escape, but I try doing the breathing technique the Friends are always on about. It sort of helps.

I sit, just breathing, and after a moment Priya makes a shocked sound. "Ness, I'm impressed. When did you learn such self-control? I expected you to be halfway back home by now."

I grit my teeth, trying not to look at the woman. "I don't know what you're talking about."

Priya rolls her eyes.

The next stop comes, and the demon woman looks up and gets off. My whole body slumps when she does, tension releasing.

"Do you ever wonder," I ask quietly as the subway starts up again, "why some people come out of their Nightmares monsters only in body and some come out monsters in mind too?"

"I thought they'd settled that. It has to do with the type of nightmare you have. If the monster in your dream has the brain capacity of a peanut, you will too. But if your fear is a person or anything as intelligent as you, you retain your sense of self, even if your body is warped."

I lean my head back against the glass. "I suppose." I tip my head, thinking of Cy, of the first vampire Nightmare from his strain. "But that doesn't explain people like Valentine Valence. His whole personality changed after his nightmare."

Priya shrugs. "Eh. Maybe that was his biggest fear? To have his personality changed?"

"And to be a vampire."

"I don't know, man." Priya waves it off. "I think trying to find logic in something as illogical as a nightmare is a waste of time. People's brains are weird, and how the nightmare affects them is weird, and I don't think there's much point wasting time debating the hows and whys."

I close my eyes, swallowing. I think of my sister, the way my father's bones crunched in her teeth. Did she wonder about Nightmares, think about what her greatest fear was? Did she think that she'd come through the other end of the nightmare retaining her identity, just mutated into something stronger, something scarier?

Maybe. I might believe it if you told me she did it convinced she'd still be herself on the other side.

But it still raises the question: Why would she *want* to be stronger or scarier in the first place?

I rub my temples.

I need to stop letting my old math teacher's words haunt me so. What the hell does he know anyway?

He's wrong. He has to be.

"It's not fair," I whisper softly, "that some people come through their nightmares ugly or monstrous but still themselves and others are just . . ."

"Gone?"

"Yeah."

Priya nods slowly. "It's not fair."

She doesn't ask me why I'm thinking about it. She knows my expressions and moods well enough to know that my sister is on my mind.

"At least you know what happened to her," Priya whispers softly, her voice gentle. "It might not seem like a lot, but it is."

I look away. Sometimes I forget about Priya's mother. She went to sleep one night and disappeared. Simply vanished. No one knows what happened.

It's actually pretty common. No one knows whether the people who disappear just become something so small they're invisible to the naked eye—though notable disappearances often correlate to a sudden rise in diseases, so there's a theory that those people were so afraid of illness that they became germs.

But others, like Priya's mom, aren't tied to any disease outbreaks. We just don't know what happened to her.

Priya says her mother's greatest fear was something happening to her family, but how do you physically become a fear of losing your family? I have no idea.

"Do you ever wonder what she became?" I ask.

"All the time," Priya replies. "Sometimes I imagine she's here with me, invisible and intangible, like a ghost."

I smile slightly at that. "Watching over you?"

"Something like that." A ghost of a smile crosses Priya's face. "I bet she'd be proud of how I took down that Nightmare the other day."

I laugh. "I'm sure she would."

The train stops, and another Nightmare gets on. This one is a giant slug, and it pools in the doorway, like a giant lump of bread dough. Priya doesn't even react, completely unconcerned.

"How do you do that?" I ask.

"Do what?"

"Stay so calm?"

She shrugs. "I dunno. The slug guy seems chill."

"But how do you *know*?" I ask. "It's not like you can tell by looking if they're evil. How do you tell which ones are going to hurt people?"

Priya rolls her eyes. "That's easy. If it's attacking me, I kill it. If it's attacking other people, I kill it. If it's not attacking anyone, I don't kill it. I feel like it's a really simple distinction."

I snort-laugh. "I suppose so."

I wish I lived in Priya's world, where everything is so easy. But instead I live in my world, where any Nightmare I see is another potential horror story, another monster just waiting to crunch on my bones.

"Speaking of." Priya leans forward, grin big and bright on her face. "I have *newwwwwssss*."

I raise my eyebrows, more than willing to be pulled from my thoughts. "Oh?"

"You remember how I heroically defeated that Nightmare lady and saved you?"

I roll my eyes at the description, but a smile tugs at my lips. "Yeah?"

"Well, Nightmare Defense thought it was pretty awesome!" Her eyes are sparkling with glee.

My eyes widen as I suddenly see where she's going with you. "Did they—?"

"They accepted me!" Priya's smile is brighter than all the lights in the subway. "I'm going to start basic training next month!"

Holy shit.

"Priya!" I shriek, raising my arms.

After all these years, all that work, all those applications, finally, Priya is actually getting what she's worked so hard for.

She's absolutely glowing with happiness. "I just found out this afternoon! They want me to come in and sign the paperwork tomorrow. I can't believe they said yes. Finally." Her whole body is vibrating. "I'm gonna kill sea monsters. And sky monsters. And fight dragons. It's gonna be *epic*."

My chest is near bursting with happiness. Priya has wanted this forever, and she's worked so damn hard. For a moment, I'm glowing as brightly as she is, her joy contagious, her happiness mine.

But beneath it, selfishly, I'm a little sad. If she's out there fighting dragons, she's not going to be here, with me. It's a dumb, pathetic, little grief, and it makes me wonder what else I have in my life besides Priya. She's my best and only friend.

Until this moment, I hadn't realized quite how badly my fear has stunted my life. I haven't made other friends at the Friends of the Restful Soul—they're not bad people, it's just that they're all, well, actually devoted to their work, and I'm there trying to cling to the safety and the free room and board.

What else do I have in my life?

Nothing. I've been too afraid to do anything else.

I think of Cy, belatedly, and his exasperated expressions. Of him telling me how to reach him.

Maybe I could contact him. Say hi. He's new to the city, and I haven't done a lot of the tourist things. Maybe that would be nice. Then I won't be alone when Priya is gone.

My hands shake a little in my lap at the thought of doing anything with a Nightmare, but I force them still.

". . . and I hear they keep Nightmares in cages on the training grounds, and so we'll actually get to fight, like, hydras and dragons during practice . . ."

Priya continues chattering excitedly the rest of the way there, and I occasionally ask questions, to which she enthusiastically goes on tangents about everything from the types of weapons they'll be given to how they have planes, actually flying war planes, to fight flying Nightmares.

Honestly, it sounds absolutely terrifying and likely to get her killed—I feel like rocket launchers from a distance are a better bet than aerial fights—but I don't say anything. Criticizing Nightmare Defense in front of Priya is a fast way to end up on her shit list. Everyone else in her life is busy trying to convince her not to join—she doesn't need that from me too.

Besides, I'm not exactly in a good position to be judging other people's life choices.

Priya continues chatting, at one point whipping out a pack of trading cards she bought with the faces and heroic feats of famous heroes of Nightmare Defense. Charlie Chambers, who slew the Great Sea Dragon. Simone Yuen, who stopped a dinosaur invasion. Davinderjeet Sharma, who blew up a zombie-flooded island.

All their faces stare up at me, majestic and brave. The exact opposite of me.

Priya's still buzzing excitedly when we get off the subway and climb the grimy stairs onto the street, heading to Adhya's apartment building.

Tucked between a tiny Chinese grocer and a post office, the

entrance to Adhya's apartment building is brick and mortar, the door painted a bright, cheery blue. It's shockingly lacking grime, given the state of the city, but this is also Adhya we're taking about, and I wouldn't be surprised if she came down every day to clean the door and make sure it looked pristine.

We clomp up the narrow stairwell to the third floor, and Priya knocks on a polished wood door with the number four on it.

It opens, revealing not Adhya but her girlfriend, Livia.

Livia grins at us both. She's Black, tall, and slim, with turquoise glasses and braids tied back with a blue ribbon. She's got a relaxed air about her, something inherently calming. Where both Adhya and Priya are high energy in completely different ways, Livia radiates calm.

In this family, they need someone like that.

"Come on in," Livia says. "Adhya's just in the kitchen. She wanted to cook dinner tonight to celebrate Priya's news and you being alive, Ness."

Priya starts undoing her combat boots but pauses. "Wait, how does she know about my news?"

Livia raises an eyebrow. "Did you forget? You gave our phone as your backup contact number in case they couldn't reach you at the cult."

"Still not a cult," I mutter as I slip off my ankle boots.

They both ignore my comment, and Priya scowls. "I wanted to tell her."

"Trust me, it's better this way," Livia says, her smile ironic. "She's had some time to let the shock wear off."

Priya's expression dims. "She was mad, wasn't she?"

Livia sighs heavily, rubbing her temple. "Your sister loves you, Priya. She's just worried about you. It's a dangerous job."

"But it's my choice." Priya's voice is passionate and angry, the fire of an old argument coming back.

"I know," Livia says gently. "So does Adhya."

Priya mutters unhappily as we step into the apartment.

Adhya and Livia have the nicest apartment I've ever been in. It has four shoebox-size rooms—a living room, a kitchen, a bedroom, and a bathroom—and by Newham standards, it's a mansion. I wish I could afford a place like this all to myself.

Of course, I never will. Adhya is a doctor, a very specialized, highly paid one. I don't have the brains for that or the money to pay for schooling. Livia is an engineer at an auto company. She's brilliant and holds multiple patents for all sorts of things, from different types of brake systems to a design for an electrical auto engine. I can't even figure out how to open doors that need two keys, so I'm pretty sure becoming an engineering genius is also out for me.

No, I'll never be as wealthy and successful as Livia and Adhya. Which is why the Friends of the Restful Soul has always been my best option for having a stable, safe life. I had my own tiny room. I never had to worry about food or rent. It had everything I needed.

And I'm losing it.

I swallow heavily, trying not to think about it as I pad over to the table. It's long and rectangular, pressed against the window so all four seats can have a view of the city skyline while we eat.

Adhya comes out of the kitchen bearing a massive pot. "Dinner!"

Adhya is the exact opposite of her sister in so many ways. She's short where Priya is tall, her hair long and natural where Priya keeps hers short and dyed. But they have the same warm brown eyes, heart-shaped faces, and skeptically arched eyebrows.

"Sit down." Adhya is smiling as she puts the pot down in the middle of the table. "It's a celebration night, so I made Newham chowder."

"Ooh!" Priya leans forward, breathing in the scent. "You splurged! There's shrimp *and* salmon!"

"I did splurge." Adhya admits it, taking off her oven mitts. "I'm happy for you, Pri."

Priya looks away, shifting awkwardly in her seat like she's not sure how to respond.

Adhya turns to me, her smile widening. "And I'm happy you're alive, Ness! My god, I can't believe you survived that!"

"Neither can I," I admit.

We all settle down to eat, and the usual questions pop up—am I all right, am I healthy, what happened on the boat—most of which I dodge and say I'm not ready to talk about.

Adhya nods with sad eyes. "Ness, this sounds so traumatic. I'm so sorry."

I shrug vaguely. "It's fine."

"It doesn't sound fine." A pregnant pause. "Have you considered seeing a therapist? I can refer you to a good one."

I roll my eyes. "If I wanted therapy, I'd use the free services at the Friends."

"Well." Adhya's lips are pursed. "I'm sure the Friends do the best they can, but I was thinking more of a professional."

That's Adhya speak for "the Friends are a bunch of con artists running a cult and I don't trust them at all."

"I can't afford that." I wave it away. "And really, I'm fine."

"I just think—"

Livia lays her hand on Adhya's arm, a small, gentle motion, and Adhya stops. Their eyes meet for a moment, some unspoken communication happening, and then Adhya looks away and sighs. Livia removes her hand and resumes eating.

"So, Priya." Adhya's smile looks more like a grimace. "Tell me more about your training for Nightmare Defense."

Her tone makes it sound like Priya has joined up with a gang.

I wonder which is worse in Adhya's eyes: a gang or a cult.

Judging from her pinched expression, they're both equally awful places for her sister.

We continue like this for a while, Adhya asking careful, slow questions, trying and failing to hide her dislike. When does Priya start? Does she have to move into some kind of training barracks? Will she still be able to come for weekly dinners? What kind of protocols are in place to keep Priya safe?

It's always an exquisite kind of pain, watching Priya and Adhya interact. I think of my own sister, dead and gone, and wonder what kind of relationship we'd have had if she hadn't become a Nightmare.

Would we have had weekly dinners together? Would we have seen eye to eye on my life choices? Or hers?

Ruby always loved building things in her spare time. Birdhouses, mostly, but she'd also built a new chair for our father's birthday, which she regularly rubbed with beeswax so it glowed. She said she found it calming, after working so hard at school, to let her mind wander while her hands created something beautiful.

My throat closes, and I try to keep my lips from trembling as I watch Priya and Adhya. They lean toward each other, their movements mirroring each other's, espousing completely opposite opinions even as they make the same motions, so perfectly in sync even when they're not.

Watching them is like seeing what I could have had.

What was stolen from me.

I stare down at the table, my chowder barely touched. Livia gently leans toward me. "Are you okay?"

I smile up at her, a little sad. "Yeah, just tired. Been a long few days."

I feel like Livia sees right through me, but she doesn't call me on my lie, just asks me if I want another portion of soup. I take a few more bites and decide that I do.

". . . which is why Coffee Brothers' pumpkin banana latte isn't as good as Tea'N'Go's cinnamon chestnut mocha." Priya finishes explaining with a flourish that nearly knocks over her bowl of soup, which she then scrambles to stabilize.

Adhya is laughing as she asks, "Have you tried every flavored latte in this city?"

"Probably."

That's not even an exaggeration. Priya loves fancy coffees and has a personal ranking system of the best ones in the city. I can't count how many places I've been dragged to so we can try some sugary, caffeinated concoction that, if I'm being honest, tastes the same as every other sugary, caffeinated concoction we've tried. Priya says I don't have a connoisseur's taste, which is probably true since, if the popularity of these shops is anything to go by, I seem to be the only one in Newham who can't tell the difference between all the fancy coffees.

"Where are you even getting money for this?" Adhya asks, still shaking her head and smiling. "I thought the Friends didn't give you salaries."

"I have a part-time job," Priya explains with a shrug. "Every other weekend."

Adhya's expression brightens. "Wonderful! Can you make it a career?"

"I'm joining Nightmare Defense." Priya's voice goes flat. "*That's* my career."

"Of course." Adhya nervously pushes a strand of hair behind her ear. "But just in case that doesn't work out."

Priya snorts. "Really?"

"Backup plans are important."

Beside me, Livia rests her head in her hands. I'm tempted to do the same. We can both see the impending fight about Nightmare Defense looming. Honestly, I'm surprised it took this long to happen.

"Sure, I suppose I could join the Montessauri gang full-time if Nightmare Defense doesn't work out," Priya says sarcastically.

"The Montessauri gang?" Adhya looks more startled than horrified. "What are you doing with *them*?"

"Getting money." Priya shrugs. "I work as a bouncer at their biweekly fight club. Pay's pretty decent."

"Priya." Adhya's voice is strained. "What are you involving yourself with a *gang* for?"

"Oh, don't give me that!" Priya snaps. "Your office pays the Zimmer gang a monthly protection fee same as half the other places in Newham."

"Yes, but we don't work at their illegal fight rings!"

Priya waves a hand dismissively. "A job's a job. And this one's fine. I just throw drunks and assholes out the door. It's good practice for Nightmare fighting."

"Why does everything have to go back to Nightmares with you?" Adhya's expression is pinched. "Why are you so obsessed with fighting them?"

"Why are you so obsessed with avoiding them?"

"I don't avoid them," Adhya counters. "I work with them every day. That's literally my job."

"Yeah, but your whole thing is that you make them less Nightmare-y."

"Yes, that is what trauma reconstructive surgeons do," Adhya deadpans.

"No, I mean you try and make them become human again. You've built your whole career around erasing the effects of

Nightmares." Priya's eyes are hard on Adhya. "You're just as obsessed with Nightmares as I am. I'm obsessed with fighting them but you're obsessed with *erasing* them."

"That's not—I'm not—"

Livia and I exchange a look.

This is getting a little more personal than the usual fights about Nightmare Defense. Adhya has always been vehemently opposed to Priya joining, supposedly because it's dangerous. But really, this is Newham—every job is dangerous, even the ones that shouldn't be.

It's never seemed more of an excuse than it does now, watching them argue over how they've chosen to respond to Nightmares in their lives—Priya by fighting the violent ones, Adhya by making the nonviolent ones look more human.

And then there's me, who can only ever hide from Nightmares, whether they're violent or not.

All of us have lost family to Nightmares, and we've all let it warp our lives in different ways.

Livia tips her head and I nod and rise from the table. We pick up the dishes and leave the room, heading for the tiny kitchen.

We start washing the dishes together, the sound of Priya and Adhya bickering in the other room a familiar music.

"I was hoping tonight they'd behave," I sigh.

Livia shakes her head. "I don't think they can. Not right now."

She puts a wet, scrubbed dish in my hand, and I towel it dry and put it in one of the cupboards.

"I love Adhya dearly," Livia says, "but she needs to accept that her sister is her own person. A very different person than herself. And there's nothing wrong with either of them because of it."

I nod slowly, drying another plate and wondering if I was as blind to Ruby and her wants as Adhya is to Priya's. We're all looking at the world through our own biased eyes. I've always thought of Ruby as a hapless victim, full of the same desires and fears I am.

But what if she wasn't?

What if I'm the one who's been imposing my own interpretation onto Ruby's actions?

What if she really *did* intend to become a Nightmare?

I dry another plate as I come back to the crux of it all, the question that everything else leads to:

Why?

15

The next few days mostly consist of me sleeping and trying to get my single room back.

I fail at both of these things.

I struggle to sleep in Priya's room, constantly afraid that she's going to come in while I'm unconscious. I can't even be in the room while she's asleep either. I try—I do. I take sleeping pills and I calm myself and practice telling myself that it's okay, she won't turn into a Nightmare, I literally saw her take the pills.

It doesn't help.

I stare at the ceiling, my eyes wide with fear, my heart racing, as she snores on the other side of the room.

Every day, I badger the Director for my old room, but he's become canny at avoiding me, and I'm only continuing out of a growing sense of desperation. He's not giving me my single room back. I know that intellectually.

But I can't accept defeat.

Which is why I corner him one morning to beg for my room back.

"Ah, Ness, I was looking for you."

I pause, my carefully prepared speech vanishing. "Wait, you were?"

"Yes." He smiles his strange lizard smile at me. "You're going to a memorial today."

I blink at him. "I am? I thought I was off memorials after the, uh, incident last week."

"You are." He massages the bridge of his snout, as though even the memory of me running away from the Nightmare and ditching Priya gives him a headache. "But that woman's memorial is being held today, and you know policy. You knew her, you're the one who needs to go."

I stare at him, horrified. "I knew her for all of five minutes before she turned into a Nightmare and tried to kill me!"

"Still better than anyone else here. Go pick up some flowers and get over there."

I groan. "What about Priya?"

He shrugs. "She's at one of her Nightmare Defense meetings. She told me she'd be out all day when she left this morning."

Ugh. Not only do I have to return to the scene of the attack, I have to do it alone?

What a joke.

But I don't want to rock the boat, especially when I'm so close to being thrown out and ending up homeless, so I do as I'm told and head down to the reception desk, where we keep the flowers stocked for disciples going out to spread the word.

Ugh. When I think of it that way, it really does sound like I'm in a cult.

Of course, because my day is doomed to be trash, Cindy is manning the reception desk. She looks harassed and tired, with bags under her eyes.

When she sees me, she purses her lips together. "The phone lines have been ringing all morning."

I glare back. "And?"

"And it's your fault."

I spread my hands. "How is it *my* fault?"

"Because," she says slowly, "the newspapers got ahold of your name. They know you're the boat disaster survivor."

Shit.

"I think every reporter in the whole city—no, the whole country—wants to talk to you," Cindy tells me, just as the phone rings again. She doesn't answer it, just gives it a look so scorching I expect the phone to burst into flames.

I groan. "You've got to be kidding me."

"I wish I were." Another phone rings. "But you're a media hot topic right now."

"How do I make them go away?" I moan.

"Eh, they'll forget about you eventually," Cindy says, in a rare moment of what I think might be sympathy. "They don't have long attention spans." She sighs heavily as another phone starts ringing. "But it's going to be noisy until they do."

"Great. Just great." A sudden thought occurs to me. "Wait, are they offering money to interview me?"

Cindy gives me a disgusted look. "You know it's against doctrine to take money for tragedy."

"Uh."

"And aside from that, profiting from a tragedy like this is just morally bankrupt," she continues, her tone casual but her eyes on me judging.

"Right. Of course. Totally agree." I give a choked laugh. "But, uh, I'm curious. You know. For curiosity. Not because I want money in case the Director kicks me out or anything." I lick my lips and lean forward. "So did they offer money?"

She rolls her eyes. "I wouldn't know. I hung up before they could offer."

"Of course you did," I say with a sigh, shoulders slumping.

I take a bouquet of flowers from the stack and head out, wondering if I should ask to be at the reception desk for a day or two. Just to make sure reporters aren't hassling anyone else because of me and definitely not to see how much they'll offer for an interview.

The walk to Mrs. Sanden's part of town is faster than taking the subway most of the time, but today seems to be an exception.

Because of course it is.

A barricade crosses the whole of Seventieth Street, simple black blockades that no one dares cross—you never know what a road is blockaded for, so it's not worth it to ignore those blockades. Sure, they might just be fixing a pipe, but there also might be a gang war going on, or a violent Nightmare on the loose.

I turn around, but more people have already come up behind me, pressing against my back, trapping me in the crowd. I'm shoved to the side by a newcomer, and suddenly I have a perfect view through the crowd of exactly what's beyond those barricades.

A massive Nightmare crouches on the pavement.

It's easily twelve or thirteen feet tall, a giant apelike thing with glittering black scales. It's mouth is open and fangs are bared, but no sound comes out, not even a grunt, as though it's incapable of making noise. It's back is arched and bristling.

In one hand, it clutches a screaming woman.

The woman flails, the only distinguishing feature from this far back her vibrant-red hair, which flies around as she bucks her head and wriggles and tries desperately to escape. She has no hope—that thing's hand is as big as she is.

The Nightmare roars silently, mouth wide, spittle flying, the violence of the motion somehow more disturbing because it's soundless.

I jerk back, but I'm trapped, pressed in the crowd now, unable to escape. Sweat slides down my forehead as panic rises, the need to run consuming my mind. I elbow and claw at people, and they bat me away and curse at me, but no one moves, the crowd packed too tightly. I need to get out of here, to run, to hide, to escape, and my eyes are fixed on that horrible visage and the screaming, desperate woman in its arms.

Boom.

The world shakes as the first explosion goes off.

The creature snarls, swinging its horrific head to one side, revealing spiny ridges on its neck, covered in blood and gore, like someone scooped out a chunk of its neck with a melon baller.

Leaning out the window across the street is a blond Nightmare Defense soldier with a rocket launcher over one shoulder and a speakerphone in the other. It's hard to tell from this distance, but it might actually be Charlie Chambers himself. That would explain the crowd. No one wants to miss Charlie Chambers killing a Nightmare.

Except me, apparently.

"It's vulnerable to missiles!" Charlie's voice booms into his speakerphone, a sharp contrast to the silent monster. "All units, *FIRE!*"

I see them now, in the windows of the surrounding buildings, on the rooftops, and in front of the crowd. People in navy suits and goggles, their belts bristling with weapons, each of them with rocket launchers braced on their shoulders.

The air is full of fire.

The monster rears, chest bare and bloody. For a moment, it looks like it's untouched by the missiles and Nightmare Defense has failed.

Then the Nightmare keels over to one side, its massive body slumping to the ground. The pavement cracks where it lands, breaking apart, chunks of asphalt flying. A pipe somewhere beneath is ruptured, and bloodstained water jumps into the air like a horrible, gory fountain.

The woman the Nightmare was holding is crushed beneath it.

She screams once, a final desperate cry for help. After that, nothing is left of her except the slowly pooling blood beneath the Nightmare, her blood and the Nightmare's mixing until it's impossible to tell which is which.

My breathing doesn't even out, my panic still rattling about me like it could rip itself right out of my body and run away on its own. But it can't because I'm still pinned by the crowd of morons who don't know the meaning of common sense.

This isn't a goddamn spectacle. They should be running, not treating this like free entertainment. But I seem to be the only one who thinks that.

Nightmare Defense holsters their rockets and starts getting the chains out to tow the body. Someone calls out for the chain saw since they'll have to remove the body in pieces. The crowd surges forward, asking for Charlie's autograph— he writes it using the Nightmare's blood. There's plenty of it, especially after the chain saw is brought out.

My eyes are fixed on the spot where the woman disappeared, a prisoner of a Nightmare, an innocent caught up in the chaos.

Now she's dead.

It's not like this is new. It's not like this isn't common. But it's very mundanity makes me all the more afraid.

Eventually, the road blocks are lifted and we're allowed to walk by. My breathing is finally back under control and the panic has eased, leaving only an exhausted feeling and the skin-crawling sensation of a narrowly dodged bullet.

What if that monster had turned on the crowd?

I shiver. I should have taken the subway. No—I should never have left my room in the first place. Nothing good comes of leaving my safe space.

It's noon by the time I arrive at the deceased Mrs. Sanden's apartment building. My panic attack has taken everything out of me, and I'm jumpier than usual, wincing at every sound, scuttling away from every strange look. I feel like a wrung-out dishcloth.

I'm wondering if I should just skip this memorial and go back to Priya's room and sleep. The Director would never know I skipped out.

But I'm already here, so I might as well put the flowers down before I leave.

I ascend the steps slowly until I reach her floor. The door is open, and my memory slips back to the moment Mrs. Sanden fell backward. When she'd fainted. When she'd become a Nightmare.

Had she done it on purpose?

Had we really pissed her off that much?

I sigh heavily. Why am I doing this, questioning every Nightmare in my past just because some math teacher I barely remember said something dumb? Not everything is intentional. Sometimes, people just turn into monsters.

Pretty sure no one wanted to be a giant ape dragon that destroyed a street and crushed an innocent woman in his fall.

I shake my head like I can shed the thoughts like droplets of water from wet hair.

The apartment has been emptied out, and the bare wooden

floor is covered in flowers. I'm not surprised it's empty. Priya and Nightmare Mrs. Sanden destroyed almost everything in it, and the landlord probably needs the place cleared anyway before it can be put on the market again.

Another woman is in the room, kneeling quietly before the pile of flowers. She's white but heavily tanned from sun, and I wonder where on earth she got a tan in Newham. Her short, sandy hair is slicked to her head, and her body is concealed by the long brown coat she's wearing.

I step into the room and carefully place my wilting flowers in the pile. Then, because I know the Director will be upset if I don't, I stack a pile of pamphlets for the Friends of the Restful Soul's therapy programs beside the flowers.

"Are you here from the cult?" the kneeling woman asks, looking up at me.

"It's not a cult," I insist, but there's no energy in my voice.

She smiles at me, a little too widely, too much teeth. "Of course not, excuse me."

I shrug it off. As the saints say, *shake it, shake it, shake it off.*

Oh no, wait, that's a pop song.

I don't actually remember what the saints said because I never really paid attention. No wonder Cindy is so scornful of me, I must look like such a transparent fraud to her.

I sigh, bowing my head. Why can't things ever be simple?

"If you don't mind me asking," the woman says. "Are you that girl who survived the boat explosion that the papers are all talking about?"

I blanch. "How did you know?"

She shrugs. "Oh, just a thought. I knew the survivor was from the cult."

Ugggggh. Everyone is going to be so mad at me. They're all probably getting accosted by random people wondering if they're the survivor. Now I get to deal with more dumb questions and every one of the Friends is going to hold a grudge against me.

The Director will probably have to kick me out just to get rid of all the calls and harassment.

Why does this day just keep getting worse?

"Oh," I finally say.

She rises slowly, stretching. "It's a pity."

"What? The explosion?" I wasn't sure pity was the right word. Travesty? Horrific loss of life? Pity seems a bit tame.

"Hmm? No." The woman reaches under her coat. "It's a pity that after surviving all that, now I have to kill you."

Then she whips out a knife and lunges for me.

16

I don't dodge the knife so much as stumble backward so hard that I end up falling on my ass.

I collapse back into the bouquets of flowers, and despite how soft they look, they don't cushion my fall in the slightest. I land painfully, right on my tailbone, zags of agony slicing up my back.

Crushed petals float around me like an advertisement for shampoo or a scene from a romantic film. Pollen lingers in the air, itching at my throat and making my nose twitch with the urge to sneeze.

The knife whistles through the air right where I was just standing.

She's trying to kill me.

Some random woman I've never met is trying to kill me.

What the fuck?

She sighs heavily and looks down at me, covered in flower petals, on my ass on the floor, and raises an eyebrow. "Come on, kid, I don't want this to be messy. I promise it'll be painless if you don't wiggle."

I stare at her, mouth slightly open.

All this time, I've been so scared it's going to be a Nightmare that gets me, my bones crunching between their teeth and my blood sinking between the floorboards and soaking into the foundation. But in the end, it's going to be some random lady at a memorial service.

Not just some random lady. In Newham, someone you don't know confirming your identity and then trying to murder you means only one thing.

An assassin.

Someone hired an assassin to kill me.

Are you *kidding* me?

She gives me an arch look, and she repositions herself, knife raised. "You gonna hold still this time?"

Hell no.

But I don't know what to do. Priya would know. Priya knows everything, and I'm sure her Nightmare-fighting skills are completely transferrable to humans.

But me? I've spent my whole life hiding. Running from everything that makes me afraid, never standing up for myself, always letting someone else fight the battles.

But running is a skill too.

And I'm *really* good at it.

My hands are shaking so badly I can barely move them, but my body knows how to run, even when I'm scared. I crab walk backward, scuttling away on the floor like the coward I am, toward the only thing my panicked, desperate mind has seized on.

The window.

The same window that I leapt out of last week, instead of calling for help. The window I'd thought back on and wondered why the hell I was such a coward, hiding and running and leaving all the hard work to Priya. The window I know has a fire escape on the other side.

The window that's going to save my life a second time.

The assassin darts forward, knife coming down toward me in a deadly arc.

I roll away.

The floor is hard and painful under me, but my roll has the advantage that now I'm not on my back but my stomach. Which makes it much easier to scramble to my feet.

"So we're doing this the hard way," the woman snarls as she whips around to me.

She must be a newer assassin, I decide. The long-term professionals murder you before you even know they're there. Or so I've heard.

One hears a lot about these kinds of things in Newham.

She lunges forward, trying to simultaneously stab me while blocking my path to the window.

I leap backward, spinning the other way—to the exit she's left unprotected in her effort to prevent me getting to the window.

The door.

She notices her mistake immediately, but she's not fast enough to stop me. I have a lot of practice running away and I'm fast, speeding out the door like ten Nightmares are on my heels, each planning on devouring a different piece of me.

Behind me, a knife thuds against wood, and I chance a glance back to see a blade embedded in the hallway wall.

If I'd been even a fraction slower, I'd be dead.

I allow myself one horrible heartbeat to realize this and then I jerk away from the apartment and race down the stairs, not looking back, not wasting those precious moments of speed just to know what's happening.

I run like there's a Nightmare chomping at my heels, like there's a boat exploding at my back. I run like I've never run before, which is saying something. I scramble down the stairwell, practically falling down the final flights of steps toward the building door.

She clatters after me, swearing viciously, but it's a distant sound, and by the time she gets to the bottom of the stairs, I'm already out the apartment building door.

I take off into the crowd, merging with the masses of people all dressed like me, various shades of browns and gray waistcoats and pants, white shirts, the aggregate mass of the city swallowing me up and consuming me until I'm only one more brushstroke in the million-stroke painting of Newham.

17

I don't stop running until I'm halfway across the city, covered in sweat, and gasping for breath.

I unbutton the top of my shirt and vest to let some air in, but nothing is going to save this shirt from the grimy sweat stains I've made in the underarms. I run my hand through my hair, pushing it off my sticky forehead and slicking it out of my eyes.

I lean against a cool brick wall in the shade and just breathe, chest rising and falling in a staccato rhythm, sucking air into my scraped throat. Around me, people walk past, unconcerned. I look like I've just run for my life, and none of them bat an eye. I'm invisible to them.

A woman walks by, carrying what I assume is a pet crocodile, given that it has a pink bow around its neck. It looks at me with murder in its beady yellow eyes as they stride past.

I want to go home.

I want to hide in my tiny room at the Friends of the Restful Soul. To curl up in a tight ball, pull the blanket over my head, and let the rest of the world disappear. To let my muscles slowly unclench in the safety of my tiny little room, just me, alone.

Except that room isn't mine anymore.

I squeeze my eyes shut, my hands clenched into fists by my sides.

I could go hide in Priya's room, but it's not the same. She could walk in at any time. I love Priya, but I need to feel like no one can get me, like I'm completely alone, completely safe, undisturbed. In a tiny coffin of my own design, with no room for anyone else.

I cover my eyes with my hand, whole body shaking. I have nowhere to retreat to. Fine. It's all right. It wasn't a Nightmare attack. I don't need to hide from the world.

No, it was just your run-of-the-mill assassin.

That's so much better.

Nightmares might try to kill you, but when you get away, you're away. When you hide, they don't come find you. Escape means safety.

Assassins? Not so much.

What the hell am I going to do if she tries to kill me again? Right now, she might be hunting me, looking for me down streets and alleyways, making a list of the places I'm most likely to run to, planning ways to break in there and get me where I think I'm safe.

Joke's on her, I don't feel safe anywhere.

I wrap my arms around myself and force myself to take deep breaths. What the hell have I done lately to warrant an assassin being hired to kill me?

Well, that's obvious.

The boat explosion.

I mean, it might not be. Perhaps a disgruntled relative of Mrs. Sanden blames me for her turning into a Nightmare and dying. And maybe this person sat there, waiting for me to show up, so they could then murder me. It would explain all the posturing. Maybe she wasn't used to the whole murder thing.

But if it was a disgruntled relative, they could have sued me. With a well-placed bribe or two, they probably would have won, and then I'd be on the hook for thousands of dollars. It's a much more profitable way to ruin my life.

So yeah. I don't think it was a disgruntled relative.

I think this is related to that damn boat.

Before I came back, people assumed that the boat was destroyed because of an accident with the fuel. Me surviving and telling the police about the explosion might have changed that conversation. Maybe it wasn't an accident, maybe it *was* a bomb, and something I said clued people in? Or maybe they only think something I say *could* clue people in.

But it seems clear to me that someone is pissed I survived that explosion.

Fuck.

I am so royally screwed I can't think of the words to describe it. My vocabulary isn't extensive enough.

Because there's another consideration here. I've already told the police about the explosion, and the papers already know. Killing me won't do shit except possibly draw even more attention to this mess.

No, if they really wanted vengeance, they'd have waited a month or two for things to die down, and then I'd have had an "accident."

Having an accident right now draws a lot of attention. Unless they need me to die now. And the only reason they'd need that is because they see me as a liability.

Which would mean that the boat explosion definitely wasn't an accident.

And the people who planted the bomb—whoever the hell they are—think I know something. That I saw something that could incriminate them. That I have some way of identifying them.

The problem is, I don't know *anything*.

I rip through my memories, searching for anything even remotely helpful. Did I see anything suspicious? Or anything that could indicate a culprit?

But I did all this with the police, and honestly, I didn't come up with anything then, and I'm not really coming up with anything now.

I bow my head. They have to know I already spoke to the police. Maybe they know I don't know anything and they're just tying up loose ends. I don't know. I don't suppose it matters.

It doesn't change that someone wants me dead.

I take a deep breath. Okay. I'm okay. I'm not dead yet. I just need to figure out next steps.

It doesn't take me long to figure out what to do, and I set out for the Newham central police office.

Sure, our police take bribes, and probably whoever wants

me killed has a few cops in their pocket, but I'm unlikely to get knifed in the police building itself—the officers tend to frown on that.

They have a nice alleyway behind the building for that.

Of course, this reminds me of the news headline from a few months ago: **COP FIGHTING TO END CORRUPTION IN POLICE FORCE DIES OF MYSTERIOUS STABBING IN POLICE STATION, NO SUSPECTS FOUND.**

Yeah. Okay. That was an awkward moment. But that doesn't *usually* happen. I think.

And on the chance the detective assigned to my case hasn't been bought off, this could be useful information.

More importantly, the police have protective services for witnesses, and I'd like a detail of armed people to protect me from assassins so I can hide under the bed while everyone else fights.

They could be bribed too though.

Ugh. Why is Newham like this?

Still, I make my way to the Newham Police out of a sense of misplaced optimism and, frankly, no idea what else to do.

But because today is just determined to suck, I'm trapped behind another blockade on Fifty-Fourth. This time at least it's not a Nightmare, just a gang shoot-out.

I stand with a group of other pedestrians, waiting for the fight to end, checking our watches and muttering irritatedly as we hide behind a brick wall and listen to the sound of gunfire.

On the street, a man in a mask is trying to singlehandedly fight off the entirety of the Montessauri gang, and it's going about as well as you'd expect.

"We are the Chaos League! We bring chaos to the villains of this city!" the man in the mask is proclaiming. "We won't allow you to steal from the people of these streets any longer!"

Great, fine, wonderful, could you please do it after I've crossed the damn street?

I needn't worry. He's just some lunatic in a mask, and the bullet that finally gets him sounds like someone dropped a watermelon on the ground.

Squishy.

The gunfire stops, and we all slide out from behind the brick wall. The Montessauri gang have holstered their guns. They're all wearing dapper white suits and matching hats, and their leader, Giovanni, is the only one wearing a color— red, to be precise. He once told reporters that he didn't like having to change clothes midday, so he always wore red so the blood would blend in.

He's a bit of a drama queen.

But this is Newham. Everyone's a bit of a drama queen.

We all cross the street when we're sure the Chaos League idiot is down. Giovanni Montessauri is laughing over the dead body, his smile stretched wide as he shares a joke with his comrade.

It strikes me then that I'm not even sweating. I just watched a man die from gunfire, and I feel nothing. How is this any different than the Nightmare I saw murder a woman earlier?

I bow my head, sighing heavily. If only I could use that logic on my brain when it was having one of its panic episodes.

The next block over, some cops are having a smoke, watching the shoot-out and making bets on how fast the Montessauri gang will kill everyone in the Chaos League.

It really inspires confidence in my choice to go to the police.

But still, ten minutes later, I'm sitting across from Detective Timmons.

The Newham Central police station is an old building, and the room I've been led to is small and cramped, with plastered white walls that are flaking in the corners and exposing chunks of brick beneath. The table is old and it tips whenever I touch it, the peeling varnish flaking off on my fingers.

Timmons has brought me tea, which I sip slowly, not because I'm savoring it but because it tastes absolutely awful but I don't want to be rude, so I'm pretending to sip when all I'm actually doing is touching my lips to the rim of the cup and not drinking.

I tell him what happened, my voice hoarse because I'm nervous and thirsty and not drinking the gross tea.

Finally, I finish, and he frowns, tapping one finger on the table and watching me with narrowed eyes.

"So," he says slowly. "You think this is connected to the boat?"

"Definitely," I tell him, fake sipping my tea. "Right before she attacked, she mentioned the boat."

"And you don't have any other enemies?"

I blink. "Not really."

Of course, that's not actually true. I don't think Cindy

likes me very much or even the Director at this point. Or really, anyone in the Friends. But I don't think they'd send an assassin to kill me. It's against doctrine.

Also, they can just kick me out. They don't have to pay money for that.

"Hmm." Timmons rubs his chin. He's giving me this look I think is meant to be hard and suspicious, but today I've already seen a gang war and a murderous Nightmare and faced down a woman with a knife. So I really don't think it's nearly as effective as he thinks it is. Especially since he's wearing a polka-dot bow tie today. You just can't be that intimidating in a polka-dot bow tie.

"See, the trouble is," he says slowly, "I'm not really sure that you're being straight with me."

I blink at him. "What?"

"Our scientists did some math." He sips his own tea, then grimaces and puts it down. "It's not possible for you to have swum to shore from the boat. No human could have done it unless they were a world champion. Not given the distance to shore and the currents that night."

Oh. Oh shit.

"So I'm left wondering: Why you'd lie?" he drawls, so slow, so easy, and suddenly I decide maybe a man in a bow tie can be ominous.

"I . . ."

"Tell me," he says, not giving me time to come up with an answer. "Did you set the bomb?"

My mouth drops open. "*What?*"

"It would have been easy to bring it in with the luggage," he continues. "And we know you boarded with a lot of luggage."

"It was *mail*."

He continues as if he hasn't heard me. "Did you use a timer or trigger it with a radio signal? You'd have needed to be a safe distance away before setting the bomb."

"I was *on the boat* when it blew up!"

"Emergency rafts are attached to the side," he muses. "It would be fairly easy to steal one, lower it into the water, and sneak away in the dark. That explosion burned so hot, no one would be surprised to never find the remains of the life rafts."

"I didn't blow up the boat!"

I rise from my seat, knocking my teacup over in the process. It spills across the bare table between us, blotchy and ugly as it soaks into the parts of the wood that aren't varnished, and drips onto the floor.

Detective Timmons doesn't move. He just watches me with his suspicious eyes, his mouth turned into something both smug and angry, like me having a reaction just proves he's right.

I open my mouth. I can fix this. I can tell them about Cy. I can explain.

But then I close my mouth.

I promised Cy I'd keep him out of this. And now actual literal assassins are coming after me. If I tell them about Cy, won't that be the same as putting a target on his back too?

If I don't say anything, they'll keep believing I'm involved in the bombing.

If I tell them about Cy to clear my name, I might be condemning him to death.

What a choice.

"So." Detective Timmons has his eyebrows raised, and his eyes are sharp on me. "Are you ready to tell me who ordered that boat blown up?"

I swear. "I didn't blow up the boat."

"I can make it easier for you. We have protective custody to keep you safe. If you give us names, we'll even waive the charges against you."

I glare. "What charges?"

He shrugs. "We'll find evidence."

He'll fake evidence. That's what he means. He's sure I'm guilty, so he'll "find" something that proves his theory so he can take me down. That's what cops do.

I'm such an idiot. I should never have come here.

"You won't find anything." I take a deep breath. "Because I swam to shore. Your experts are wrong."

I straighten, adjusting my waistcoat and shirt so they're sitting just right on me, doing up my loose top button and rolling down my sleeves.

"I'm leaving now," I tell him. "I've given you everything I know. I hope you catch the criminals responsible for this. If you need to reach me, you know where to find me."

Then I stride from the room. My back is straight, and even though my heart pounds and my palms are sweaty, my hands don't shake.

Part of me expects him to grab me from behind and arrest me right then and there. Smash me into a wall and cuff me, drag me into the cells, somewhere it'll be even easier for an assassin to take me out.

But he doesn't try to stop me, just watches me with narrowed eyes as I leave.

I keep my straight-backed, stiff posture all the way down in the elevator, even though I'm alone, and all the way across the main lobby as I leave the building.

I don't know why he doesn't arrest me. Maybe he's questioning his conclusions or maybe he just thinks he can follow me until he finds the real culprit. I don't care. He won't find anything on me, and I'm not going to admit to a crime I didn't commit. And I'm not going to throw Cy under the bus to save myself either.

I may be a coward, but I'm not a monster.

I don't sign death warrants for people who save my life. Even if they are bloodsucking Nightmares.

But as I walk away from the police station, I can't help but throw a glance over my shoulder, fear coiling in my chest.

How many enemies will I make before this is over?

18

I stand outside a restaurant in the south end of the city. It's got that grimy, sort of unkempt look that most things have in Newham. A brick facade with a smooth, old wooden door. It has a more classic look than a lot of the places in the city, a more homey, old-world feel. Or rather, what the people fantasize about the Old World being.

Hanging above the door is a wooden sign with black letters scrawled in cursive: *The Lantern Man's Restaurant.*

I slip inside, my shoes clicking on the hardwood floor. It's a small, cramped place, but most buildings here are. Tables line the walls, and barstools perch around the counter. Braced above the counter is a massive, boxy television. Koval Enterprises' newest invention, a household model that's actually too expensive for most households. I bet watching it is a big draw for people—I've not seen one in a restaurant before, and my first instinct is to say whoever runs this place has great business sense.

The TV is on, and an advertisement for a new drink that promises to make you immortal flashes across the screen. I snort, wondering who's dumb enough to buy into that kind of scam.

The restaurant is empty right now, and the sound on their little TV is off.

A Black woman comes out from the back room smiling. "Hi, sorry, we're not open for another half hour."

I blink. "Oh. I'm not—I'm not looking to eat."

"You here about a job?" She eyes me speculatively. "We're hiring a night server."

Night server. That's side speak for someone to work in a speakeasy. I glance around, but I don't see where their hidden entrance is, though it wouldn't be much of a speakeasy if I could see the door to it.

I actually agree with prohibition—alcohol stops the drugs that prevent Nightmares from working. So I'm generally against the existence of speakeasies and anywhere else that sells bootleg liquor.

But I'm pretty screwed right now, and money does sound good.

"Oh? What's the pay?" I shake my head. "Ah, no. I mean, maybe. But I'm actually here to see someone. Do you know Estelle?"

The woman nods. "Yeah, sure. You a friend?"

"A friend of a friend." I hesitate. "I need to talk to her. Is she here?"

The woman shakes her head. "Not yet. But her shift starts at opening, so she'll be here in the next ten or so." She nods to one of the empty tables. "You can sit over there and wait if you want."

My shoulders loosen. "Yeah, thanks. I will."

I seat myself at the table indicated. A newspaper has been forgotten on the chair, yesterday's issue. I spread it across the table, running my hand over the grainy black-and-white images, ink smearing on my fingers.

The first page is still about the boat explosion.

My skin crawls, and my mind flicks back to the assassin, the way her blade whistled through the air. And before that, the heat of the air as the flames licked the boat, the cold of the water.

I don't want to think about the boat explosion right now.

I flip to the next page and find more standard articles. Some branch of the military caught experimenting on soldiers, trying to engineer the ideal warrior, which backfired when their experiments killed everyone. A prison break from a high-security prison for the dangerously unstable, who are now loose in Newham. Yet another child trafficking ring exposed—this one feeding kids to some horrific Eldritch horror Nightmare in the basement.

My eyes are drawn to an article about a man with a fear of human contact who had a nightmare and woke up with skin that was addictive to the touch, like a drug. And this drug spread on anything he touched, and within a week he'd been eaten alive by all the people in his apartment building who pushed the same elevator button as him.

After the news had come out about his death and his nightmare, there'd been a wave of people having the same nightmare. They'd read the story and become afraid of that happening to them, and then, well. Next thing you know, there's a pandemic of people with addictive skin who are terrified to touch anyone for fear of addicting them.

Nightmares can be contagious in multiple ways.

"Hello?"

I look up, and a white girl with a massive mop of curly red hair looks down at me. She's more freckle than girl, and her face has something a little hungry and fey about it. Something about the hollow of her cheeks and the lines around her eyes that says she's seen hard times and come through them stronger.

She also has two perfect punctures in her throat.

I swallow, eyes darting between her face and her bite marks. "You're Estelle?"

"I am." She tips her head to the side and puts her hands on her hips, assessing me. "Who's asking?"

"I'm—I need to get in touch with Cy." My eyes flick to the bite marks. "He said you had a way to contact him."

Her eyebrows rise farther, and her eyes flick to my neck, as if checking for bite marks.

"Hey," she says in this gentle voice, before sliding into the seat across from me. "Are you okay?"

"I—I'm fine. I just need to contact Cy."

"Look," she says slowly. She bites her lip. "I know that it can seem like an easy answer, selling blood. It's not sex. It feels less—less intimate. But it's not safer."

Wait. She thinks I'm—?!

This is possibly the most humiliating moment of my life. She thinks I'm an aspiring blood worker. Or sex worker. Or both.

Well, at least I know where Cy gets his dinner now.

"I'm serious," she continues. "Vampires are no joke. They can drain you dry so easily. Or bite an artery—you can't survive that." She leans forward, hands flat on the table between us. "You could *die*."

The words rattle around my head.

He could kill you.

You could die.

And for a moment, the fear comes back, like it never left. It hadn't, really—it's always been there, tight in my chest, waiting for its chance to slip out into my mind and send me running.

This time, I push it away.

If Cy was going to eat me, he'd have done it on our miserable trek. I'm not planning on selling him blood either, despite what this woman thinks. I'm *not* going to die.

I take a deep breath. "Look, I appreciate your concern . . ."

"But you're going to ignore me." Estelle rubs the bridge of her nose. "At least take a spotter."

"A what?"

"A spotter. Someone to make sure things don't go too far," Estelle explains. "I always ask Felice over there"—she gestures at the Black woman at the bar—"to spot me. To make sure that he stops when I ask, that he doesn't take too much. She brings silver and garlic, just in case he tries anything."

That is . . . very practical, I have to admit.

"Has he ever gone too far?" I ask. Now I'm curious.

"Never," she admits. "And honestly, if I thought he would,

I wouldn't be selling him blood. But you can't be too careful. Always take precautions, even if you don't think you'll need them. Never get arrogant. Arrogance kills."

I let out a long breath. Am I being foolish, going to Cy? She's not wrong—he is dangerous. I know it.

But I need to talk to him. He was on that boat too. He deserves to know that he might be in danger. No matter how all this shakes out, I have to talk to him.

"I'm not selling blood." I rub my temple. "Seriously. I'm not. I—I know Cy from somewhere else."

She seems skeptical. "Then why didn't he give you his phone number directly?"

Because he could be traced with that, I realize. He hadn't completely trusted I wouldn't turn on him and give him to the police. He'd been protecting himself, in case I turned out to be the monster in this story.

It should make me feel sad, that he's afraid of me betraying him. But weirdly, it actually makes me like him more. Because it shows that he was afraid of me, afraid that I could ruin him, that I had power to hurt him. And he still let me go and live my life. He didn't try to hurt or control me. He didn't dispose of me, though that would have been easier.

In a city like Newham, honestly, I'd say at least half the population wouldn't have made those choices. Common decency, we'd called it back in my hometown, to not murder people in your way. But here in Newham, decency isn't so common, and morals are always for sale.

So even common decency sometimes seems like a grand thing. Even when it really shouldn't.

I slump. "It's a long story. Can you please call him and say Ness is here. It's important."

"I can call him," she says. "But it's not even close to sunset yet."

"I know."

She gives a resigned sigh. "You sure there's no one else I can call for you instead?"

I want to call Priya. I want to hear her voice, strong and assured, telling me that everything will be all right. I want her to come rescue me, to fight the monsters while I hide.

But I can't.

For one thing, Priya is out all day at Nightmare Defense. I have no idea when she'll be back, so even if I called, I probably wouldn't reach her.

And of course, there's the problem that the only way she can be reached right now is by calling the Friends of the Restful Soul.

And I don't want the Friends to know that I called.

Because someone there had to be in on my assassination attempt.

After all, how else would the assassin have known where I was going today? And when?

No. This was planned, and only a few people could have tipped the assassin off. And all of them are part of the Friends of the Restful Soul.

Priya wasn't in on it, that much I'm sure. Priya wouldn't

do that, and besides, I don't think she even knew today was the day of the funeral. Even if she had, I just don't believe Priya would do that to me, no matter what she was paid. Even if she were promised a position in Nightmare Defense.

But everyone else? Cindy hates me. Always has. The Director has always been kind but frustrated. He was so chipper today too, telling me where to go for the funeral.

Who else knew?

Other Friends, probably. I don't think any of them hate me—or I didn't think that before—but I don't think anyone there *likes* me either.

Everyone is nice to me because that's who they are. But they look at me and I know that most of them can see through the thin veneer of believer I've painted myself with. They expected me to wash out years ago, like most other initiates who stay a year or two doing good works that look good on their applications for bigger, better places.

But not me. Year after year, I stay, and I continue to insist I want to be a lifer. And they continue to be baffled because it's clear that I suck at the doctrine and the only thing I believe in is saving my own skin.

So yeah, I don't have the best relationship with most of the people there. I've never really cared. I just wanted the safety they provided. Finding Priya there was a bonus.

But now I feel adrift, like I have no one to rely on. Priya is still there, and I don't know how to reach her. I don't know who at the Friends betrayed me or why, and I don't know what to do.

And I have no one else in my life.

"No," I whisper to Estelle. "No, there's no one else to call."

Finally, after a long look at me, she rises and heads toward the phone.

19

Cy gives me directions to an apartment building. I don't
know if he hears the shaking in my voice or the desperation
clinging to my words when I tell him I need to see him *right
now*, and no, it really cannot wait for evening.

When I finally hang up the phone, Estelle has her arms
crossed beside me.

"You're not going to his place, are you?" she asks, her eyes
narrowed with concern.

I wince. She doesn't even have to say the words. I barely
know him. I shouldn't be going anywhere with him, especially not to his apartment. I'd be trapped. He could do
anything to me.

But, I reason, he had plenty of time to show his hand after
the boat explosion. I'm probably safe.

Probably.

But it doesn't make the fear go away, coiled in my chest.
Nothing does.

This fear, I think, is actually rational. Sometimes it's hard,
with my fears, to tell where the line is. It all feels the same,
the sweaty palms and hollow, beating heart. I have to try to

think each one through—am I being smart and cautious with this fear, or am I being ridiculous?

But I think this is a reasonable fear. Going home alone with a vampire you barely know is a bad idea. It just is. If I said that to someone on the street, they'd be absolutely right to call me insane.

The fear isn't unjustified.

But at the same time, it sort of is. Because it's not like I don't know Cy—I know what matters about him, which is that he dragged me to shore, woke me from a nightmare, and helped me to the train station. He never gave me any reason to fear him, and I've been spending the past week debating if I can conquer my fears enough to reach out and see if we can become friends.

But I'm still scared because the fear is insidious, especially when it's rooted in real concerns.

"I know it's a bad idea," I say softly. "I'm not dumb."

Estelle bites her lip. "Look, if you're in some kind of trouble, there are better options than blood selling."

"I'm not—that's not why." I rub my temples. "I need to talk to him about something else. Something we both accidentally got involved in."

Her lips thin, and she doesn't look like she believes me, but she sighs and turns to the table, writing something on a pad of paper and then handing it to me.

"Here," she says. "Give this to him."

I raise an eyebrow. "What is it?"

"Read it for yourself."

I do. The writing, clear and bold says, *You're not welcome back here unless this girl, alive and well, comes back and tells me you didn't hurt her.*

I meet Estelle's eyes, and I'm surprised how grateful I feel. Cy will probably be hurt by this, the lack of trust we all have in him, because it's not deserved. He's never done anything to earn this kind of caution and fear.

But the problem is, others have.

Cy may not be responsible for the terrible things other people have done, but he has to accept the precautions that people like me need to take because of them.

"Thank you," I say to Estelle. "I appreciate this."

She smiles at me, but it's a tight expression. "Just be careful. He's never been anything but kind to me, but it's always better to be safe. You don't want to find out someone has a bad side the hard way."

I nod and promise her "I'll be careful."

I leave the bar and head toward the address Cy gave me.

Because I'm paranoid and because I was attacked by an assassin earlier today, and because Cy clearly doesn't want his address known, I take a winding, confusing route there, weaving through crowds on the subway, even though it's an easy walk from the bar.

You can never be too careful.

Says the person walking into a Nightmare's lair.

I'm turning a corner, and I hadn't been paying attention to what street it was, because I've ended up in a place I've tried to avoid ever since coming here.

Newham Academy. The school Ruby got her scholarship to.

It's an old Gothic building, with tall turrets and stone lions out front, brick wall surrounding a lush garden area. On the front of the building, a Latin phrase I don't understand is positioned under their school crest, an eagle diving over a cityscape. Students in neat uniforms swarming through the wrought-iron gates, laughing and chatting, their faces flushed with life.

My throat tightens. That was supposed to be Ruby. Should have been Ruby. Would have been, if only she hadn't forgotten her Nightmare medication.

If she did forget it.

I walk past it quickly, trying to tamp down my pain. I have enough to deal with, I can't be thinking about this right now.

When I finally arrive at Cy's address, I'm surprised to find it's in the nice part of town. The part of town that's full of tall, white town houses that sparkle with cleanliness. A massive park sits across the street, and it doesn't even look like it's full of homeless people—which probably means the neighborhood bribes the police to violently beat them out, which makes the pretty, pristine park look kind of ugly, when I think about it that way.

I press the buzzer on the building, and the door unlocks. I open it and come face-to-face with the largest man I've ever seen.

He's a Nightmare—there's no questioning it. He looks human, mostly, with freckled, white skin and a shock of dark hair, but he's easily nearly seven feet tall and all muscle. His arms hang down past his knees like a gorilla, and they're exaggeratedly muscled, his fists as big as an auto tire.

My fists clench at my sides, and I try not to shake.

He could crush me with one fist.

I'd never have a chance.

"Name?" he asks, his voice bored.

My mouth opens, and to my shock, my voice is steady when it comes out. "Ness. Here to see Cy."

He bobs his head, his security uniform straining against his chest. "He called down to say he was expecting you." He opens the door wider and steps aside to let me in. "Eleventh floor."

I want to run. I want to be halfway down the street, fleeing back to my tiny room at the Friends and barring the door behind me.

But I take a deep, calming breath, and I step into the apartment lobby. Because this fear isn't rational. This man is clearly in control of himself, and he's just doing his job, watching the door. He's not a mindless monster.

I let out the breath. My hands are still shaking, my heart is still slamming in my chest, but I'm still here.

I walk quickly to the elevator and get inside. The security guard returns to his chair by the door, taking out a paper and reading it.

The elevator doors close, and I slump against the wall, running my hand through my sweaty hair. I release a long exhale of relief.

It must suck being that security guard. His type of Nightmare is obvious—he was afraid of someone. A specific person. Nightmares can't literally turn you into an already-existing person, so instead, they warp and twist your body into a caricature of that person. Especially among kids who have Nightmares, thuggish appearances that reflect their bullies are common.

The elevator dings as it arrives on the eleventh floor, and I get off.

The hall is short, one door at each end. The floor is smooth, white stone that isn't marble but looks like it wishes it were. The tiny hall has a mini-chandelier just above the entrance to the elevator and a painting of a pot of flowers on the wall.

Heart thudding in my chest, I knock on the door with the number two on it.

The door opens, and Cy stands there.

His dark brown hair is fluffy, no hair gel or salt to ruin it. He's no longer wearing the black shirt and trousers I first met him in, but a much more standard white shirt, black waistcoat, and black trousers, like he could be anyone in this city—a librarian, a gangster, a mayor. His eyes are lined with eyeliner again, and it makes them glow green.

"Hey," he says. His expression is worried.

"Hey." I swallow, ducking my head, feeling awkward. "Sorry to intrude."

"It's all right." He smiles faintly, but his expression is still concerned. "I was hoping you'd call."

My voice cracks a little. "I was thinking of it. I thought we might go to one of the new films or something next week. But then . . ."

"Then . . . ?"

I shake my head. "Oh, before I forget, Estelle wanted me to give this to you."

He takes the note, skims it, and sighs softly, before pocketing it.

"You read it?" he asks.

"Yep."

He nods but doesn't say anything else about it. "Sorry, where are my manners? Come in. You don't need to stay standing out in the hall."

He steps aside to let me in, and I slip into the apartment and then freeze, gaping.

It's not like I hadn't figured out this place was on the posh side, given the door guard, the hall chandelier, and the general feeling of fanciness. But it was another thing to see Cy's apartment.

It's like a whole other world.

The room is large, big enough for a couch and bookshelves and a table and still enough space for at least ten people. There's a massive window along the wall, covered by a thick curtain to make sure no sunlight gets in. Lamps on every corner are on, and the room still feels warm and lit, even though there's no natural light. I can see a door to a bathroom and what might be a bedroom.

I stumble inside, and he closes the door behind me.

"Wow," I say numbly.

He shrugs but has a small smile, as though he's happy I like it. "It cost way too much for something so small."

I stare at him. This isn't small, not in Newham. "You own this place? Not even renting?"

"Nope. No renting." He laughs at my expression. "You act like you've never seen an apartment this big before."

"I haven't."

He flushes, then looks away. "Oh."

I turn around, taking it all in. The spacious room. The

couch, which looks somehow both artistic and incredibly comfortable. The rug, which is fluffy and soft and perfect. And on the eleventh floor, I bet when the windows are uncovered, it's a beautiful view.

It's paradise. I want this apartment. I would kill to have this place.

"How?" I ask softly. "How did you get this?"

He runs a hand through his thick, black hair and shrugs. "I, uh, might have robbed my father."

I turn around to face him. "What?"

He clears his throat. "My dad. He's pretty, ah, loaded. Real loaded. And when I ran away from home, I might have . . ." He considers his words carefully. "Pocketed a few little trinkets."

"A few little trinkets," I deadpan.

He shrugs. "Can't run away from home with nothing. He had cash to spare. I took everything I could fit in my bag that wasn't nailed down. Sold it all when I got to Newham and bought myself a new identity and an apartment."

"No wonder you think he wants to kill you," I mutter. I can't fathom how much Cy must have stolen to afford all this.

He shrugs, looking away. "He probably would have wanted to kill me whether I robbed him or not. Just the fact that I left him would have made him . . ." He shudders. "Well. I left for a reason."

I hesitate, but my curiosity is too great and I ask, "Will you tell me about it?"

Cy hesitates, then sits on the couch, clearly nervous. "I . . ."

I sit beside him. "You don't have to. If you don't want."

"No," he whispers, bowing his head. "It's not that. It's just." He grimaces. "Where to start?"

I tip my head. "Wherever you want."

Cy seems to come to a decision, and his voice, when he speaks, is slow and soft.

"My father is very rich. He's always been rich—old money. And he's only gotten richer." Cy licks his lips. "And he's very absorbed in himself. He wanted to be handsome and rich for eternity, so shortly after I was born, he went out and paid someone to turn him into a vampire."

I blink, stunned. "He *what*?"

Cy shrugs. "He never really saw the use for daylight anyway, so it was a good bargain for him. And despite being raised Catholic, I doubt he's ever spared a thought for his immortal soul." He smiles bitterly. "He's never really cared about hurting people to get what he wants."

I can't imagine going out and actively paying someone to make you into a bloodsucking monster. Sure, becoming powerful and immortal would be cool, I get that, but being forced to prey on other people for all eternity?

"But . . . there are other ways to be immortal," I protest. "He could have tried to become one of the endless sages!"

"They're invisible," Cy snorts. "I think he'd have gone mad if people couldn't see him. No, he didn't mind the cost of becoming a vampire." Cy's mouth twists. "I think he liked it, actually."

My voice is dry. "Liked it?"

Cy nods. "He—he always liked . . . hurting people. He

was a predator before he ever became a monster." His eyes flick to me to see if I understand what he's trying to say.

I do.

I wish I didn't, but I know *exactly* what he's saying, and it makes me sick.

"After he became a vampire, he got to do all the awful things he did before but pretend that it wasn't him. That it was this 'curse.'" Cy's voice is bitter and disgusted. "He loved it. The tortured tragedy. He'd really ham that shit up. 'I don't want to hurt you, but I just can't help myself.'" Cy swallows. "Of course he could stop himself. He just didn't *want* to."

My skin crawls, and I find I'm clutching my own arms, like I'm trying to hug myself.

"My father has always gotten what he wants, and fuck everyone else." Cy licks his lips. "But he's also a terrible narcissist. He needs to be admired and romanticized, no matter what he does. No matter how horrific."

A chill slithers down my spine, tiny, icy fingers sliding down each vertebrae one by one.

"So early on in the film days, he bought up a bunch of the studios. And he had them make films about vampires. Films about the kind of vampire *he* was." His eyes flick to mine, then away. "And he had them romanticize him."

"No," I breathe, starting to see things come together.

"Yes. My father, he . . . he got his blood a lot of ways." Cy swallows heavily, clearly uncomfortable with this topic. "He used drugs to knock women in clubs unconscious and then bite them. They'd wake up, knowing they'd been violated, that someone had . . . had done things to them while they were unconscious but with no memory of it."

Cy is staring at the floor, unable to meet my eyes, as though he feels stained by association.

"My father ordered the movie execs to make that seem sexy. He wanted to see himself as impossibly romantic. He wasn't killing these girls. He was humane. He wasn't even forcing them to experience the pain of being bitten. They'd never even remember what happened to them."

I feel sick, my whole body slimy with oil. The sheer violation, the way it's glossed over and covered up. How many people saw that portrayed as sexy and let it twist their mind, devaluing their trauma or feeling encouraged to perpetuate those crimes?

"He drugged and assaulted them," I whisper. "And then he had movies made that romanticized it so no one would ever think he was doing anything wrong?"

Cy nods once, sharply. "And the worst part is, it *worked*."

I think of all the sexy vampire romances I've seen on the ads at the cinema, how popular they are, and my skin wants to crawl right off my body, leaving my muscle and flesh exposed while it runs away.

"Media is powerful," Cy whispers. "And when you portray something as good and romantic, people believe it. Not all people, but enough. It becomes a trend, a view. When you picture a vampire biting a woman and wiping her memory, you don't think of them as evil. Because you're used to it. Accustomed to it. You don't think about it anymore."

"But it is. It's evil. It's assault." His voice cracks. "And then you take even their memory of it, and leave them there, knowing something has been done to them but not what. It's sick."

He meets my eyes. "And because of him, it's become normal."

I look down, staring at the rug, fluffy and dark green. I wonder what it was like growing up with a father like that—and what things a father like that might have done to his son.

"I—I can't believe he went that far to excuse his abuse," I whisper, even though I very much can.

"He's gone further." Cy's voice is dark. "The way films show relationships, the way they laugh off sexual assaults, the way they never discuss consent—that's deliberate. That's him, making sure that his victims never feel like they can get help. Making them doubt their own experiences because the movies make it seem fine. Making them feel the police will doubt them when they come in to report it."

My voice is soft. "And how many men see those things and believe that's acceptable behavior and then continue the abuse cycles?"

"Sometimes I wonder," he whispers, his voice strained, "if I hadn't been raised in that house, if I hadn't known what was happening, would I have been brainwashed by it too? Would I have hurt people and never thought I'd done anything wrong?"

I want to tell him he wouldn't, but the truth is, no one knows what kind of person they'd be in another life. That's not a reassurance I can give, and it's not one he'd believe.

"I think," I tell him, "it doesn't really matter what you might have done if you weren't raised there. This is the life you're in, and what matters is how you behave in this one." I cock an eyebrow. "And so far, you haven't followed in his footsteps, have you?"

"God, no." He blinks, then his face twists in an ironic smile. "Though I am a vampire now. Which sure feels like it."

"Well, have you been drugging and assaulting girls for blood?"

"*No!*"

"I didn't think so." I tip my head. "So I'm not sure how you two are anything alike."

He swallows and looks down, his voice pained. "We both prey on people. I prey on people."

I hum in consideration. "He certainly does. But I don't know that the relationship between you and Estelle could be considered predatory. It's more transactional, and everyone involved seems all right with it." I shrug. "Estelle seems cautious of you but also seems to generally like you, so I imagine you haven't been awful to her."

His expression has relaxed a bit, like my words have stolen some of his tension. Finally he admits, "I've tried to not be an asshole."

"Seems like you've done all right." I grin. "Honestly, it was a bit of a relief meeting Estelle. I was worried you were eating small animals or something."

"What do I look like to you, a budding serial killer?" His voice is horrified. "What, you thought I was going to pet shops and eating the puppies?"

"Well, not the puppies." I shrug. "Maybe the rats?"

He looks revolted. "I'm not eating rats."

"More ethical than puppies."

He just gives me a look.

"Sorry." I clear my throat. "How did it happen? The nightmare?"

His eyes lower. "I ran away. And that night, the night I left, I forgot to take the pills."

I wince.

"We'd always had the medicine in the water to keep us from dreaming," he explains. "But I was on a train across the country and I didn't think to take the pills. I'd never had to remember before."

"And you had a nightmare," I finish quietly for him.

He nods sharply. "I didn't even realize what was happening at first. Not until this creepy guy appeared, with these terrifying, black eyes . . ."

He trails off and the hairs on my skin rise as I recall the strange Nightmare Phantom and his toothy smile, the way he laughed and told me that he was helping us.

I guess I'm not the only one who saw him.

"Anyway." Cy brushes this away, though the image of the Nightmare Phantom lingers in my mind. "One night away, and I'd already failed. I'd turned into my father."

"No," I say decisively.

He raises his eyebrows. "No?"

"You haven't." I meet his eyes. "Would your father have towed me to shore?"

"Maybe," he says, then admits, "but he'd probably have

eaten you when you got there."

"Precisely." I tell him. "You're your own person. Just because you have the potential to become him, doesn't mean you have to. Lots of people own knives, but not all of them become that serial killer who slashed little boys' kidneys out."

He snorts, a half smile on his face, sort of twisted, like he's not sure if he's allowed to smile at such a gruesome comment. "That's true."

I hesitate, then lean closer and put my hand on his shoulder. I've never voluntarily touched a Nightmare before and I try to quell the nerves. "You make your own choices, Cy. He doesn't make them for you, no matter that you're both vampires now. He can't control you."

Cy bows his head, and he whispers, "I hope so. I really do."

"I believe in you."

He pulls away. "No, you don't."

I lean back, lost for words.

"You're terrified of me," he points out.

Right. That.

"I'm not, actually." I put my hands in my lap and look down. "I have a phobia of Nightmares. It's not a rational thing—I know I don't have to be afraid of you, or the door guard or lots of other people. But my brain plays tricks on me. It paints all Nightmares with the same brush even though, intellectually, I'm perfectly aware that's not the case."

I take a deep breath, not looking up, too worried about what expression he'll have. "But I want to be friends with you. Because I like you." My lips quirk. "Even if I am still a little terrified."

He's silent after this admission, staring at me with large eyes. I finally lift my head a little, and his expression is hard to read, confusion and hope and fear and sadness all mixed together into something that's impossible to figure out what he's thinking.

Finally he says, "Why on earth were you chasing me down on the boat if you're that scared?"

"I was trying to be brave." I stare at the floor, face flushed. "It didn't exactly work out well."

His smile quirks up. "I think it worked out all right."

I snort, staring at my hands still fisted in my lap. They're still shaking. But maybe I'm less scared, or maybe I'm just getting better at ignoring it because I also feel another emotion, a different, completely unexpected one.

Sitting next to Cy on the couch of his ridiculously nice apartment, I almost feel like everything is going to be okay.

20

It takes me a while to tell Cy about the assassination attempt.

Not because there's a lot to say, but because I keep going on tangents where I talk about the funeral for Mrs. Sanden and have to explain how Priya and I were there when she became a Nightmare, which rambles over to how I ended up on the boat and then back to the assassination.

When I get to the part where the police told me that they thought I was involved because I couldn't have swum to shore on my own, Cy purses his lips worriedly but doesn't stop me. I know he's worried that they'll figure out he survived too—or that the assassins already have. After all, they know I didn't blow up the boat, which means they'll also have figured out I had help surviving.

Cy is in as much danger as I am.

Well, almost as much.

When I finally finish, words trailing into nothing, we sit beside each other on the couch for a long moment, silent, letting our situation hang in the air, the slow acceptance of just how much shit we've somehow gotten ourselves in.

Finally, he asks quietly, "Are you okay?"

I blink, then nod. "I'm not hurt."

"But are you okay?"

I raise my head, then sigh and wrap my arms around my knees and tuck my chin in. "No, I'm not okay. But there's not much to do about that."

He slumps back, running a hand through his hair. "Shit."

"Yep."

"So in summary." Cy starts counting with one hand. "The police suspect you bombed the boat. The people who *actually* bombed the boat are trying to kill you—and they likely know that you had help getting to shore and therefore might not be the only survivor."

"Pretty much," I agree. "I knew I had to tell you immediately when I realized there was a good chance they'd be onto you soon too."

He nods, as though that's a perfectly reasonable explanation for why I had to come over. As though I couldn't have warned him over the phone and skipped town.

But I hadn't wanted to tell him over the phone and skip town.

Firstly, because I have no money to skip town.

Secondly, because for all Newham's flaws, this is my home. I don't want to leave.

And lastly, because I'm tired of running. For once in my life, I want to face my damn problems head-on.

The irony of me discovering this when my problems include assassins who blew up a boat and are trying to kill me instead of, you know, any of the mundane issues I've had in my life isn't lost on me.

"So about your cult . . ." Cy hedges.

"Still not a cult."

He rolls his eyes. "Okay, so about your not-cult. Someone there has to be in contact with the assassins, right? Otherwise how would the assassin have known where to wait for you?"

"That's what I was thinking too," I admit. "The problem is I don't know who at the Friends would have known. The Director, for sure, and maybe Cindy. Probably any of the other people around when I was talking to Cindy. Anyone the Director told, I guess?"

He frowns. "That's a lot of suspects."

"I know." But I think of the Director and his secret room and his smile when he was handing down the assignment and I wonder if there are actually a lot of suspects. Maybe there's more than just filing cabinets in that room.

"I don't think it's safe for you to go back to the Friends until we know what's going on," Cy says slowly, his voice concerned.

I grimace. "I know."

He takes a deep breath, as though steeling himself. "If—I don't know if you have a place to go, but if you don't, you can stay here."

He looks away as he speaks, his shoulders tight, as though he's afraid of my reaction. Afraid I might misinterpret it or afraid I'll discard it out of fear or some other reason altogether, I don't know.

But the truth is I don't have anywhere else to go. Priya is my only friend, and she lives with the Friends. What am I going to do, show up on her sister's doorstep, ask Adhya and Livia to take me into their tiny apartment?

No. And besides, anyone who knows me would know that's the first place I'd go. I can't put them in danger that way.

"Thanks." My voice is a whisper. "I'll be out of your hair as soon as possible."

He lifts his head, blinking. "Wait, you're staying?"

I stare at him. "Well, you offered . . ."

"I didn't think you'd say yes," he confesses.

I tip my head to one side. "So . . . are you rescinding the offer?"

"What? No!" He waves his hands. "It's fine. You're more than welcome here."

I raise an eyebrow. "You're awfully enthusiastic now."

He rolls his eyes. "Yes, I promise not to bite."

"I didn't say anything." My mouth quirks up into a half smile.

"You didn't need to." He laughs and rises. "I'm going to see if I have some spare blankets and stuff. You can have the couch."

"Um, actually." I hesitate and then point to a door. "Is that a closet?"

He frowns. "Um. Yes?"

I walk over and open it. It's empty.

"I only got this place a couple of months ago," he explains. "I haven't really collected enough crap to put in it yet."

I test out the bottom, and there's plenty of room for me to curl up and close the door. It's perfect.

225

Cy stares at me as if I've lost my mind. "You're not actually planning to sleep in the closet, are you?"

I flush. "What's wrong with that?"

"It's a closet."

"And?"

"And I have a couch?" He tips his head. "Hell, if you don't like the couch, I'll swap you and you can have the bed. I'd offer to share the bed, it's king size, but I feel like that would send the wrong message."

I blush and cough. "Yeah, that sends a very different message. I'm, uh . . ."

"Not sleeping with me." He winks. "In either meaning of the word."

I cough a laugh.

"Anyway, you're welcome to the bed and I'll take the couch if there's something wrong with it," he insists.

I shake my head. "No, seriously, I *like* the closet." I bow my head. "I, um, can't sleep in the same room as other people."

He frowns. "I'll close the door between the rooms?"

I shake my head. "It's . . ." I swallow. "What if someone comes in through the window? What if they break open the front door? What if—" I cut myself off. "Sorry. I—I haven't been good at sleeping around people. Or open spaces. Or anything, really. Not for a long time."

He's quiet awhile. "Because you're afraid of Nightmares?"

I nod.

"I've already become a Nightmare," he says gently. "I can't be changed again."

I shake my head.

"Is it the vampire thing? Because I promise . . ."

I shake my head. "I just . . . I like small spaces. Places I can hide. They make me feel safe."

He considers me for a long moment, then sighs. "All right. The closet is yours."

"Thank you."

"I'll go grab those blankets."

He slips into the other room, what I assume is the bedroom. I can see the corner of the bed, the rumpled blankets hanging off the edge, as he bends over something, muttering to himself as he tugs things out of the way.

I wander away from my closet, padding around the apartment. It's fairly sparse, and it does have an almost catalogue feel to it, now that I'm paying attention. Like someone just moved in and bought all new furniture.

I pause by the coffee table, which is covered in newspapers, and pick one up. The front story is about the people who died on the boat, and it lists their names and a little bit about them. Some people only have things like *Aaron Adamu, mail delivery boy, 17.* But others have much more.

Vilhelm "the Knife" Guntz, age unknown, leader of the Guntz gang, arrested twice for racketeering, human trafficking . . .

I'd never seen the Knife in person, but he'd controlled a whole bunch of territory near Forty-Third, made the shopkeepers in the area pay "protection fees." He was notorious.

227

I frown. That area was now controlled by Giovanni Montessauri, if the shoot-out I'd passed was any indication. It hadn't taken long for Guntz territory to get divvied up.

My eyes fall back down to the paper, to another name.

Constance Wang, mayoral candidate, 47. She built her platform on a promise to clean up the crime in the city, including pressing charges against current government officials for corruption . . .

It was early for a mayoral candidate assassination, but not that early. Not outside of the realm of possibility.

Catherine Cortez, actress, 33. A rising starlet who recently stole a leading part . . .
Angelina Van Vels, heiress, 21. Heir to the Van Vels fortune . . .
Ambassador Emma Sorenson, 63, a keen political mind . . .

The names blurred together, so many victims, swirling and twisting and morphing in my mind until they crystallized into a moment of perfect clarity.

"Ness?" Cy has returned with a pile of bedding. "Is something wrong?"

I look up at him. "Cy."

"Yes?"

"The boat explosion." My mouth is dry. "If it was an

assassination, who was the target?"

He frowns. "I don't know. There are so many possibilities."

"There are *too* many possibilities."

He shakes his head. "I don't follow."

"This boat goes to Palton Island every day, three times a day." My finger shakes on the paper. "Why did this specific one have so many important people on it?"

He frowns, brow wrinkling. His voice is slow and thoughtful. "I don't know."

"What if we've all been looking at this wrong?" I whisper. "What if it's not one target?"

His eyes widen in understanding.

"What if they were *all* targets." I lean forward. "What if someone lured all their targets onto the same boat and then blew it up?"

The blankets fall from Cy's fingers, and his expression is ill. "Lured?"

I look down, suddenly remembering how Cy ended up on the boat.

"I didn't mean—"

"No," he whispers. "You're right." He swallows heavily. "It makes sense. It makes complete sense. It's the only thing that does make sense. Because so many people died, and it's so inconvenient, no one thinks it's an assassination. But it's actually a mass assassination of dozens of targets."

I bow my head, realizing what this means for him. "I'm sorry."

He gives me a sad smile. "I told you my father wanted me dead."

"Maybe your friend didn't know he was luring you to your death," I try.

He shrugs. "Maybe."

He doesn't sound convinced.

I look out the window, and I realize what I need to do. I don't have the knowledge or resources to catch an assassin or group of assassins who have the resources to blow up a boat.

But I don't have to.

I just have to make sure that this information gets to people who do.

21

I sit in the Lantern Man's Restaurant as the morning light slants through the windows. They're open for the breakfast and lunch crowds, and the place is buzzing, the chatter a low hum, since so many of the people who come here come for the TV on the wall above the bar.

I'd been hoping to see Estelle again, reassure her I was fine, but it looks like she only works afternoons and evenings, so I'll have to come back.

Instead, I sip on a soda and watch the news, like everyone else in the restaurant.

On the screen, the Mayor is being interviewed. She's white, her long, dark hair is pulled back into a high ponytail, and she's wearing a tuxedo that hugs her curves. Her eyes are heavily outlined in black and her lipstick is dark red in her campaign posters, but on the monochrome television, just looks black.

Behind the Mayor is a giant pterodactyl.

It's not what a real pterodactyl looks like, I imagine, since the leathery wings and iridescent skin looks eerily like the film poster for *Dinosaur Attack*, which was probably what inspired the poor sap who Nightmared his way into this. A thick chain hangs around its neck, and it screeches at the sky, its long, toothy mouth open wide.

It snaps at people who get too close, and the Mayor jerks the chain, as though showing it who's boss.

I try very hard not to think of the moral and ethical implications of keeping a monster that used to be a person on a chain while it tries to eat people. If I go too far down that rabbit hole, I'll start imagining my giant spider sister in chains, the Mayor riding her like a monstrous mount, and I really don't want to think about that because of how viscerally sick the idea makes me.

"Miss Mayor!" calls someone on the television screen, one of the many reporters in attendance at the press conference. "What do you say to the *Post*'s exposé this morning, claiming that the boat explosion was a mass assassination?"

The Mayor smiles, her teeth white and shiny. "I say that it's an interesting theory but lacks evidence."

Not that the papers had needed evidence.

I'd called up the *Post* after talking with Cy yesterday and arranged an interview. They'd been willing to pay for an exclusive with the one and only survivor of the boat explosion. Not enough, if I was being honest, but something, and for someone with no cash, something was a lot.

I'd simply told them that when I was being interviewed by police, I'd seen a piece of paper on the detective's desk outlining a theory that it could have been a group assassination.

The dots were pretty easy to connect from there.

"If it's true, doesn't that mean you had Constance Wong assassinated?" asks another person.

"I don't need to resort to assassinations." The Mayor waves the insinuation away. "I know the people of Newham will make the correct choice to reelect me." Her smile widens. "Of course, the other people running for my position might not have the same confidence. If she were assassinated, I'd look at them."

Behind her, the pterodactyl screeches.

"Miss Mayor!" A reporter pushes forward at the edge of the screen. "How do you respond to the people that believe you facing jail time means you're not fit for office? That the people need a mayor well-connected enough to avoid criminal charges?"

The Mayor raises an eyebrow, then smiles.

"How do I respond to them?" she muses.

The pterodactyl lets out a screech, swinging its long neck around and grabbing the man in its jaws. The reporter screams, and the pterodactyl tips its head back, tossing the man up so his feet stick up into the air.

Then it gulps.

Its throat works as it swallows the man, a foot at a time, slurping him down like a worm. His screams are audible right up until he's fully consumed.

The Mayor smiles into the camera, wide and sharp. "That's how I respond."

The screen cuts away to the news anchors. The press conference is officially over.

I down the rest of my drink in one go, like it's a shot of whisky and not a strawberry lemonade. My hands shake a little as I put the empty cup down, ice rattling.

Sometimes I really hate Newham.

The volume in the room rises into angry chattering. I'm not the only one thinking about drinks because people swarm the door at the side of the room that probably leads to the illegal speakeasy in the back where all the liquor is.

"Can you believe the nerve?" someone mutters. "A whole boat of people? We all know that assassinations happen, but a whole boat? What's next, someone taking down a whole apartment building for one person?"

"Well, I wouldn't use that assassination company again," another person was saying. "Can you imagine how embarrassing this must be for all their clients? Especially since I bet they all paid to make it look like an accident, and now it's all over the news."

Yes, it is.

And those clients will be furious.

I've very glad right now that my name isn't connected to that article. The *Post* had decided that it looked much better if they connected the dots themselves, and I had wholeheartedly agreed. They hadn't even put the writer's name on the article. We all knew how Newham works.

So the wrath of all these clients, whose assassinations were now all over the media, would likely fall on the one group that they could hold responsible.

The assassins they'd hired.

Who would assassinate the assassins first? Would it be the Mayor, who didn't need this kind of attention leading up to her reelection campaign? Would it be notorious gang lord Giovanni Montessauri, known for his bloody vengeance on his enemies?

The bookies are probably already taking bets.

I don't have to do shit to stop the people who tried to assassinate me—their own clients will do that for me.

Some might call this a coward's plan. And you know what? I am a coward, so maybe it is.

But I'm also not stupid enough to believe that I could find and take on these people by myself. I mean, look at me. I run from Nightmares by jumping out windows and hiding under couches. The one time I managed to be brave, I ended up blown up.

I'm not Priya, who's trained her whole life to fight monsters, who's capable and fearless. I'm not Cy, incredibly strong and near impossible to kill and rich enough that he could probably hire an assassin himself.

I'm just me.

And maybe I don't have to be strong or an amazing fighter because this is a much cleaner, less risky solution, and I'm okay with that.

The door to the pub jangles open, and Priya walks in.

She's wearing her usual baggy fatigues and a long trench coat that hides the dozens of weapons I'm sure she's carrying. Her eyes have shadows under them as they scan the room.

When her eyes land on me, they widen in shock.

"Ness?" she cries, barreling over, not noticing or caring about the people she plows through to get to me. "How are you here? Where have you been? I was worried sick all night! Wait, did you call me here?"

I had, actually. I'd asked Cy to phone the Friends and make up an excuse to meet Priya because I was feeling paranoid and no one there would recognize Cy's voice.

"Sit down," I laugh, gesturing to the seat across from me. "I'll explain everything."

And I do. I finally have a chance to talk to her, and the words burst from me as though they've been waiting for their chance to explode outward. I tell her about Cy, how he rescued me on the boat, the assassination attempt at the funeral, why I decided to run to Cy instead of back to the Friends, all of it.

She listens, her brow furrowed, her expression getting angrier and angrier as I speak, her fists clenched on the table like she's getting ready to beat the shit out of the assassin herself.

"The fuck," she says when I'm done. "I'm going to kill that assassin bitch."

"No, you're not," I insist. "We don't even know where to find her. Let the Mayor kill her. Or Giovanni Montessauri. Or some other psychopath running around the city."

Priya glowers, clearly displeased with this, but sighs and unclenches her fists, giving in.

"The part I find most incredible," she tells me, "is that you went and hid in a vampire's apartment last night. What happened to the Ness I knew? The one who'd jump out a window before going to a vampire's home, never mind sleeping there?"

I shrug awkwardly, looking away. "Cy's not so bad."

"I'm sure he's not." Priya waves this away, clearly unconcerned about Cy. And why would she be? I'm the only one here who's irrational about Nightmares. "But I bet you still checked your neck out in the mirror when you woke up this morning, didn't you?"

I flush. She's right—I did.

No bite marks. Obviously. Not that I expected there would be. But I still had to check—just in case.

Priya shakes her head, smiling slightly. "So do I get to meet him?"

I shrug. "It's daylight."

Priya sighs dramatically. "So it is."

I smile slightly. "I'm glad you're taking this so well. I was a little worried you'd go all wannabe Nightmare hunter on me."

She rolls her eyes. "I want to hunt sea dragons and man-eating pterodactyls." She waves her hand. "I'm not some asshole who's going to stab some guy minding his own business. Especially one who saved my best friend."

I grin at her. I shouldn't have bothered worrying.

Her smile falls. "But I *am* worried about who at the Friends sold you out to these assassins."

I bow my head. "Yeah. Me too."

"Who knew?" Priya asks. "About the funeral."

"Uh." I shrug. "I mean, the Director, obviously. But Cindy

did too. And I assume other people, but I couldn't say who."

Priya frowns. "Cindy's always been kinda suspicious. She's so . . ."

"Pious?" I offer.

"Isolated," Priya finally says.

I blink. "Pardon?"

Though now that I think about it, Cindy is always on her own. Sure, she talks to people, but she eats her lunches alone, and she spends her evenings writing in her notebook, lost in her own world.

"It's always been strange to me," Priya says. "She clearly knows the doctrine in and out, and she certainly does everything right. But she's always so distant from everyone. Like there's a layer of glass between her and the world. She reminds me of you."

"Of me?" I repeat, incredulous. Cindy and I have *nothing* in common.

"Yeah. She makes all the right noises, does all the right things to stay with the Friends, but she doesn't seem to actually connect with people there. If I didn't know better, I'd say she was doing what you are, using them for the free food and rent. Except that her clothes are always nice, and she has some great hair products, so she can't be broke." Priya taps a finger to her lips. "She just doesn't quite *fit*."

"I thought she was just really pious," I admit.

"I'm not sure about that." Priya grins. "If she was so pious, you and she would never have ended up in your ridiculous passive-aggressive rivalry nonsense."

"We're not in a rivalry," I protest, but my voice is weak.

Priya snorts. "Sure, Ness, sure."

I bite my lip, looking down. I never really got along with Cindy, but thinking of her as someone willing to sell me out to assassins still hurts. "So you think it was her. You think she sold me out to get back at me for the ankle thing."

"I don't know," Priya says. "I think the Director is looking just as shady right now."

I jerk my head up. "The Director?"

"Oh, come on, Ness. A fake wall with a mysterious room? That didn't raise any flags for you at all?"

I shrug. "It's Newham. Everyone has a secret room. There were no bodies, so I figured, you know . . ."

Priya just looks at me.

I flush. "Yeah, okay, maybe it's a little suspicious."

Priya rolls her eyes.

"Look, he was always sketchy as hell," Priya insists. "He's running a cult, for god's sake."

I wince. "Even you think it's a cult?"

Priya snorts. "Ness, the only one who doesn't think it's a cult is you."

I look away awkwardly.

"But it's been around for nearly a century," I insist. "It's well respected. Having worked there helps your résumé."

"And that in itself didn't tip you off?" Priya asks. "This is Newham, Ness. The only things that earn any kind of respect in this city are wildly corrupt."

The worst part is, she's right. She's absolutely right. All the signs were there, the red flags practically smothering me, and I'd just closed my eyes and refused to see it.

Because if I saw it, could I cling to my illusion that my safe place was still safe?

"So what if it's a cult?" I say quietly. "Or if it's corrupt? That doesn't mean the Director sold me out."

Priya gives me a long, tired look before she finally says, "True. It doesn't." Her eyes narrow. "Which is why we need proof."

I blink. "What?"

"We need to know who sold you out, Ness," Priya explains patiently. "Even if this all blows over, will you ever feel safe there again, not knowing who gave you up to assassins?"

She's right.

I wouldn't feel safe. I'd never be able to go back. I'd lose my safe space forever. Everything I'd built up for the last three years, everything I'd worked so hard to cling to—my little room, my hidey-hole, my home.

I take a long, deep breath.

"Fine," I whisper. "What did you have in mind?"

And Priya grins, wide and fearless, and I know I'm not going to like whatever this plan is.

22

Priya and I return to the Friends of the Restful Soul.

For three years, I've walked up to this facade, the smooth, aged marble-and-brick front, and I've seen home. The crack in the second step, the smell of incense and herbs from the small shrine to the saints, the disciple giving out pamphlets on the street to passersby, all of it is familiar, a comforting sameness. Each thing reassures me that nothing will change, that this place will be as it always has been: home.

This building is where I could hide away from the world. I know every nook and cranny, every hiding spot, every corner. And high up is my own room, just for me, my little closet that no one but me can enter. Or could enter, I suppose, now that they've given it to someone else.

For the last three years, this is the only place in the world where I felt safe.

Now, for the first time, I feel trepidation as I ascend the steps.

Everything is wrong. I've lost my safe space, my little room, my home. I've spent the night fearing for my life, and the comforting safety of the building now feels smothering and confining, like I'm walking into a prison. All because someone in the Friends of the Restful Soul sold me out to assassins—which I'm pretty sure is super against doctrine. You know. Not that I'm bitter or anything.

Well, to be fair, this started before I was sold out. But the selling out really didn't help.

A yawning loss sits in my chest, like a piece of my soul has been carved right out of my body, devoured by my fear and the feeling of betrayal that lurks beneath it all. I try to tell myself that it'll be better when we confirm who sold me out—when I know they've been assassinated themselves, everything can slide back to the way it was. I can feel safe again.

Except I don't think I can.

I don't think I'll ever be able to get that feeling back, that complete and utter trust I once had, the knowledge that, in my tiny room, the world could never get to me. The feeling of contentment that came—I have to admit now—mostly from ignorance.

But I'm trying not to think about that.

Which should be easy, since, according to Priya, I'm an expert at ignoring things I don't want to see.

We traverse the familiar halls, Priya in the lead, her eyes gleaming like this is all a grand adventure. She's practically skipping as she gives everyone we pass suspicious and knowing looks.

I roll my eyes. She's acting like she's a hero in a penny novel, on the verge of uncovering a dastardly and villainous plot that will shock and scandalize the reader. Which, honestly, this is Newham—I'm pretty sure I trip over villainous plots, like, six times a day.

No one stops us, and most people just roll their eyes when they see Priya and I. Yeah, we both have reputations unfortunately. And not good ones. Honestly, now that I think about it, I feel like half the Friends would have probably sold me out just to get rid of me if it wasn't so explicitly against doctrine.

It's a bit of a sad thought. I really love it here, but here does not love me at all.

We reach the Director's office, and Priya tugs me into a janitor's closet across from the room. We spy through a crack in the door at the office, Priya's body vibrating with excitement beside me.

"What are we doing?" I ask.

"We're waiting for him to leave," Priya explains. "He's got that seminar every day at three. When he leaves, we're going to break into that room, and we're going to find out what's really going on here."

I sigh. "And if it turns out it really is just boring paperwork and there's nothing nefarious?"

"Then we wait for him and question him ourselves!"

I rub my temples. "And if it's not him?"

"Then we kidnap Cindy and ask her questions!"

I groan. Maybe we're the villains of the penny novel.

"That sounds way too dangerous." I consider. "And like too much work."

Priya is undeterred. "Come on, Ness. We're investigating!"

"You're going to get us both killed," I mutter under my

breath, but my words won't stop anything. Priya is on a mission, and honestly, she usually finds what she's looking for on a mission.

And I'd rather be looking for answers with her by my side than alone.

People go in and out of the office, and Priya checks her watch impatiently, waiting for the Director to leave for his seminar. She looks so confident there, like nothing could go wrong.

"How do you do it?" I ask all of a sudden, the words slipping out before I can catch them.

"Do what?"

"Be so fearless." I look away. "You're not afraid of anything."

Priya snorts. "Really? You think I'm some sort of superhuman with absolutely no fears in the entire world?"

I blink. "Um . . . yes?"

Priya rolls her eyes. "Give me a break, Ness. Everyone's afraid of something."

"What are you afraid of?" I ask, curiosity piqued. What could scare someone as strong and capable as Priya?

She's quiet a long moment before softly saying, "Isn't it obvious?" She looks up into my eyes. "I'm afraid of loss."

The word hangs heavy in the air.

"I'm afraid of losing all the people I love." She swallows painfully, and her words scrape out like they've been run over sandpaper. "And being left completely alone."

Oh.

I bow my head. Of course. I'd seen how devastated she was

when she thought I was dead, the chinks in the armor around her soul. But it hadn't really clicked that meant she was *afraid* of losing people.

Priya's voice is soft. "I'm afraid that if something does happen, it'll be my fault. I'll mess up, not stop a dangerous Nightmare or something, and it'll go on to kill my sister or you or Livia." She shakes her head. "I couldn't live with myself if that happened."

My heart breaks a little at the words, at the glimpse of fear and insecurity that I've never realized lurked in Priya's heart. And I understand now why we're here, why she's so hell-bent on breaking in and finding out exactly who sold me out right this second, no matter the risk.

She's worried if she delays, it'll be too late, and the assassin will strike again.

Right here, right now, Priya is afraid.

"So, yeah." Priya gives me a crooked smile. "I'm not fearless."

I try to give her a smile back. "You're still braver than me."

"That's not hard."

"Ouch." I clap my hand to my chest, mock wounded.

Priya laughs. "Sorry, I had to. You set it up so well."

"I thought we were having a moment."

"We were." Priya grins. "And now I'm ending the moment because things got way too serious for a minute there."

I roll my eyes, but I'm smiling. Priya uses her humor like a weapon and I haven't realized until this moment how much I appreciated that. There's something about making a mockery of serious things that takes their power from them, makes them less frightening, less painful.

The door across the hall opens and we both fall silent instantly, turning to watch our quarry.

The Director steps out. The sunlight coming through a nearby window makes his green scales gleam, and his forked tongue slides out, tasting the air. He's wearing a long, monkish brown robe, like always. His lower half can't really handle trousers, what with the different way lizard legs work, so he always wears robes of some sort for decency.

He adjusts his spectacles, then pads down the hall, his webbed feet making soft smacking sounds on the tiled floor.

We wait a few moments, until we're absolutely sure he's gone, before sneaking out of the janitor's closet and down the hall to his door.

Which is locked.

I turn to Priya. "Slight flaw in this plan."

Priya smirks. "Is it?"

She takes out a long wire, and I lean against the wall.

"Where'd you learn how to pick locks?" I ask.

"I didn't," she admits.

Then she wraps the wire around the door handle, hooks it over the nearby windowsill for leverage, and *yanks*.

The whole doorknob rips out and clatters to the floor.

Priya grins at me. "This is much easier."

I cover my face with my hands, but I follow her through the now-open door.

The Director's office is empty. The desk, old and distinguished, sits on one side of the room, papers neatly stacked, pens in their holders, everything perfectly in place. The chairs on either side of the desk are pushed in, and the only thing out of place is an open bottle of Dr. Almansa's Scale Oil and Shiner, which looks like it was forgotten mid-oiling.

I tsk. I've been taken to task over all sorts of doctrine I ignored, but here's the Director himself, blatantly ignoring the "no vanity products" rule.

I wonder if I could use this to blackmail my way back into my room. Probably not.

Priya places her hands on her hips. "Okay, which wall is the one that leads to the secret room?"

I point at it, and then we commence the fun game of trying to figure out how to open the secret door. We take out all the books on the shelf, hoping one of them is a trick book, but it's not. Then we try pushing in various places on the bookshelf, which also fails. Then Priya leans on the wall casually, over and over, while I stare at her, baffled.

"What?" she says. "It works in the films."

I sigh heavily and then go to the desk and sit down. The chair is shockingly uncomfortable, probably because there's a huge hole in the bottom for the Director's tail. The level is also all wrong for human anatomy, and I end up with my knees whacking the bottom of the desk and I'm not exactly tall.

My feet slide across the floor and catch on something. I look down, curious.

There's a button on the floor.

Well.

That was easier than I expected.

I push it with my foot, and sure enough, the wall swings inward.

Priya grins. "Awesome."

I'm glad someone's having fun.

The secret room is much as I remember it. Wall-to-wall filing cabinets made of mahogany with gilt trim. A desk on the far side, with another of those weird chairs designed for the Director. A large, incredibly detailed painting of Saint Irving hangs on one wall. The room is organized and neat, much like the front office. It looks completely innocuous.

Except that it's behind a secret wall, of course.

"So what are we looking for?" I ask Priya as we walk in.

"Something incriminating," Priya says.

"How specific."

"We'll know it when we see it," Priya insists, opening one of the drawers.

"If you say so," I tell her skeptically, opening a drawer of my own. I'm not exactly a forensic accountant—or any kind of accountant. I wouldn't know money laundering if it beat me up and robbed me in an alley.

And honestly, I don't know what other crimes a bunch of paperwork would show us.

But I gamely pick out a file and flip through it, as though I know what the hell I'm doing.

"They're personnel files," I say slowly, as I flip through the file I've pulled out. It has a picture of a young man, with his name, birth date, and age. Below that is information on when he became an acolyte of the Friends, what jobs he did, and when he did them.

The next page is an overview of his therapy sessions, which list his fears, and some details about past trauma that fed into them. I stop reading when I realize what it is, since that seems private.

On the top corner is a note that says *Transfer NB*, followed by a date last year.

After looking at him another moment, I remember him. He was with the Friends for a few months before the Director asked if he'd be willing to transfer to the New Bristol branch. He had, and we hadn't heard from him since, to no one's surprise, given that New Bristol was way up the coast.

"What do you have?" I ask.

"Also a personnel file," Priya says. "Some guy transferred out before we ever got here."

"So this room is just full of everyone who worked here?" I stare at Priya. "How . . . nefarious."

Priya shrugs. "We've only just started. Let's look around a bit."

So we do. At least ten filing cabinets line the walls. It doesn't take us long to realize there aren't just files on acolytes of the Friends, but patients and volunteers and everyone who's walked in the door since the place opened decades ago.

I have to admit, it's getting a little weird. Who needs this many cabinets of just . . . people?

The files stretch back years, and there's just so *many* of them. Each one is essentially the same. A page with biographical details, and then notes on their therapy tucked in behind.

And on the top corner of every file there's a note with their current status.

There's a lot of statuses, most of them indecipherable abbreviations—PB, NPS, NE—most of them gibberish to me, with no hope of guessing what they could mean. But others are more obvious. *Transfer NB*, for example, which I assume stands for "transferred to New Bristol." *Transfer OC* is similarly obvious, though I'm not sure if the abbreviation refers to Old Castle, O'Conner City, or Out of Country.

I pick up another file, and the black-and-white face of a Nightmare stares up at me, some sort of fishlike thing with bulbous eyes and long whiskers. I remember him—he was in the group therapy for Nightmares that time I nearly set the room on fire. You don't forget a face like that.

On the top corner of the page, it says *Transferred OC*.

My brows pull into a frown. Why would a voluntary patient be transferred somewhere else? Staff would be, sure, but the people who came in casually for the group meetings? That's weird. Maybe he'd moved.

Frowning, I go back through the files, looking for other transfers.

Most of them aren't staff.

Have I misinterpreted something? How can so many non-staff end up transferred?

My fingers flip through the files, and I pull out a familiar name.

Priya.

I open the file, but it's sparse. She's never been for therapy, and so she only has one page with biographical information and an NE on the top corner.

"Ness?"

I turn to Priya. "Yeah?"

She holds out a file. "I found yours."

I hesitate, then take it. "Swap you. I've got yours."

She takes it, opening it and rolling her eyes when she sees how bare-bones it is. I look down at my own, which is thicker. I swallow, then open it.

The top corner has a *Transfer NB (pending)*.

I stare at it a long moment. I think of all the times the Director encouraged me to consider transferring to the New Bristol branch. All the times I turned him down.

Unsettled but not quite sure why, I flip to the back to the therapy notes, feeling no compunction about reading what they wrote about me. There's only a few lines.

Generalized Nightmare fear caused by sister turning into Nightmare and slaughtering father and others.

Progress: Fear has successfully been focused away from the specifics of the spider and onto the general concept of Nightmares.

Recommendation: Extremely promising candidate for SRP, transfer to NB as soon as possible. To avoid overwriting current fear, ensure transfer is voluntary.

I read it again. And again.

The first part isn't that much of a red flag. It just states what I have, a fear of Nightmares, and how it's evolved over the years. I remember the early years, panicking at the sight of a single tiny spider, arachnophobia taken to the extreme. It's been a long time since I've had an issue with spiders—the fear transferred over to Nightmares in general.

Except it also says *avoid overwriting current fear.* If I reread the first part with that in mind, it could be read as if the Friends overwrote my spider fear with a fear of Nightmares.

But no. That can't be right. Why on earth would they want me to be afraid of Nightmares? That makes no sense.

But.

It also says "ensure transfer is voluntary."

Which implies, you know, that some people go involuntarily.

Have I ever seen any of the people who've been transferred again?

I wrack my mind, but it comes up blank. I haven't.

No one ever returned after being transferred.

I'd never noticed because I never cared. I'd never been friends with anyone here except for Priya, too trapped in my own little world, hiding in my room from the big bad world outside.

I should have guessed. I should have figured out something was wrong so long ago.

I've been so blind.

"Priya . . ." I choke out, my heart beating faster and faster as the pieces all click together and build into something too terrible for me to put into words.

"Priya is occupied."

I turn around haltingly, like the world has slowed down for me and every second takes an hour. I know that voice. And I know, whatever I see, it will be bad, and things are already very, very bad.

Because I'm starting to think something terrible might be happening to the people who "transfer."

And I have a feeling that the Friends will have no qualms about doing even more terrible things to protect that secret.

Palms sweaty, fear choking my breath, I turn around.

The Director is standing in the doorway, pointing a gun at Priya's head.

23

This isn't the first time someone's pulled a gun on me.

The first time was about two weeks after I moved to Newham. I was eleven years old and still raw from my sister's transformation and my father's death. It was a simple mugging, but when the gun came out, all I could think was that I'd escaped death once, I wasn't likely to do it again.

I collapsed.

I screamed and bawled my panicked little head off, begging for my life. The mugger, who'd been hoping I had money, was shocked by the vehemence of my response, and ended up running away. But I couldn't leave the spot I'd collapsed in, rocking back and forth, weeping and mumbling, begging for life from someone who'd long left.

My aunt found me there an hour later and brought me home. We had to have the Talk about Newham, about safety and violence, about what a threat was and how to handle it. She told me to remember that on the other end of a gun was a human. They might be bad, but they weren't mindless, like the monster my sister had become.

I don't know how she knew what to say, but it did the trick. When I was mugged again a week later, I mostly maintained my composure and just handed over my fake wallet, which had a few cents in it—my real wallet, of course, was hidden in my belt.

Over the years, I'd faced down more guns than I could count. But I'd always survived, albeit minus some cash.

So it's been a long time since I've been afraid of a gun.

But now, as my heart rate slowly rises and my eyes fix on the gun, I remember why I was so scared of them that day in the street when I collapsed into tears. I remember that they can kill instantly, that you can't duck out of the way of a bullet.

And this time, unlike all my previous times facing a gun, I don't think it's money the wielder wants.

The Director's webbed hands are tight on the smooth surface of the pistol, and his yellow eyes are narrowed as he looks between us. His scaled face is twisted, lips curled back to expose his small, sharp lizard teeth.

"What do you think you're doing in here?" His voice is hoarse and raspy, and his forked tongue flickers out, tasting the air, as though he can divine the truth from the texture of our words.

"We're . . ." I trail off. What the hell can I say to explain this?

And what can *he* say to explain why he came in with a gun? Because unless this room is full of things exactly as horrible as I fear I've discovered, why come in armed?

Priya is glowering at the gun pointed at her, as though it's a personal insult. She knows that if she goes for it, she'll get shot, so she can't fight back. I can almost hear her grinding her teeth.

The Director raises a scaly brow. "Find anything interesting?"

I look down at the files in my hands. My hands, which I've trained for so many years not to shake in front of the Director. Because he's a Nightmare, but it's not his fault. He's not a mindless monster like my sister became.

No, he *chose* to be a monster.

I look up at him, my eyes steady. "What happens to the people who get transferred?"

The Director smiles. "Why, they start working at the branch they're transferred to."

"Then what about all the people who don't work here who've been transferred?" My voice is hard.

"They moved. We transferred their treatment plans."

I stare at him steadily, waiting for him to blink, but he doesn't flinch.

"If it's all so innocent," I ask softly, "why do you have a gun?"

The Director raises a scaled eyebrow. "Shouldn't I? I caught two people breaking into confidential patient files."

He has a point.

But I'm not going to let him manipulate his way out of this. Not this time. Because I'm starting to suspect I've been the subject of a lot of manipulation over my time here.

"You know, a lot of these files say the transfer was involuntary," I say quietly. I don't actually know if this is true, but my file did say they should ensure I went voluntarily. Which implies other people didn't. "That sounds a lot like kidnapping."

The Director is silent for a long time before finally shrugging. "Some patients need a bit of a push to get the help they need."

I blink. "A push."

"That's right."

"So you kidnap them."

"Kidnap is such a strong word."

"Not as strong as the stench coming off your bullshit."

He snorts, still completely unbothered. And why should he be? No matter what we've found here, he'll just deny it. This isn't some penny novel where, when the villain gets caught, he reveals his entire dastardly plans. Real villains are way too smart to get tripped up monologuing their plans to their enemies.

No, he's just going to use that gun he's holding to make sure we don't cause any more problems.

I swallow, bowing my head, trying not to let my heart crack right down the center. It feels like it's shattering, like someone has taken a hammer and smashed my chest and it's fractured into a spiderweb of cracks.

I've never been safe here. My room, my home, my love for this place—all of it has been a lie.

My safety has never been more than a cleverly spun

illusion, built on my own ignorance and desperation for a place to hide from the world.

I think back on all those times the Director asked me if I'd be willing to transfer. It seemed like every few weeks he'd bring it up, and every time, I'd panicked, too terrified at the prospect of somewhere new, somewhere I might not have my tiny room to myself. I'd clung to the known security of my current situation, too scared to try anything new, to change and evolve, no matter how he pushed.

I'd thought that was a flaw. A piece of my cowardice that was ruining my life, not allowing me to move forward.

And maybe it was—but it had also saved my life.

Because looking back on it all now, it was painfully clear the Director had been trying to send me off somewhere I'd never come back from.

I wonder now if he'd ever actually planned to kick me out. I'd been so scared of losing my home. Had that been intentional? Had he planned to make me so scared of losing everything that when he offered to transfer me later on, I'd say yes out of sheer desperation, clinging to the last scrap of certainty left?

The worst part is that it would have worked.

I would have taken that olive branch, would have transferred rather than risk ending up homeless and broke on the streets of Newham. I would have done anything to avoid that.

And he knew it.

I wonder now if he engineered it. If he never meant for me to grow a spine, if all those therapy sessions I'd had growing up had all been meant not to help me, but to steer me toward the Friends of the Restful Soul, to make me feel safe and comfortable here and nowhere else.

Like a spider luring in a fly, I'd been wrapped in a web that I couldn't even see. A web that trapped not my body, but my mind.

But just like any other spiderweb, at the end of the day, everyone trapped in one gets consumed.

And the spider lives to spin another web.

I swallow heavily, throat choked. I can't think about this right now. I can't handle this.

So instead of asking about what he planned to do with me in New Bristol, if my whole life was a terrible manipulation, I ask an easier question, though painful in a different way.

"Why did you sell me out to the assassins who blew me up on the boat?" My voice is numb.

He blinks slowly, slitted eyes baffled. "I didn't sell you out to assassins."

"Come on," I say, my voice tired and my eyes burning. "You've got a gun. I'm not going anywhere. Just let me have the satisfaction of knowing who blew up the boat."

"I told you," the Director says testily. "I didn't sell you out to them. What a waste that would have been."

"Forgive me if I don't believe you," I whisper, voice hoarse.

He shrugs. "I don't really care what you believe."

"Are you going to kill us?" I ask softly.

He rolls his eyes. "Of course not. I thought you said you read the files?"

I open my mouth, then close it. "You're going to send us to New Bristol."

He smiles broadly. "I think the both of you would benefit from an aggressive therapy program."

My heart tightens, and I want to cry, want to mourn the loss of every piece of foundation that kept me standing, that kept me moving, that kept me sane after my sister died. But I don't. I can't.

In that moment, Priya meets my eyes.

The Director has been pointing his gun at her, but his focus has been on me. On my questions, my accusations. Priya has taken that opportunity, and inch by careful inch, she's maneuvered herself just close enough. It wouldn't be close enough for most people, but Priya has long legs, and people forget that.

I know exactly what she's planning to do. She nods at me once.

I don't hesitate.

I just duck.

In an instant, Priya flattens and her leg shoots out, swinging around in an arc.

Her boot catches the Director right in his knees. Or rather, where his knees would be if he had human anatomy.

Unfortunately for us, he doesn't.

He yelps and stumbles, but he doesn't go down, and the gun doesn't leave his hand. He swings it around, aiming at Priya, and she dives behind one of the solid wood cabinets.

BANG.

The shot embeds itself in the wood, and Priya presses herself against the wall, eyes wide, staring at the bullet hole where she'd been a heartbeat before.

I'm still on the ground, frozen, hiding, hoping no one notices me, when I realize I have a clear line to the door.

I can escape.

I can run, leave all this behind, run all the way back to Cy's apartment and hide in his closet, cowering like the coward I am, and leave Priya to fight this battle.

I don't move.

I've spent my whole life running. My whole life avoiding everything that makes me afraid, and what has it done?

It's just made me more afraid.

The more I run, the more I build up my fears, the more I solidify my own certainty that I am a coward. But no one made me into a coward, though if those files are right, the Friends might have helped. But at the end of the day, no one can make you into something you're not. I made myself into a coward. The Friends just helped me do it.

But I don't want to be afraid anymore.

Just like I made myself into a coward, I can make myself brave too.

So instead of running, instead of fleeing into the world and hiding, I crawl over to one of the filing cabinets. Priya and the Director don't even notice me, both of them caught up in their epic battle, which is mostly Priya using various pieces of furniture to protect herself from gunfire.

I yank a drawer out, files spilling across the floor, the

heavy wood weighing me down until my arms drag. No one pays me any mind. Why should they? Everyone knows all I ever do is run from trouble.

But not this time.

I heft the drawer, and then, in a terrible, terrifying moment, I swing it.

My heart is racing, and sweat trickles down my spine, and my mind is screaming at me, telling me to run, not to be a hero, to just save myself, live to fight another day.

But I ignore it—ignore everything that isn't the Director and the drawer.

Then I bring the massive wood drawer down on the Director's green, scaly head.

24

Silence reigns, everyone in the room frozen in complete and utter shock.

The drawer is heavy in my hand, a little fleck of blood on it where it struck the Director. A green scale has fallen to the rug.

The Director's hand slowly lowers, and the gun clatters to the floor. He sways, just for a moment, before following suit, tumbling to the ground in an unconscious puddle.

My breath comes hard and fast, and I hold the drawer menacingly, like I'm going to need to hit him again. But he doesn't move.

I did it.

I faced him. I was terrified, but I didn't run. I stood up to him, and I took him down.

I've never done that before.

A feeling is swelling in my chest, a powerful, unfamiliar sensation. It's warm and expansive, like I'm filling up with light.

Pride.

I'm *proud* of myself.

I never want this feeling to end, never want to let go of the glow that suffuses me, the way my heart is still racing but in a good way, a satisfied way, like I've just won the lottery. Like I've just made a miracle happen all on my own.

I've spent so much of my life feeling small and scared, I never knew what it was like to feel this way.

Capable.

Brave.

Worthy.

I close my eyes and slowly lower the drawer. It falls from numb, shocked fingers and clatters to the ground on top of the gun.

Priya's eyes are wide, and she stares at me like she doesn't know me. But it's not a look of judgment—it's a look of pride.

"Damn, Ness. I didn't know you had it in you." She grins, wide and bright. "We'll make a Nightmare hunter of you yet!"

I bark a stunned laugh. "Yeah, no thanks."

I did one brave thing, but already my mind is backing away, going back to the fear, slipping away and musing over how lucky I was that worked, and how lightning doesn't strike twice. Sure, I stood up to my fear once and it ended okay, but who's to say that next time it will work out this well?

Fear exists for a reason. It warns us not to do stupid shit. It keeps us safe.

It only becomes a problem when it consumes our lives.

But I push those thoughts away and cling to this moment because I did it. I saved Priya for once. I was the hero for the first time ever.

My chest is rising and falling rapidly, and I think I might be grinning a wild, manic grin, and Priya is grinning back at me and we're okay, we're going to be okay—

The door opens.

Priya and I both whirl around, Priya with her fists up, ready for a fight, me, crouching, like I'm already making myself small, preparing to run. So much for my newfound bravery.

Cindy stands in the doorway, her notebook in hand, her eyes wide, fixed on the unconscious body of the Director.

We stare at her.

She stares back.

"I can explain," I say weakly.

Cindy looks at me, one eyebrow raised. "Oh?"

"He was evil," I tell her. I gesture at the file cabinets. "He was kidnapping people."

"And doing what with them?"

"Uh." I rub the back of my head. "I don't know."

Cindy pinches the bridge of her nose. "Really?"

"You have to believe me!" I step forward. "I didn't just randomly attack the Director."

"Oh, you never attack people randomly," Cindy agrees easily, wiggling her ankle pointedly.

I wince. "He started it."

Cindy steps into the room, her fingers skimming over the files. She flips one open.

"You know, I've been looking for these for months," she comments.

"I—wait, what?"

Cindy blinks and looks up to me. "You're sure it doesn't say where the missing people are going?"

Priya and I exchange a look.

Priya leans forward. "It almost sounds like you knew they were kidnapping people."

"Of course I knew. Why do you think I'm here?" Cindy sighs, running her hand through her hair. "I guess I should start over. My name is Cindy Lim, and I'm an investigative journalist with the *Newham Gazette*."

My mouth drops open.

Priya is nodding though. "I should have suspected. I'm guessing that notebook isn't poetry."

"No, it's research notes." Cindy shrugs. "I write it in a multilingual cipher so it's harder to crack. I tell people it's poetry because people *expect* they won't understand poetry, so if they see some of my notes, they won't be suspicious if it looks like nonsense."

Wow, have I judged Cindy wrong.

"Why didn't you say anything?" I ask.

She rolls her eyes. "I was undercover." She shrugs. "And besides, I couldn't be sure you weren't in on it."

"What?" I sputter. "Why would you think I was in on the kidnapping?"

She shrugs. "You've been here awhile, and most of the long-term staff are accomplices."

Oh god. Did everyone know this place was evil except me?

"Is that why you've always been such a bitch to me?" I ask.

Cindy glares. "No, I've been a bitch to you because you do things like break my ankle."

"I didn't *actually* break it. Maybe sprain it."

Cindy doesn't look impressed by this excuse. "I'm still not convinced you weren't in on this," she says, eyes narrowed. "How do I know this whole thing isn't some power grab?"

I raise my hands in exasperation. "I'm not involved in this, Cindy! I found out about ten minutes ago, when I broke in here because I thought the Director sold me out to assassins for finding his secret room."

Cindy's expression sobers a little. "Did he hire assassins?"

"I don't know!" My hands fall and my head bows. "He denied it, but he's a liar."

We're all silent for a moment, staring at the Director on the floor, as if we can get answers from his unconscious body.

"If you knew this was happening, why didn't you stop it?" I finally ask her.

Cindy sighs heavily. "Because I didn't know what was happening to the people who disappeared. I've traced dozens of disappearances over the last decade to the Friends, but I can't figure out what's happening to the victims. And without knowing where they're going, what's the point of stopping them?"

"You stop the kidnapping," I reply, my voice deadpan. This seems kind of obvious.

Cindy sighs. "No, you stop the *Friends* kidnapping. There's a difference."

I'm not seeing it.

Cindy rolls her eyes at my expression. "All right, so what if they're selling the people to a third party? Then that third party will just keep hiring other people to kidnap for them, and I'll have lost my only clue that could have led me to them."

Oh.

"My point is"—Cindy raises one hand in a half shrug—"this clearly has been going on awhile, and I don't think the Director is just some run-of-the-mill serial killer. This is an organized operation. And if I don't know what happens to the people, I can't stop it permanently. I needed to gather intel before I took action."

We all look back to the Director.

"So um, that plan's probably out now," I admit.

"Well, he didn't see me. So I could probably stay on." Cindy looks over the files, a grin spreading across her face. "But now I have *these*."

"You really think you can figure out what's happening from some files?" Priya asks, sounding skeptical.

"No idea!" Cindy admits cheerily. "But it's going to be a lot of fun trying. Paperwork is my favorite part, you know. It's like you're searching through puzzle pieces and you don't which ones fit in the puzzle and which don't."

"Sounds tedious," Priya says.

"Oh, no, I love it. I love puzzles." Cindy opens a folder, her eyes bright. "There's something wonderfully satisfying about solving them."

She starts wading through the piles of paperwork, her eyes bright, her notebook out.

"Um, before you get all involved in that," I say. "What are we going to do with the Director?"

Cindy blinks, then looks at us. "Oh, leave him. I'm going to call some friends and pack all these papers up. We'll be gone before he wakes." She considers. "But we should tie him up for good measure."

I blink. "Shouldn't we call the police?"

"Oh, no, he'll bribe them out of charges and into charging you." Cindy snaps her fingers. "That reminds me. The police came by this morning. They were looking for you, Ness."

My heart stops, then restarts, faster than before. "Wait, what?"

"You pissed off someone big-time." Cindy shrugs. "Enough for them to pay for you to get arrested."

Somehow, in the chaos of the confrontation with the Director, I'd lost sight of the real reason I'd come here: to figure out who set the assassin on me.

And for everything that happened here, not one piece of it has got me any closer to safety, to being protected from the people who want to kill me.

I've failed.

I was so wrapped up in the small picture, I didn't see the big picture, and in the big picture, I'm still an incompetent coward.

Fuck me.

"You guys should make sure not to forget the stuff in your room," Cindy tells us, pulling me out of my thoughts.

It takes me a moment to understand.

Of course we need to get our stuff.

Because we're not coming back.

It's all falling apart. I won't ever get my room back. I won't ever get my little safe haven again. It's gone from me forever. The life I've so carefully built over the years has been overturned, and no matter what I do, I won't be able to get it back.

I'm homeless.

I'm wanted by a bunch of psychopaths that blew up a boat. They've hired assassins to kill me, probably bribed the police to arrest me, and who knows what else.

My hands shake, and I bow my head, the true extent of everything I've lost finally hitting me like a ton of bricks. My shoulders tighten. I don't know what I'm going to do. I'd been thinking in terms of a "when this is over" solution where I returned to the life I had. But that won't happen now.

My life is gone.

I have nothing left.

The massiveness of the loss is incomprehensible, and all I want to do is crawl into my room and hide from the world, block it all out and weep, protected in my small closet room.

But I can't.

And I never will again.

25

Priya and I grab our trunks from her room before we leave.

On the way out, I stop in front of my door. Or the door to the room that was once mine. I press my forehead to the old, heavy wood and take a long, deep breath. It hurts more than I thought, to say goodbye. Even though I know now that the safety of this place was only ever an illusion. Even though even if I could come back, I wouldn't be able to feel safe here.

But this was my home for three years, and saying goodbye makes my chest constrict, like my ribs are closing around my heart.

All I've ever wanted was to feel safe. To have a place I could hide from the monsters of the world, where the Nightmares couldn't get me.

But I wonder now if such a place exists, if nowhere in Newham is truly safe. If safety as an entire concept is an illusion.

Finally, I turn away from the door.

My throat has choked up, and I'm silent as we drag our trunks through the familiar halls. Priya doesn't say anything, letting me stew in my grief, wallow and roll in it.

Outside, the sun is still high, and it's so bright that it feels fake. I hate it instantly. Maybe I should go nocturnal like Cy so I never have to see it again.

Priya and I separate on the subway. She's taking her stuff to her sister's cramped apartment, and is going to have a hell of a time explaining to them why she's suddenly moving back in with them for a month before joining Nightmare Defense.

"You'll be okay with your vampire?" Priya asks, avoiding my eyes.

I can tell she wants to invite me but also knows she can't invite me to an apartment that's not even hers—especially given how small their place is. I doubt I'd even fit.

"I'll be okay," I tell her.

It's better this way, I tell myself. I can't risk putting them in danger, and there's still a target on my back.

No one knows about Cy, and he's also a lot harder to hurt than Adhya and Livia.

"Call me," Priya insists. "I want to be sure you're all right." She considers. "Though maybe not until Adhya is done yelling at me. I'm sure there's going to be a lot of I-told-you-so's."

I laugh, imagining Priya sitting on the couch, not at all contrite, as Adhya paces back and forth in front of her, alternately yelling *What were you thinking?!* and *Haven't I been telling you?!*

Ruby used to do that when Dad was working late. These exasperated lectures, how she was the big sister, the responsible sister, and why couldn't I fall in line? She was only trying to protect me, after all.

The memory is like someone gently running a blade over an old scab, tugging at pieces and drawing small pinpricks of blood.

Sometimes I miss Ruby so much I can't bear it. Sometimes I'm so jealous of Priya and Adhya I can't even look at them.

No, it's better I'm not there for that conversation.

So I drag my trunk back to Cy's place, hoping that he'll be okay with another night of me. I don't think he'll call me a leech and kick me to the curb after only one night, but I've been wrong about people before. Like the Director.

Even worse than being kicked out—he might ask for rent.

Given that all I have is the measly amount of cash I got for talking with the *Post*, I can't imagine I'd ever be able to pay for space, even that little closet, in a place as nice as Cy's.

Or maybe he'll want the rent paid in blood.

My skin crawls at the thought, but it's less terror inducing than it would once have been. Before, I'd have lived on the streets and risked the Nightmares. Now I'd consider the idea seriously. If it comes to it, I don't know that I'd say no.

I'm not sure if that's a sign that I'm not as afraid as I once was or a sign that I'm more desperate than I've ever been before.

The security guard at Cy's building lets me in without questions. It's the same man as before, and I'm so exhausted and emotionally strained already that I don't even twitch at the sight of his Nightmare-mutated form this time.

I haul my trunk up in the elevator and down the hall, the sound of it scraping the fancy fake marble floor high and grating, like fingernails on a chalkboard.

Finally, I make it to Cy's door and knock. "It's me."

He opens it.

His hair is ruffled, but he's still put together, and his eyes are soft, the green brilliant against the eyeliner.

He takes one look at me, my disheveled appearance and my trunk, and his expression melts into concern. "What's happened now?"

My mouth trembles and my eyes water and before I realize what's happening, I'm leaning forward into his chest, crying into his shirt, the whole story spilling out as I cling to him in a pathetic, desperate hug.

He makes soothing sounds as I speak, gently reassuring me I can stay with him until I get back on my feet, it's no trouble, don't even worry about it, it's all going to be okay, you're going to be okay.

He leads me inside and settles me on the couch, grabbing me a glass of water, which I sip miserably but cling to, just to have something solid to hold on to.

"I understand what it's like," he whispers. "To be alone here."

"No, you don't." I sniffle. "You're rich. You have no idea what it's like to be broke and trying to find a way to survive in Newham." I laugh jerkily. "Never mind the fact that you're one of the dangerous parts of the city. No one's going to prey on you—you're—"

I stop.

"I'm what?" he snaps, eyes flashing. "I'm the one preying on them?"

I shrug, looking away. "That's what they'll assume. It keeps you safe."

He glares at me a long moment, then sighs heavily, shoulders slumping. "No, you're right. It's not the same." He swallows. "I'm sorry. I don't know what it's like to be poor and powerless in a city full of monsters."

I nod, accepting his words. "I'm sorry for implying you were one of the monsters." My eyes flick to him. "Before too."

He looks away. "It's not a wrong assumption. You had no reason to give me the benefit of the doubt."

We sit in silence a long time, and I sip my water. I'm feeling a bit better, more balanced. Yes, my life as I knew it is over. I won't get my home back, and I'm caught in a web of assassins that I don't know how to get out of. But it could be worse. Cy will let me stay for a bit. I've been in worse places.

I mean, I didn't end up in a cult because I was doing *well* in life.

I sigh heavily. "What the hell am I going to do about the police?"

He frowns, considering. "You can't get caught. I'm sure they've been bribed."

"Me too." I rub my temples. "And they must suspect you exist by now because I couldn't have swum to shore myself. It's only a matter of time before they figure out who on the passenger manifest could have swum to shore."

He grimaces. "I know."

I take a deep breath. "But we don't need to hold out for long, just long enough."

"You think one of their clients will take them out for us because of all the bad press."

"I do." I shrug. "The Mayor will probably feed them to her pterodactyl. We just need to hold out until then."

"Yeah." He agrees, then hesitates. "But how long will that be?"

I bow my head. "I don't know."

"What if they find us before the Mayor finds them?"

My shoulders slump. "I don't know."

We're silent a long moment before I ask, "Do you think we should try to find them ourselves?"

"And do what?" He tips his head to one side. "Even if we figured out who they were, what would we do with that information?"

"Publicize it?" I shrug. "If they're named, the competition might take them out. Or maybe those stupid Chaos League people will butt in. Try to make the streets of Newham safer and cause chaos to villains or whatever it is they do."

"Ugh, the last thing we need is those clowns involved too."

I snort. "At least they're a good distraction."

He laughs. It's a nice laugh, warm and soothing.

I'm feeling a lot more relaxed now, even though I'm still in the middle of this mess. There's something grounding about having Cy here, about not being alone in this.

"If we figured out who was after us," I finally say, "I bet we could send that information to the families of the victims too."

Cy's eyes widen. "You mean the gang that lost their leader in that strike."

"Yeah."

"The violent, vicious, incredibly homicidal gang that is furious their leader was taken out in such a cowardly way."

I sip my water, smiling. "Yep."

He stares at me, his expression going from shocked to thoughtful to tentatively hopeful. "You know, that might actually work. Better than the papers or the law or any of that."

"It might."

He leans back. "Of course, there's the issue of how you find this assassin group in the first place."

I bite my lip. Here comes the awkward part. "I have an idea."

He tips his head. "Oh?"

I hesitate, then take a deep breath before just plowing through my nerves and getting the words out. "The friend who wrote you."

Cy's expression twists, pain and confusion in his eyes. "Dev. His name is Dev."

"Dev, then," I say.

"What about him?"

"Do you know where to find him?" I lick my lips. "An address in Palton? Where you were supposed to meet?"

He hesitates, then nods. "He gave me an address." His eyes flick to me. "He might have left though. Since the boat exploded."

"Maybe."

"He might never have been there at all." He swallows, then looks at the floor. "I mean, if it was a trap, he had no reason to actually . . ."

I lean forward. "Do you think he knowingly would have killed you?"

Cy flinches. His eyes are full of pain, and he's looking off at distant memories I can't see. Finally, he bows his head, and whispers, "No. No, I don't think Dev would have willingly tried to have me killed."

"Which means one of two things. One, you weren't a target, in which case we go have a nice visit with your friend." I fold my hands on my lap. "Or two, we talk to him and find out who knew about your meeting and who could have hired the assassins. And then we find them."

He seems uncertain. "I'm sure it's my father. We can't face him. He—" Cy shudders. "I can't."

"Cy, for all you know, Dev will give you an unrelated name, like one of the assassins themselves. Your father may have hired them, but they're the ones who would have stalked Dev to find you all on their own. There's a good chance he can lead us to them. Or one of them."

Cy closes his eyes.

"Even if it doesn't work," I tell him softly, "I think getting out of town until this blows over is a good idea. For both of us. So it's a win-win."

He hesitates a long moment, his expression pained and hopeful at the same time, before finally bowing his head. "All right. Let's get on that damn boat again."

I hope this time we actually make it to the other side.

26

I try calling Priya to get her to join us and because it's past time she and Cy met, but when Livia picks up the phone, she informs me that Adhya and Priya are having the fight of the century and she doesn't think Priya will be able to go anywhere or do anything anytime soon.

I admit, I'm a little disappointed. I always feel better when I have Priya with me.

But maybe it's for the best—if this doesn't work out, Cy and I will probably go into hiding somewhere until things blow over, and Priya is way too excited about joining Nightmare Defense to disappear too. And hiding was never Priya's strong suit anyway—that's my thing.

So it's only Cy and I who make our way to the docks just after sunset.

I'm not sure what I expect when I get there. A memorial for everyone who died? A calm, solemn atmosphere about the tragedy? A lot of people too hesitant to get on the boat?

But no.

It's exactly the same.

Crowds push and pull all around the dock, and the line to board is around the corner. People carrying suitcases of mail check their watches and yell at the people in front of them to hurry up. Paper boys and girls run around, trying to hawk the latest edition of the *Post*, and uniformed police stop random people to write them tickets, in hope of being bribed to tear them up.

It's like the explosion never happened. Everything is the same.

It's only me who's different.

Cy and I go to the counter to buy tickets, which Cy pays for and I pretend not to notice so I don't have to face the awkwardness of actually acknowledging that he's the one who has to pay for everything, even though we both know that's how it's got to be.

Then we line up with everyone else.

"It's eerie," Cy says suddenly, "how little things changed."

"I was just thinking that," I reply.

"I guess to them, it hasn't." He sighs. "Especially with the reveal that the boat was bombed. Because there's no reason to be afraid of the boats or that it'll happen again. Assassins aren't an engineering problem, they're just a Newham problem."

I snort. "And after all the publicity, I doubt they'll try blowing up another boat anytime soon."

The ticketer checks our tickets and waves us up the ramp. It's the same guy as last time, though he clearly doesn't remember me, and I decide not to remind him.

I hesitate at the bottom of the ramp, swallowing. It's like I'm back in time, and I'm ascending the same boat that blew up. It looks exactly the same—massive city on the water, black prow, wood paneling on the top, smokestack towering high above. I know that it's not the same boat, just the same model, but my hands are shaking at my sides, and I'm suddenly really regretting this whole idea. We should just go back to Cy's apartment. I shouldn't have come here.

Cy grabs one of my shaking hands in his.

I blink and look up at him.

"It's gonna be okay," he says gently. "We survived the last journey, and we'll survive this one." He winks at me. "Though hopefully this one will be less dramatic."

I give him a choked laugh. "It better be."

Cy's hand is warm in mine, anchoring me, and I take a deep breath and ascend the ramp. Even though my heart beats too fast and my breathing is shallow, my fear leaking out through involuntary motions. But still, I ascend.

Because I am *not* going to be a coward anymore.

The top deck is much as I remember it. Oh sure, the bar is on the other side of this boat, and the tables are a little different, but it's the same vibe. The music has already started, and the dancers are sweeping the floor, preparing for the moment we set off and they can start sneakily spiking their drinks and partying all night long.

We settle against the rail of the boat, watching as the dockworkers pull up the ramp and lock the gate, trapping us all on board. And then, without any announcement, we're off, the boat pulling away from the dock, the only sign of anything happening the faint hum of the engine beneath my feet.

The people by the bar scream in excitement as the boat leaves the dock and the law of the land. They start gleefully spiking their booze, still trying to be surreptitious but mostly failing in their eagerness. The music cranks up, louder and louder, so loud I can feel it like a second heartbeat in my chest.

People are starting to drink and dance, and a girl is making eyes at Cy, her eyebrows waggling suggestively as she nods him over to the dance floor.

But Cy doesn't move, remaining settled beside me, leaning against the railing.

I nod at the dancers. "You don't want to join?"

Cy shakes his head. "I'm good."

I raise my eyebrows. "I don't mind if that's what you're worried about. I'm all right."

I'm actually a bit of a nervous mess, but that's a me problem. I really don't see why Cy should avoid having fun just because I'm twitchy being on a boat again.

He waves my concern away. "Don't worry, you're not keeping me from it."

"You seemed to be having a lot of fun on the last boat before I ruined it," I point it.

His expression sobers as he watches the dancers. The light from the radium glow sticks the partiers are waving glints off his dark hair and makes his eyes seem to glow even greener, almost otherworldly.

282

"You can find so many different people at a party like that," Cy says.

I tip my head, not sure where he's going with this.

"Some people dance for pure joy. They hook up for casual fun. They aren't running from anything or searching for anything, they're just looking for an evening that will entertain and bring them joy. They live in the moment, and they're happy."

I think of Priya, hungry for all the different experiences just because they're fun.

"Yeah," I say. "I know someone like that."

He nods absently. "But not everyone is like that. Some people go to forget. They're running from their own lives, either from where they are now or from a past whose claws they can't extract from their mind. They drink to numb the fear and self-awareness of how deeply unhappy they are, and they hook up to chase brief highs that they can't get in their normal lives."

I watch him, silent now.

"And some people," he says slowly, "come because they're lonely. Because in a wild, turbulent night of dancing and drinking and sex, no one knows who they are. Everything is live in the moment, anonymous. No one knows if you're a bloodsucking Nightmare. You don't have to see the fear creep into their eyes and the dread slide in. For that night, you're best friends, no strings attached, no knowledge needed."

I wonder how many people react the way I did when I first saw him—with fear and suspicion. And the people who don't are probably fans of those vampire romance movies, so every time he talks to those people, he's reminded of his father.

No matter who he meets, the moment they know what he is, things change.

I'm quiet for a long time before I say, "How long have you been in Newham, Cy?"

"Two months."

"Have you made any friends?" I ask.

He shakes his head, then hesitates. "Unless you've changed your mind?"

I've never been good at making friends because I'm so scared of people becoming monsters, because I'm scared of trusting people only to lose them to their nightmares.

But that's just been another form of cowardice.

So I lean my shoulder against his and grin. "Well, I *suppose* I could be convinced."

"Is that so?" he says, a slow smile beginning to creep across his face.

"Well." I wink at him. "There *are* some conditions, you know."

He raises his eyebrow, but he's smiling. "Such as?"

"You can't forget my birthday," I tell him. "That's a fireable offense."

"I didn't know I was being hired."

"Of course. This whole time we've been together has been the job interview."

"Has it now?"

"It is."

"All right then, when's your birthday?"

"June eighth."

He nods solemnly and presses his palm against his chest. "I promise to keep that date in my heart."

I match his solemn expression. "You better."

"Well, if we're to be friends," he tells me, his voice light and teasing, "I have to inform you of something *very* important."

"Oh, do tell."

He leans forward, his eyes on mine, fake dramatically. "Are you ready?"

"I'm ready."

"Are you sure?"

"Totally."

"Well then." He lowers his voice to a faux whisper. "I have to be honest—I like romance films."

I stare at him, then burst into laughter. "Seriously?"

He grins. "Seriously. And being my friend means you have to watch them with me."

I'm doubled over with laughter, grinning so wide it hurts. Finally I rise, wiping my eyes.

"You want to know something funny?" I ask him.

"What?"

"I hate romance films."

He bursts into laughter. "Well, that's it, we can't be friends."

"It's a tragedy." I can't hide my smile. "But you know what? I think I can make the sacrifice to watch a few with you."

"I promise, I'll only show you the cheesiest, funniest, most cringeworthy ones," he informs me.

"I'll endeavor not to curse your name."

He grins, and there's something so light and happy in his expression, and I'm grinning back.

And I realize—my hands have stopped shaking. I'm not scared anymore, even though we're still on the boat and nothing's really changed.

But I'm not afraid.

I feel safe.

Not because I'm in a safe place or I'm tucked away, hiding from the world where nothing can find me. No, I feel safe because I'm with Cy. Because Cy makes me feel safe.

I've always felt safe with Priya. I never would have gone back to the Friends today if I didn't. I trust her to be there for me, to protect me and keep the danger away. Just like I trust Cy.

I always thought I was safe at the Friends of the Restful Soul, in my room. That safety meant a place to hide from everything that frightened me.

But the real safe place is with my friends. It's not where I hide, but the people around me who make me feel safe.

I lean against Cy, and he wraps his arm around my shoulder to tuck me against him. Our voices twine together, laughter rising up into the dark as the neon lights of the boat cut through the shimmering water and we head toward the future.

27

It's the middle of the night when we arrive, and the city is awake and *alive*.

Palton is considered the party city because while they have laws against alcohol consumption, they're even more lax than Newham, which is really saying a lot. Palton is a city of casinos and gambling halls, and those places would murder anyone who took their drink sale profit from them.

No. Really. They murdered every government official who voted for the prohibition laws.

All around us, massive casinos rise up, each one more elaborate and ostentatious than the last, lining the boardwalk of the city. The largest and glitziest is the Koval Kasino, which is plated entirely in gold and shaped like a giant dragon egg, complete with neon-lit dragon head breaking out of the top of the egg. That's the high rollers suite. Supposedly the dragon's eyes are windows and you can look down on the whole city like some sort of megalomaniac god.

People stand outside every casino, advertising various jackpots, some of them with numbers so big I can't believe they're real. The neon lights are so bright and ubiquitous, it feels like daylight even though the dawn isn't for hours.

We make our way down the street, past groups of drunk partygoers who scream in delight at nothing and everything. The boardwalk is crowded, and Cy and I have to push through the crowds. There's something electric about it all, an energy that crackles against my skin and makes my lips dry.

It takes Cy and me a while to find the address he has for where Dev is staying. But we do eventually find it, just off the main strip.

A towering casino-and-hotel combination, it looms, glittering and golden, covered in neon signs advertising multimillion-dollar jackpots and drinks to die for. All the neon is so distracting it takes me a while to realize that the glitz is turning eyes away from the flaking paint on the front door and the way one of the bulbs in the sign has burned out.

We're not on the really rich, shiny part of the boardwalk anymore. These are the tier-two casinos and hotels.

Cy hesitates at the door. "He might have left already."

"He might," I agree.

"That might be better," Cy says. "That he's not here. I don't—I don't know that I want to know if he set me up to die. I—"

"Cy." I put my hand on his arm. "It'll be okay. Whatever happens."

He meets my eyes and I give him an encouraging smile, letting my hand fall to his and squeeze gently in support, letting him know I'm here for him.

He nods once, sharply, and takes a deep breath.

Then he walks through the door.

I trail behind, eyes wide as I take in the interior of the building, the plush red carpets, the large, glamorous arrows pointing to the slot machines, the roulette games, the poker tables. The reception desk is marble, and the people standing behind it are all dressed in red-and-black suits with the casino logo on them.

By the time I arrive at reception, Cy has already convinced the receptionist to check if Dev is staying there.

"Yes, here he is," the receptionist says, a pretty Asian woman with film star Anna May Wong's signature eyeliner and slicked hair. "Would you like me to call up to his room?"

"Please," Cy says, smiling nervously.

She calls up, and Cy's fingers tense on the counter, waiting for an answer.

"Hello?" The receptionist smiles, even though you can't see that over the phone. "Yes, you have a visitor? Someone named Cy. Yes. Oh lovely, I'll let him know."

She puts the phone down and smiles at Cy. "He says he'll be right down. Why don't you take a seat?"

Cy's smile is tight and nervous. "Thanks."

We walk over to some chairs by the door, high-backed, elaborate things, and sit down to wait. Cy's foot taps nervously on the ground, and he keeps looking around, biting his lip. He has to be careful about that—he has fangs now, they'll probably draw blood if he keeps it up.

"So how did you and Dev meet?" I ask him.

"School." He shrugs. "We met on the first day of school and clicked instantly. Never looked back."

I smile faintly, my eyes lowered. I don't remember much about school. I went when I was a kid, me and Ruby, walking down the road every day to the town schoolhouse. Ruby would hold my hand and smile down at me and tell me that I was to study hard because kids that studied got scholarships to go bigger and better places.

But I never wanted to go bigger, better places. I just wanted to be wherever my sister was.

Of course, after she died and I came to Newham to live with my aunt, I didn't really have time for school. I went occasionally to the local one, but I mostly skipped. I just never saw the point. When in my life was I going to need to know about protons and electrons in molecules or how photosynthesis worked?

But now I'm thinking about school and my sister, and my mind turns back to my old teacher's words again.

Maybe he's not wrong. Maybe I've just been too afraid of what I'd find if I actually looked.

"Cy!"

Cy and I both turn at the sound of the voice. Cy's expression is a complicated mixture of hurt and hopeful, and I really hope Dev genuinely isn't connected to the boat explosion for Cy's sake.

"Dev," Cy whispers.

Dev comes over. He's maybe twenty, with dark brown skin, an aquiline nose, and thick, tousled black hair. He has a wide mouth that's currently stretched into a broad, genuine grin.

"Cy," he says, his long legs eating the distance as he hurries toward us. "I didn't think you'd come!"

Cy blinks. "Um."

"I waited all week." Dev is rattling on, his smile nervous and hopeful. "I thought . . . I thought maybe you'd decided against coming."

Cy looks away.

Dev turns to me, his smile nervous but determined. "Is this your friend?"

"I'm Ness." I hold out my gloved hand, and he shakes it vigorously.

"Nice to meet you!" Dev shifts on his feet, his nervous chatter getting faster. "I was worried when Cy ran off that he'd be lonely. He's such a people person, you know, so I'm glad he's making friends."

I blink and nod, my mind trying to catch up with how fast Dev talks. I'm not sure what I expected Cy's friend to be like, but I don't think it was this.

Cy's head is bowed. "Why did you contact me, Dev?"

Dev blinks, then looks away. "I wanted to apologize. To fix things." He runs his hand through his hair. "I . . . I miss you. You're my best friend. And I just . . . ."

"You told me you didn't want to see me anymore," Cy says.

"I know." Dev's expression falls. "It was wrong. *I* was wrong." He swallows. "I was so unhappy without you. Really

291

miserable." He bows his head. "I felt awful, like I'd sawed off my arm." He blinks rapidly. "That's kind of a gory metaphor, I'm sorry, I'm not good at this, but the point is, I felt really bad and I missed you a lot."

Cy is speechless, mouth open. He's shocked, but I can see the hope blooming in his eyes, a desperate, small thing that he's clearly scared will disappear in a heartbeat.

He clears his throat and swallows convulsively and asks, "What about Beth?"

Dev brightens. "She understands now, really! When she realized that we were still corresponding in that magazine, it was her idea to go on a vacation here so you could come visit. So I could see you and make things up to you."

Cy blinks, then frowns. "Wait. Coming here was . . . Beth's idea?"

Oh no.

"Yeah." Dev grins broadly. "She's really gotten better, Cy. She's much more relaxed, I swear. No more jealousy."

I have a bad feeling he's wrong about that.

Cy's expression of confused horror doesn't change. "So you're here with Beth. And my father doesn't know?"

"Your father?" Dev looks baffled. "What? No! Are you insane? What kind of crazy would I have to be to be in contact with that monster?"

Dev doesn't understand, but I do. And Cy does.

Someone *did* put a hit on Cy.

But it wasn't his father.

"Turn around slowly."

It's a woman's voice, and I already know whose it will be, even though I don't recognize it, have never heard the voice before. Because the moment Dev told us whose suggestion meeting on Palton was, Cy and I both understood the truth.

I turn, and sure enough, a woman who can only be Beth stands just behind a ring of masked, armed men, all of whom have very large, very deadly looking guns trained on us.

"Beth?" Dev whispers, his eyes wide and frightened as his gaze flicks from one armed and masked assailant to the next.

Beth smiles. She's white, skin so pale that she looks like she's never seen the sun in her life. Her long, dark brown hair falls loose around her, like a sleek, perfect cloak, and despite it being the middle of the night, she's dressed like she's just stepped out of a soiree hosted by the Mayor, in a long, elegant black dress that makes her look more like a vampire than Cy.

Really, what is it with evil people dressing like they're posing for a pin-up calendar of Villain of the Month?

"Beth . . ." Dev's voice drops in terror. "What's going on?"

Beth's eyes are smiling even as her mouth twists into a sneer. "I'm doing what I should have done ages ago. I'm getting rid of the toxic element in our relationship."

28

I stare at Beth, and my first thought is that it was really dumb of me to not realize this was a possibility. I mean, Cy told me she was a jealous creep. What did any of us think would happen if Dev tried to get back in contact with Cy?

Man, I really wish I were better at this whole figuring-out-who-the-villain-is thing. It always seems so obvious in hindsight.

Some people walk by, completely ignoring us and our predicament. This is a common enough scene, and no one is going to intervene, even if our guts end up on the pavement. The worst that will happen is the hotel will bill Beth for the carpet cleaning.

Dev's eyes are wide and confused as he stares between his girlfriend and the men with guns surrounding us. "I don't . . . I don't understand."

"Oh, baby," she says softly, her hands out. "You don't have to worry. I'm taking the temptation away." She walks over to Dev and loops her arm through his, leaning against him. He pulls away, but she's determined. "I'm sorry you had to see this. It was supposed to be solved last week."

"Last week?" he says. "Last week, like . . . like the boat . . ."

"Of course." Beth ignores the horror on his face and turns to Cy. "How the hell did you manage to survive that?"

Cy just stares at her, still in shock.

"Hmm." Beth's eyes narrow speculatively. "I wonder if you take after your father now?"

Cy flinches and looks away, unable to meet her eyes.

Beth's smile curls up.

"Be careful," she calls to the armed people surrounding us. "I suspect he's a vampire."

They don't respond, except to tighten their grips on their guns, their eyes, visible through slits in their face masks, narrowed in focus.

The man in the lead, still masked, tosses a pair of handcuffs to me and Cy. I fumble the catch and one set smacks me in the chest before falling to the ground in a puddle. Cy, on the other hand, catches his set automatically, only to yelp in pain and drop them instantly.

Silver.

They want him to put on silver handcuffs.

His fingers are red and burnt where he touched the handcuffs, and our eyes meet for a moment, an acknowledgment of how extremely screwed we're about to be.

"Put the cuffs on," the muffled voice of the masked man says. "These bullets are loaded with silver shots as well. We heard about your father and we came prepared, just in case."

Cy flinches, his eyes flicking around, looking for an opening to escape.

There isn't one.

If he runs, they'll shoot him, and no matter how fast he is, he's not faster than a speeding bullet.

"You too, girl," the man snaps. "Put the cuffs on."

Right. So I guess I'm not getting out of this either.

Not that I thought I would.

When neither Cy nor I move toward the cuffs, the man hefts his gun threateningly. "If you don't have those cuffs on in thirty seconds, I'll kill you right here. I'd like to take you alive, but it's no skin off my teeth if you die now."

He's dead serious.

I put on the handcuffs.

Cy does too, slowly and with clenched teeth as the metal scalds his fingers and wrists like its coated in acid. But he doesn't cry out, just sucks in a long, whistling breath and grits his teeth against the agony.

Dev is still standing there, stunned. Beth has wrapped her arm around him and he's stiff in her grasp, like he's trying to pull away from her touch but is too afraid to move.

"Beth . . . you . . . you really hired people to kill Cy?" he repeats, as though he still can't believe it, despite ample evidence.

"Shh," she whispers to him, running a finger down his cheek. "Don't worry about it. I did it for us. He was taking you away from me. You couldn't stop thinking about him—it was driving a wedge between us."

Yeah, pretty sure the only one driving a wedge between you and your boyfriend is yourself, Beth.

"Now it's just us, no complications," Beth whispers into Dev's ear, her fingers running up and down his chest in a way that's probably meant to be sexy but just looks like she's writing her name on her property with her finger.

Dev's expression is crumpling fast, like his whole world is coming down around him and he has absolutely no idea how to stop it.

Cy looks resigned, his head bowed, his muscles tight, trying not to cry out from the pain of the cuffs.

I weigh my options and then decide I'm screwed anyway, so I might as well go out by being an absolute bitch.

"Do you know why people become jealous?" I ask Beth, my eyes on hers.

Beth looks at me, head tipped, like I'm a pile of dog shit that decided to start talking.

"It's because they're afraid." I hold Beth's gaze. "They're afraid of their partner leaving them. Afraid of being alone again." My lips curl in a sneer. "And do you know why they're so afraid?"

Beth doesn't say anything, but her lips tighten.

"It's because deep down, they're insecure. No matter what their partner says or does, they don't trust them. Not necessarily because their partner is untrustworthy—but because they're afraid they're not worth anything themselves. That if their partner has a chance to find someone else, they'll take it, because who wants to be in love with someone like you? You're not worthy of love."

Beth reels back. "Shut up."

"But the irony is, Dev *did* love you. And Cy didn't ruin it. *You* did. You clung so tight that you strangled your own relationship." My eyes hold Beth. "You're a coward. And it's ruined everything you love."

Beth sneers, her fingers curled tight in Dev's shirt. "You don't know anything!"

But clearly someone else is listening, and he thinks I'm right. Because Dev finally breaks free from his shocked state and shoves Beth away from him, hard.

Beth stumbles back, and Dev takes several steps away from her.

"Dev?" Beth's voice is small and confused.

"Fuck you," Dev whispers, broken pain and kindling hatred in his eyes. "I never want to see you again."

Beth swings to him. "Dev, no, I—"

The men in black surround Cy and I, blocking my view of the drama playing out between the former lovebirds. Gloved hands grab my arms and force me to turn around, marching Cy and I toward the door in rough steps and rougher voices, hissing at me to move move move, or they'll cut their losses.

I manage to look back once. Dev is trying to chase us down, screaming for Cy, and Beth is clawing at his shirt, yanking him backward, trying to hold him back or pull him close. Her words aren't audible, only the cadence of her voice, rising and falling with panic and desperation, as their fragile relationship shatters into a million pieces.

Fear destroys.

It destroys everything it touches. It destroyed my life—I can see that now, the cracks and fissures like a spiderweb across my life, breaking it apart and then devouring the pieces.

Fear led me to a cult, desperate for even the illusion of safety. And the more I hid away, the more my fear grew, trapping me in a lifestyle that only served as a crutch, propping up my terror instead of facing it. Instead of fixing it.

Cy and I are roughly loaded into a van parked in front of the hotel. It's black, with no distinguishing marks, and people give it a wide berth, as though they can tell it's up to no good. Given that we're chained and being death marched into it, they're right to steer clear.

As the door slams shut behind us, sealing us in the complete darkness of the back of the van, the fear curls its long tendrils from where it slumbered in the depths of my soul. Because I can't see a way out of this, a way to break free of these chains and run, and wherever they're taking us, well, it's not going to be good.

Regret tastes like ash and cheap casino perfume as I finally understand that sometimes you run and run and run, and when you finally stand up and fight—

—you fail.

29

As soon as we start driving, Cy heads to the back door to try to break it open. He smashes against it with his painfully swollen hands, the shackles digging in and burning his flesh with each beat. He makes small sounds of rage or pain or both as he smashes his fists uselessly against the metal.

"It looked armored," I say quietly. "I'm not sure even you can break through that."

He swears, hits it a few more times, and then finally slumps, flopping beside me. The engine rumbles beneath us, and occasionally we thud or bump over something that sends us up in the air for a moment.

I lean against Cy, feeling the steady in and out of his breath and the thump of his heart. I'm glad he's one of the vampire strains with a heartbeat. The ones without are also cold to the touch, so it really would have been like resting against a corpse. No thanks.

We don't drive long before the car slows to a crawl and then finally stops. Cy and I both tense, preparing for the back doors to open. My heartbeat is so loud I can't hear anything else, and I'm not even sure I'm staring at the back doors because it's so dark.

We wait.

And wait.

And wait.

At some point, I slump to the side of the car, accepting that while we have stopped, those doors aren't going to open anytime soon.

Cy occasionally bangs on them to no avail, and eventually he slumps down too. It's not like there's much else we can do except wait.

Time passes. It's hard to tell how long it's been in the dark with no watch, but it's long enough that I'm wondering if they're ever planning to let us out. Certainly, it's been hours, though how many, I couldn't say.

Eventually, I doze off.

My sleep is uneasy, but dreamless. It's almost like I can feel the dream, waiting for me, kept away by a slowly thinning wall, like melting ice. It feels like if I just pressed hard enough, it would crack apart and I could step back into the world of my nightmares.

Not that I want to.

I'm jolted awake when the engine starts up again. I rub my eyes, wondering how long I slept. Beside me, Cy mumbles sleepily and turns over. The soft crunch of wheels on pavement is the only sound in the enclosed truck, and we're moving again.

We drive a long time. Long enough that I'm starting to

half doze again, lulled by the rumble of the engine and my own exhaustion and fear. But eventually, we do stop.

I nudge Cy awake, and he rubs his eyes blearily, the motion barely visible in the continued dark.

"Where are we?" he asks.

"No clue." I hesitate. "But I think we're here. Wherever that is."

He swallows heavily and gets to his feet. I do the same. Whatever faces us on the other side of the door, we're going to face it on our feet.

Though if there were a place to hide, I'd probably use it. But there isn't, so I might as well try to continue this attempt of mine to be brave, I guess.

When the door finally opens, Cy takes a step forward, and I think he means to rush our captors. But he takes less than a step before he stalls, eyes wide.

A dozen people with guns trained on us stand at the back of the truck.

This time, no one is wearing face masks, which I suspect is a bad sign. You don't usually take the masks off unless you're not worried about your prisoners surviving and ratting you out.

"Come out of the van slowly," says one of the men, his eyes dead and cold. I recognize the voice from earlier, which means this is the same crew that kidnapped us. Which, I mean, obviously, but you can never be certain when everyone's wearing masks.

"Out, now," he repeats.

I am absolutely sure he'll have no problem killing us if we act out.

Cy and I exchange a glance and then slowly shuffle out of the back of the van, bound hands in front of us. The cuffs have chafed my wrists a little, but as we walk into the light, it becomes brutally apparent that they've absolutely destroyed Cy's wrists. His skin is melted and pus covered, and something whitish peeks out from the pink sludge of his arm, something that looks suspiciously like bone.

I look away quickly, swallowing my nausea.

We need to get those cuffs off him. Vampires can heal from most damage, but not if the cuffs are still worsening it every moment.

As we step onto the concrete, I get a good look at where we are. It's a warehouse of some sort, certainly not the kind of thing that's on tiny casino-and-resorts-only Palton Island. Which means that long time we weren't driving was probably because we were parked on a boat, heading back to the mainland.

Other than that, there's no indication to show where we are.

The soldiers gesture us forward, and we march across the warehouse-like room full of trucks, large metal cages, and a few autos. My eyes are massive as they take in all of it—this operation is huge, much bigger than some normal assassination company. This is like a military base.

We're led into a narrow concrete hallway that leads to a long stairwell down, deep underground. Nothing good ever happens in basements. That's something the penny novels and the news all agree on.

Too bad I don't have a choice.

My heart thuds in time with my steps as I descend, my mind whirling, part of it occupied with wondering who these assassins could be, given all their hardware. But mostly, I want to know why they've taken us prisoner instead of killing us.

In my experience, you don't take people prisoner when you want them dead—not unless you have a much worse ending in mind for them than death.

All I did was escape a boat. Why is everyone so *mad* about it?

Though maybe they don't know I escaped the boat. Maybe I'm just collateral damage from Cy's capture.

But if they didn't know who I was when they captured us, I'm sure they do by now.

When we reach the bottom of the stairs, there's a door, locked and sealed. The man in the lead turns a metal hatch and flips a switch before pressing in a combination lock. The door swings open, thick steel groaning at its own weight as it swings wide, revealing a long hallway.

One of the soldiers nudges me with the butt of his gun and I stumble forward. My feet echo eerily in the smooth steel hall that looks like it's out of someone's fantasy of a space station. On each side of me, thick metal-rimmed glass doors look into empty steel rooms.

No, they're not all empty.

A red-scaled creature that looks like a cross between a dragon and a half-melted tree spits acid at the walls of its steel cell, shrieking up at us, red eyes slitted as it hisses. A massive, human-size hornet buzzes in a cell across from it, banging its body over and over against the walls. In another, a completely human-looking person stares at us, but when he smiles, his mouth stretches up and out, all the way around his head and then over the top, his entire head falling into the smile like a wilting flower. A massive, gaping maw is all that's left.

"What the hell?" Cy whispers, eyes wide.

"They're catching Nightmares," I whisper.

"But . . . why?"

I don't have an answer.

We're led down the hall, and then turn onto another, twisting through narrow, mazelike hallways, each lined with cells housing Nightmares. We pass rabid house-size wolves that barely fit into their cages and a cell full of an entire swarm of red-and-black bees that work together to form into the shape of a giant middle finger, which is really very impressive coordination.

Finally, we reach two empty cells, across from each other.

"Inside."

"I—" I swallow. "I think there's been a mistake. I'm not a Nightmare."

Someone behind me snorts. "Not yet you aren't."

His words are like ice dropped down the back of my shirt.

Not yet.

Someone shoves me from behind, and I stumble forward, into the steel cell. Across from me, Cy is now in his own cell, his eyes wide and his face creased with pain from his cuffs.

In the cell beside him is . . . something.

It's impossible to see what's in the cage because of all the webbing. The entire cage has been coated in a sticky spider-web, so much that it's a shield, hiding whatever's inside.

But I don't need to see inside to know what's in there.

A giant spider.

Just like my sister.

It can't be my sister—I know because I saw what happened to her body after the townsfolk finally stopped her rampage. I remember the bloody streaks on the road, the leg, hacked off, long and hairy, that someone had forgotten to clean up.

And the smell as they burned her body, the stench of charred hair and meat, like the world's most unappetizing cookout.

But it doesn't stop me staring at the spider-silk webbing in the cage, thinking of my sister, who became a spider just like that.

And the horrible fear that, shortly, I'll end up just like her.

The thud of boots on pavement and the way the soldiers all straighten and salute shifts my attention to the person coming down the hall.

He stops in front of the cells, surveying Cy and me.

He's tall, with straight, silver-blond hair that's been slicked into a sleek side part, dark brown eyes, a sure jaw, and a smug expression. Unlike the men who picked us up on Palton, this

306

man is actually wearing a uniform, navy blue with a series of gold stars pinned to one shoulder.

I recognize him.

I've seen him all over the Nightmare Defense recruitment posters—that smile and melted-chocolate eyes looking out at the viewer, encouraging them to sign up to fight monsters, to be a hero to the people. I've seen him staring up out of Priya's trading cards. I saw him the other day signing autographs in blood.

Charlie Chambers. Slayer of the Great Sea Dragon.

He's the embodiment of everything that the people of Newham believe is truly heroic.

I really should have known better than to trust anything or anyone good in this fucking city.

He smiles at us and waves his hand at the cages of Nightmares, as though sweeping it out before a bow.

"Welcome, Vanessa Near and Cyril Coates III, to the Newham division of Nightmare Defense."

30

Nightmare Defense.

The words crawl into my mind, a name for the organization that tried to blow me up, to assassinate me when I survived. The people who have hunted my steps and haunted my mind since the boat went up in flames.

Nightmare fucking Defense.

Thinking it through is like watching terrible puzzle pieces click into place. Because I'd wondered: Who would have the power and influence to make sure everyone ended up on that boat together? Gang lords and ambassadors, scientists and heiresses—it's just a lot of coordination and a lot of influence. I should have seen, right from the start, you needed a massive organization with a lot of political power to do this.

And to have the money and access to the number of explosives and a sophisticated detonator that could take out an entire boat? That kind of weaponry doesn't grow on trees.

But I just don't understand why the hell Nightmare Defense would be working as assassins for hire. Why they'd be blowing up boats.

It just doesn't make sense.

But maybe, I realize, it doesn't have to. Maybe I'm the naive one, or maybe Priya's hero worship has rubbed off on me. We've all idolized Nightmare Defense at one point or another. Who doesn't? They keep people safe. They fight sea monsters and demonic entities. They keep the city clear of uncontrolled violence caused by dreams as much as they can.

But no one ever said they couldn't be corrupt. They have the weapons and training to be phenomenal assassins if they want to be. Maybe that's all this is—just money and corruption, the same as everything else in Newham.

I shouldn't be surprised, and I guess I'm not. I'm just disappointed.

Everything I've ever put any bit of faith in has turned out to be evil. Maybe I'm just a shitty judge of character.

Priya's going to be so disappointed though, when she finds out what's going on here.

If she ever finds out.

Cy and I are both staring, unresponsive, at our captor. He frowns, clearly having expected us to say something.

"Do you know who I am?" he asks, expression smug.

Cy shakes his head.

"You're Charlie Chambers," I say. Look at Priya's trading card hobby coming in handy in real life.

"The one and only." His chest puffs out, his smile widening. Then his eyes cut to Cy in disgust. "At least one of you is educated."

Cy bristles, and I find it absurdly ironic, since I suspect Cy is wildly more educated than me. Just not in celebrity monster hunters.

My eyes turn to Charlie Chambers, and I smile, all sweet sincerity. "But of course I know you! You stopped the dinosaur invasion last year!"

"No." His smile drops a little, just a fraction. "That was Simone Yuen."

"Oh." I purse my lips, then snap my fingers. "The zombie apocalypse on Creekwood Island!"

"That was Davinderjeet Sharma."

"Oh."

I stare at him. He stares back, as if waiting, but I just give him a blank look.

"The swarm of giant killer moths?"

"NO!" he snarls.

Finally, Priya's obsession with Nightmare Defense and their famous hunts is actually serving me well. Sure, all it's doing is helping me enrage my soon-to-be murderer, but you know what, if you can't use your knowledge to needle your killer, what's even the point of it?

"The person who turned into a living volcano?" I ask.

His face is as red as lava as he explodes, "THE DRAGON."

I just stare at him. "The flying one over New Bristol?"

"THE SEA DRAGON." He's practically frothing at the mouth. People like him, you gotta poke them where it hurts—the ego.

"*Righhhhhhhht.*" I give him a smile from behind the cage. "Um. I knew that."

His eye twitches.

"So, Mr. Sea Dragon," Cy interrupts, his voice flat and angry. "Aren't you supposed to be out hunting Nightmares?

The hell are you doing kidnapping us?"

"And blowing up boats," I add.

I wait for him to deny it, but he just shrugs. "We do that too. But, well. You know what this city is like. This is an expensive operation. Do you know how much explosive it takes to get rid of a dragon as big as a city?"

"A lot?" I hedge.

"A lot," he agrees. His smile is cold and insincere. "And our budget is nothing. Oh, on paper, it looks good, but somehow, on its way over to us, it seems to just . . . go missing." His face twists in a sneer. "Everyone on the chain skims some off the top, and by the time we get it, there's not even close to enough to actually do our goddamn job."

My mouth is hanging slightly open. "So you decided to do a little freelance assassination?"

"We've had to get . . . creative about acquiring funds."

"By killing people."

"Well, we *are* good at killing things." He grins, tilting his head at a photo-perfect angle. "And I'm a hero. I deserve so much more than scraps."

Why is Newham like this? Can literally *anyone* in this city not be a pile of murderous trash?

Cy is muttering something under his breath, but I don't catch it. It might have been something like *I ran away from home to escape people like this*, and I resist the urge to tell him he really should have run anywhere but here, then.

"Did you say something?" Charlie paces over to Cy's cage.

Cy just looks at him and snorts. "Nothing worth repeating."

"What are you planning to do to us?" I interrupt.

"Honestly, we were going to leave you alone after you survived the explosion. You weren't one of our targets," Charlie admits, examining his manicured nails. "But you had to try to get us in trouble. That news article? Bad idea, kids."

I glare at him. "You sent an assassin after me first."

"The boat explosion? You weren't even supposed to be there." He makes a disgusted sound. "We were supposed to be killing the other girl. I don't know how you ended up on the boat instead of her, but she sure dodged a bullet." His teeth gleam in a smile. "At your expense."

"Wait," I whisper. "You were planning to kill Cindy?"

"Of course." Charlie shakes his head. "She pissed off someone real important. You know, we actually planned this whole operation around her damn mail run and then last minute, you showed up instead of her."

Cindy Lim. Investigative journalist. Spy in the Friends. What the hell had she found out to end up having people putting hits on her? To plan an entire assassination operation around her?

And after all that, she wasn't even on the fucking boat.

The entire explosion, everything that's happened since— all of this mess is Cindy's fault.

I'm going to kill Cindy myself when I see her next.

"So," I say. "How about we forget all this, then? You let me go, and I murder Cindy for you?"

He laughs. "No deal. But I like your spunk."

I slump. Too much to hope for.

Then I frown. "Wait, you said you decided to kill me after I talked to the papers. But I was attacked by an assassin before then."

He shrugs. "Wasn't us." He grins. "We wouldn't be having this conversation if it had been."

"I—"

He's lying. He has to be.

But why would he?

"Are you sure you haven't pissed off someone else?" he asks.

I roll my eyes. "Who the hell else would try to kill me?"

"That's between you and whatever god you believe in."

One of the soldiers comes up and whispers something in his ear. He tips his head to one side, and his smile widens, pulling across his handsome face so he looks just like the recruitment posters. Suddenly, it doesn't look nearly as friendly and inviting of an expression as it used to.

He nods sharply to the soldier. "Do it."

My skin prickles as the soldier slips away. I have a bad feeling our time is almost up.

He turns back to us. "I'm a busy man, so we're going to get this started."

"Get what stared?" I ask.

He smiles, all teeth. "Why, making you into a Nightmare, of course."

No.

The sound of hissing air fills the room.

"You've been isolated long enough that the Helomine

should be out of your systems," he continues smoothly.

He can't do this.

"Why?" I whisper, my voice small and broken. "Why would you want more Nightmares?"

"Oh, they have many uses." He grins. "We use some for training the new recruits, of course. But most of them are pure profit. Interesting ones we sell to collectors—though most people we sell to aren't as flashy as the Mayor is with her pterodactyl. And, of course, the Friends of the Restful Soul can always be counted on to buy in bulk."

Wait. The Friends are buying Nightmares?

I want to ask why, but my mouth won't seem to open. My body isn't listening to me—it's just slumping slowly to the floor, my muscles turned to Jell-O.

"Sleep well." Charlie laughs. "I'll see you on the other side. Try to become something useful."

I want to yell, swear, rip through the clear wall of the cage and strangle him.

But it's too late.

My body is already slumping to the ground, the energy of sitting up too much for my wobbly muscles to bear, and even though I try to keep my eyes open, fight tooth and nail against the drugs sliding through me, eventually I give in, mind swirling into oblivion as sleep takes me.

And I dream.

31

The Nightmare begins the same as it did last time.

I'm sitting in the small kitchen of my childhood home. The window is open, and a breeze slips in, rustling my hair, which was longer back then. My father is sitting across from me, wearing his faded pants and fraying shirt, the ones that he refused to throw out because they were still wearable but that were also too ratty to be seen in public. He's humming softly as he reads the paper, his lips curled in a self-satisfied smile.

Ruby is there this time too. She sits on the floor, staring out the open windows at the birds on the porch. They chirp and twitter as they hop from birdhouse to birdhouse, as though thanking Ruby for setting them up. Usually, watching the birds on the porch cheers Ruby, makes her smile, soft and hopeful, and she'll call me over and tell me a little bit about each type of bird.

But today, or rather, in whatever day the nightmare has taken me to, she doesn't. Her eyes are flat and distant, as though she can't even see the birds in front of her. There's something terribly empty about her expression. She looks like she's already in her own nightmare.

She's been so excited the last few weeks, talking nonstop about the scholarship, about her new school and new life in Newham, that the difference is stark—and child-me hopes, desperately, that Ruby is finally rethinking her choice to move away, to leave me behind.

Maybe she'll stay, child-me thinks, a selfish little thing even back then.

I wonder, as I watch the scene in front of me from the side, like a spectral observer, *Is this actually a memory?* It feels like a memory, complete with believable child-me thoughts. But I have to wonder if my mind is creating these "memories," putting a new face on a girl based on the questions that have been swirling in my mind.

The scene shifts, and I'm in a different memory.

This is a memory of afterward.

I'm sitting on the grass, a blanket draped over my shoulders. Someone is talking to me, but I'm not listening, my eyes vacant and dead. Blood covers my hands, where I had to crawl through a pool of my dad's blood to get to the cupboard, and I managed to smear it all over my face as I covered my mouth to prevent myself from screaming.

A middle-aged Asian woman is sitting next to me, stroking my back. Miss Truong, a teacher at my school. She's wearing pajamas, and her long, black hair is messy and windblown, so unlike the respectable bun she usually wears.

"Ness," she's whispering gently. "It's going to be okay."

But child-me isn't listening, still lost in the horrors of the night before.

A man comes up to us, his face fuzzy in my memory and blank in my nightmare.

"How's the kid?"

"Shocked, but not injured," Miss Truong says.

"She was lucky," the fuzzy man says. "We have two confirmed dead, two injured so far."

Miss Truong covers her mouth, gasping softly. "Who?"

"Her father and Nicholas O'Leath are both dead. Nick's wife lost her arm trying to pry it off Nick, and the sheriff is badly hurt from taking it down."

It was a small enough town that everyone knew everyone, so no one needed context for the names. No one needed it explained that Nicholas O'Leath was our postman, a pot-bellied man with a large gray mustache and a booming voice. He and his wife, a friendly woman with a permanently startled expression, lived above the post office in the center of town.

Ruby used to wait in front of it every day, her whole body buzzing with energy when the mail truck arrived, hoping for a positive response from the scholarship committee. Nick would laugh and promise the first thing he'd do would be to check for her.

Child-me doesn't react to the names, but this me, the me watching this scene like a ghost, reels back at the words, the reminder that my sister killed multiple people. That she devoured them until nothing but blood smears and the occasional gnawed bone were left. That she killed Nick, mutilated his wife. That it wasn't just our father who met a gruesome end.

I stumble back and turn away, as if I can pull myself from this memory by sheer willpower, from the vacant child-me's eyes, the sad voices of the people in my hometown.

And I do.

The world swirls around me like smoke, and suddenly I'm back in the kitchen of my childhood home again. My father is alive again, and he's swearing viciously at some papers on the table.

I close my eyes and lean back against the wall. He's alive again. It didn't happen.

But child-me's devastation haunts me.

And so do the names.

Nick, who always gave candy with the mail at Christmas, even though we all knew that money was tight.

My father, who'd done his best to raise two girls on his own in the aftermath of his wife's murder by rampaging Nightmare and in one of the greatest recessions the country had ever seen.

And my sister, twisted and monstrous, who managed to ravage her way through our home on the north side of town all the way to the main street.

I frown slightly, and my eyes open.

That's a long way.

A lot of houses sit between those locations.

Why didn't my sister attack any of the people in them?

"Shit!"

My dream-father smashes his fist against the table. He runs his hand through his hair and takes a deep, shuddering breath.

"Daddy, what's wrong?"

Ruby and I are both peeking around the corner, looking at our father with wide eyes. I remember this now—it was a few weeks before Ruby died. I'd forgotten after everything else. The mines had been laying people off, and Dad was constantly stressed, terrified he'd be next.

He wasn't, of course. He even got a raise, which we'd all been incredibly relieved by.

Which, now that I think about it, it's kind of strange that he got a raise when they were laying people off.

"Nothing's wrong, sweeties," he says, his smile strained. "Go to bed."

And in the memory, I do, and everything swirls away again, before coalescing into another day, another memory of my father in the kitchen.

Except this time, he's in a great mood. He's even bought candy.

I remember the rose-flavored candy—not because it tasted amazing, but because I had a bloody wrapper from it stuck to my arm for hours after they pulled me out from the cupboard under the sink.

This is the night my father died.

The night my sister became a Nightmare.

The memory is the same as always, the same one I've played over a million times before, asking myself if I could have changed things, done something different, wishing I'd reminded my sister to take her sleep pills, so she wouldn't dream.

The room is frozen, just as it was, Ruby and our father by the table, about to start the last conversation they'll ever have. Ruby's scholarship papers are on the table, the corners curled and yellowing from all the times she'd flipped through them, read them over and over again, obsessed over them and everything they meant to her.

The ghost me, adult me, who is watching the scene, approaches the table, my hands hovering over the papers. How many times had Ruby shown me the pages, read me the words of acceptance, burning everything about them into my memory?

My smile is sad and soft with memory as I reach out for the top page.

And pause.

The top corner of the paperwork has a large emblazoned crest, an eagle, wings spread wide, over a cityscape. Underneath are the words Newham Academy, written in cursive.

Except.

Except I just walked past Newham Academy a few days ago.

That's not their logo.

Their logo is an eagle diving over a cityscape. Diving. Wings tucked away, head pointed down. It looks nothing like this outstretched eagle.

A sick pit of pain slides through my chest. Why would they have the wrong logo on there? Had they changed logos?

No. Schools like Newham Academy, centuries old and full of distinguished alumni, didn't change their logos.

And they certainly wouldn't put the wrong logo on their scholarship acceptance letters.

Before I can fully think through what this means, the dream continues, like a film on pause that has just resumed.

I'm in the memory of the last conversation Ruby and my father had before they both died. A memory I've replayed over and over, wondering how I could have missed Ruby forgetting her pills.

But now, today, it looks different.

Maybe I'm making it look different. Maybe my questions, my wondering about my sister, have changed the way I see the memory—or maybe my mind is simply writing over the memory.

Or maybe now I'm finally seeing what it really is.

"You're still driving me to the school next week, right?" Ruby asks, her tone careful.

"Of course!" Our father looks up from his abacus. "I wouldn't let you go alone."

"I could take the train," Ruby hedges, eyes narrowed slightly.

He gives her a stern look. "Ruby, you're thirteen. You're not taking the train to *Newham* alone. Nick is loaning us his auto." Our father's expression is pleasant and a little impatient, like he's humoring her. "Maybe we'll even have time for some sightseeing before I drop you off!"

There's a beat of pause here. Ruby's expression is frozen in something I can't read.

"Sightseeing!" Ruby grins, her smile huge and bright. Too bright. Too huge. So big I feel like it might shatter her face at any moment and reveal something much darker beneath. "Can we go to the top of the famous clock tower?"

Our father smiles back. "Of course!"

The conversation over, Ruby turns away, slipping out of the room and halting in the hallway to cast one look back at our father.

She looks devastated.

Her hands are shaking by her side and her eyebrows are doing this thing where it's hard to tell if she's enraged or brokenhearted. When I was younger, I thought she was mad that our father didn't trust her to go alone to Newham.

I've been so blind.

Ruby turns away, down the hall.

Something deep in the pit of my soul clenches. Because I know now, and it's clear to me that Ruby had figured it out too.

The scholarship was fake.

So where was our father planning to drive Ruby in Nick's car?

I stare after Ruby, at the empty spot where she'd been standing.

Ruby turned into a monster and killed two men and injured anyone who tried to stop her. She'd had targets, and those targets had been the two people in town who *had* to know the scholarship was fake—my father, because he was taking her to school personally. And Nick, because he ran the postal service in town and would have received any correspondence from Newham Academy. He also, conveniently, was loaning our father his auto to take Ruby . . . wherever it was they were *really* going.

Wherever our father had sold her.

The realization is like a blow, and I fall to my knees as I let the thought crystallize. How often have I heard of child trafficking in Newham? Kidnapping for experiments or fed to Nightmares. Hadn't the Mayor been kidnapping child slaves for her sweatshops?

And yet I never imagined my father would stoop to that.

But if living in Newham has taught me anything—finding out the Friends are kidnappers, Nightmare Defense is assassinating people for hire —it's that people are always so much worse than you expect.

Especially people you trust.

And that there are a *lot* of different groups willing to buy and sell people.

A long, hairy spider leg thuds into the room, the rest of the body hidden by the wall. But where once this sight would have struck me with a soul-deep terror, sent me screaming into the cupboard, made me run from it all, this time, I don't. I just stare at the leg, and I don't feel fear.

I only feel grief. An aching, awful pain that comes from deep within me, jagged and sharp, an old pain of loss that never really healed, just lingered there like a bullet wound.

Because my sister wasn't a mindless monster.

My sister never would have hurt me.

And to my sister, who was small and fragile and weak, Nightmares weren't a curse. They were her only way to gain power in a world where she had none, her only way to fight back.

Her only way to save herself.

Her only way to stop what was going to happen short of

running away. And if she'd run, I'd have followed. After all, I was planning on following her to the academy, wasn't I? And if she'd disappeared one night and my father had told me she'd left early, I'd have believed him.

And Ruby had to know—if he was willing to sell out one daughter, he'd be willing to sell out another.

Ruby wasn't just avenging her own grief and betrayal, consumed with pain and loss. She was doing what she always did—protecting me. Keeping me safe the only way she could think of.

The spider thuds deeper into the room, and I finally accept the truth.

This wasn't done to her—she did this to herself.

The memory dissolves, vanishing into the darkness, as though no longer solid enough to keep its form. As though its hold on me has slipped away, the fear that held me for so long morphing and changing, the hooks dropping away.

Nightmares are based on our fears, and I'm not afraid of what happened to my sister anymore.

The nightmare world vanishes into smoke and darkness, a void with no beginning or end.

And from within the void, the Nightmare Phantom appears.

32

The Nightmare Phantom looks the same as he did the last time I saw him. Colorless white hair that hangs straight and thin, so fine it seems like it would fall apart if I touched it. Black eyes, inky darkness covering the whites, irises, and pupils, so it's impossible to tell what he's looking at. Smooth, blemishless skin that has no color or texture, white like a piece of paper. I can't even see shadows on his skin, as though he can't cast them. It makes him look almost two-dimensional.

He smiles at me, sharp shark teeth dominating his face.

"Welcome again!" He spreads his arms and laughs. "I almost never get repeat visitors."

"I wonder why," I deadpan before I can think better of it.

"Well, most of them aren't lucid dreamers like you are." He smiles wider. "And they usually get what they came for the first time."

I want to say that most people probably don't come here on purpose, but the words die on my tongue. Because do I really know that anymore?

After all, my sister did.

"Can I ask you something?" My voice is soft.

He shrugs. "Sure."

"Do you remember everyone who comes through here?"

"Of course not. Not even I can remember *everyone*."

"Do you remember the girl I keep seeing in my night-mares?"

He considers, then waves his hand, and we're back in my memory. That familiar kitchen table of my old home, and Ruby and I both hunched over one of my schoolbooks, trying to solve a math problem. Our faces are scrunched in concentration, and Ruby is biting the end of the pencil with nerves.

"Her?" the Nightmare Phantom asks, tipping his head to the side. "Hmm. No. She doesn't ring a bell."

"You turned her into a giant spider."

He shrugs, indifferent. "I give many people gifts."

"Gifts?" I can't help the barking laugh that comes from me. "Is that how you think of it?"

"Of course." He tips his head to the other side, cocking it, almost birdlike. "Everyone wants to be strong enough to defeat the things they're afraid of." He smiles, sharp toothed. "And I even the playing ground."

I stare at him a long moment. I think of my sister, who needed to be stronger to fight back. Who I'd assumed for years had been nothing but a victim of her dreams, when in reality, she'd been making a choice that would ensure she wouldn't be a victim—and I wouldn't be either.

I suppose, in a strange way, he *had* given her a gift.

But that's not true for everyone. Cy never wanted what happened to him.

"Not everyone wants to become what they fear," I tell him quietly.

He gives me a sly look. "Don't they, though? You know, I had a serial killer in here the other day, and his greatest fear was that he'd be punished for what he'd done. Which means his greatest desire was to kill without consequence. Don't you see?"

I do not see.

"All his nightmares were about being jailed and trapped and unable to move and escape. So I took his legs and his arms and everything that gave him power to move and speak."

I shudder, even though I shouldn't feel bad for a serial killer. "So what, you made him a gross mouthless ball of flesh with eyes?"

"Well, no, I didn't let him keep his eyes. I did let him keep the mouth. He needs to eat, after all." The Nightmare Phantom laughs. "I turned him into a flesh-eating worm, actually."

The Nightmare Phantom continues laughing, and I'm just struck by the horror that now there's probably going to be a flesh-eating virus outbreak somewhere soon, some insane serial killer eating his way through the population.

The Nightmare Phantom sighs heavily, clearly annoyed I don't see the perfect beauty of what he's done. That I don't understand.

"I've made him his fear and given him his dream!" the Nightmare Phantom insists. "Now he can kill without judgment or consequence!"

Oh god.

"Our greatest fears are warped reflections of our greatest

desires," he explains. "Fear only has power when what we're afraid of takes away the things we value most."

"I—" I feel like he's talking in a different language, like his brain is working in a way that I can sort of see but can't truly understand. "I'm not sure how that's relevant. Especially since so many Nightmares are mindless after they come out."

The Nightmare Phantom shakes his head as though disappointed. "None of them are mindless. I can't change what's in people's heads, just their outsides."

"But . . . so many of them go on killing rampages—"

"And what makes you think that they didn't want to do that?" He leans forward. "That the nightmare didn't just remove their inhibitions, take the things that kept them from embracing their true desires?"

I open my mouth, a sick, twisted feeling in my stomach.

Because I don't know that.

I've lived in Newham for years. I know that humans can be monsters. I know that there are people who get off on murder, that there are people who are only barely contained by laws and many that aren't contained at all.

How do I know that the Nightmares lost their minds? Because they killed people?

But Ruby killed people, and she was very much in her right mind.

"I suppose you're right," I say slowly. "I was assuming that people wouldn't want to be killers. But that's not a good assumption, is it?"

"Not at all." He laughs. "So you understand now. I don't take people's minds. I give them the strength to face their fears by becoming them."

I want to point out that isn't true in so many cases. That Cy isn't somehow stronger now that he's a vampire. Now that he's forced to share the same curse as his father. He's not happier.

Is he?

He never wanted to be like his father, and in his mind, that meant not becoming a vampire. But it wasn't really the vampirism that made Cy hate his father. It was what he *did* with it. It was the actions his father took, the way he used what he was to hurt others for his own gain.

And Cy hasn't done that. In fact, he's worked hard to be the opposite.

He was so afraid he would become his father, but now that he has in every real way become the same monster, it's all the clearer to me that he's *not* his father. He has all the same curses and flaws, and he still chose to be a better person.

If Cy hadn't become a Nightmare, would he have lived his whole life in fear that he was only a nightmare away from becoming just as awful as his father?

"You understand now," the Nightmare Phantom says, smiling.

And I do.

I understand that the nightmare can twist your body, but it can't twist your mind. No matter what he does to me, no matter what terrifying form I take, I will always be me inside. *I* will be the one who chooses what to do with my new, twisted form. Not him. Not anyone else.

And with that, my fear slides away, draining out of me and drifting away. Let him change me. Let him morph me into something terrible—because no matter what he does, it won't change *me*. It won't make me a murderer. It won't make me into something I'm not.

At its core, that's what's always scared me the most about becoming a Nightmare. Turning into something else and hurting the people I care about—losing my identity until there's only a monster left.

It seemed like death, but you end up taking the people you love with you.

But no matter what I become, I won't let that happen.

That is something within my power to control and always will be—my own actions.

He can't take that away from me.

"I understand now," I tell him. "I see what you're doing. But I still think it's wrong—and if you think you're doing it for them, you're deluded."

He laughs then, a deep, throaty laugh, head thrown back.

"Oh, no, I'm not doing it for *them*. Of course not. I'm doing it for *me*." He grins, wide and sharp. "Do you have any idea how *boring* it is here?"

I blink. This is not what I was anticipating. "What?"

He spreads his hands to the void around us. "I've been here for *a hundred years*. The only entertainment I get is human nightmares."

There are a lot of things in that sentence I should probably focus on. His creepy ideas of what "fun" means. The way he views us as no more than entertainment.

But that's not what catches my attention.

"Then why don't you just *leave*?"

He smiles, and even though he has no iris or pupil, I can feel his gaze on me, intensifying. "Why do you think?"

I swallow, my hands sweaty, even though that's impossible in a dream. "Um. Can you leave?"

"In theory."

He waits, clearly hoping I'll ask the right thing, but I'm way out of my depth. I feel like I've stumbled onto something very important, and I'm the last person who should be dealing with it.

"How can you leave?" I finally ask.

His smile widens, broad and gleeful. "I thought you'd never ask."

He steps forward, still smiling, and a long, old-fashioned piece of vellum appears in his hand. Fancy writing in red ink slides across it, but I'm not close enough to read it.

"A number of conditions must be met for me to be released," he tells me. "Of those, there are two that are relevant to you. The first is that I cannot tell anyone that I'm trapped here. They have to figure it out on their own, after which point, I can explain the details."

Well, that explains a lot.

"Which of course means they have to be aware enough to converse in a dream." He sighs heavily. "Do you know how hard it is to find lucid dreamers these days? Even if you find them, they *never* want to talk."

"I can't imagine why," I deadpan.

"The second," he continues, ignoring me, "is that once aware of conditions of my imprisonment, the human can, without coercion, voluntarily agree to sacrifice a part of their body to release me."

Wait, what? Volunteer a *body part*?

"Whoa, whoa," I say. "You're not—"

"Implying we make a mutually beneficial deal?" His smile is back in place, and the vellum is gone. "I absolutely am."

I just stare at him.

"You want me to free you," I repeat.

"Yes."

"Into the world."

"Yes."

"Where you would . . . do what?"

He shrugs. "Oh, I don't know. I'm sure I'll find myself something entertaining to do."

Right. Entertaining. "Isn't your idea of entertaining turning people into monsters?"

He shrugs. "I work with what I have."

"So you won't turn people into monsters when you're out in the real world."

"I never said that."

I just stare at him, eyes wide. I imagine him walking down the streets of Newham, unrestrained, casually turning every passerby into a monster, twisted and warped into a

Nightmare in the middle of the day, wide-awake.

"Yeah, I don't think—"

He interrupts me. "You're in a pretty bad situation now, aren't you?"

I blink. "What?"

He waves, and the void shifts and changes, melting into a scene of me, unconscious on the floor of my cell while armed people wander the halls of caged Nightmares.

"Do you really think that they'll let you live?" he asks.

I don't answer.

"Let's say you wake up, unchanged, just as you are now," he starts.

I snort, interrupting him. "You really expect me to believe that if I refuse you, you won't turn me into some horrifying thing out of vengeance?"

He blinks, startled. "I can't."

I stare at him. "What?"

He shrugs. "I can only grasp extremely strong fears here. Dreams are too—" He waves his hand vaguely. "You know."

The world around us melts and shifts even as we speak, strange and amorphous, changing moment by moment. A giant sea serpent swims in the distance up some sort of mountainous pig's nostril. What is my subconscious even doing over there?

"Yeah," I reply. "Dreams are weird."

"Exactly." He continues, "You have many fears, all humans do. But not all of them are strong enough to carry through. I need strong emotions to penetrate the layer of unreality between us—the kind of emotions you only really get in the worst kind of nightmares." He grins. "Of course, once they're in their nightmare, I can play with it, shift it into more interesting shapes."

Right. Of course he can. How charming.

He shrugs. "But right now? You're essentially immune to me."

I hesitate, not quite believing him. "You really can't change me?"

"That's right." He raises a hand in a half shrug. "Becoming a Nightmare was your greatest fear for a long time. You've let go of that specific fear, and your mind hasn't yet adapted enough to replace it with a new greatest fear."

He tips his head to one side. "Once your mental state settles, your mind will inevitably latch on to something else to be your greatest fear, and I'll be able to turn you into that."

His eyes are on me, an eerie feeling when he has no pupil or iris. "But I'd rather you didn't for now."

"Why?" I ask. "Don't you want power over me?"

"No."

"Why?"

"You couldn't free me then," he explains patiently. "It's in the contract. The human who agrees to free me can't be doing it out of any form of coercion—including fear."

My eyes widen. "No one who's afraid can free you. Because the threat of becoming their fear is hanging over them."

"Yes."

"That's why you've been trapped so long," I whisper, marveling. "I wondered, if you just needed someone to agree to it, why you were still here."

His lips purse. "It's hard to find people who don't fear me, are lucid enough during dreams to understand what's happening, and also are willing to free me. It's a rare combination."

No shit.

"Have you considered that you might have had more luck finding someone willing to help you, who wasn't afraid of you, if you, you know, didn't turn people into their worst nightmares?" I ask.

He gives me a blank look.

I stare back at him.

"Well." He waves his hand, voice light and airy. "What's done is done, isn't it?"

Wait. Had he really never considered this? I refuse to believe he's so clueless he didn't think that turning people into monsters might be hurting his chances.

He's looking away from me now, toward the vision he's created of the real world. In it, I'm slumbering in the cell, and a soldier outside checks in on me from time to time.

Cy is in the cage across from me, sleeping away. He won't change, at least. Nightmare Defense probably hasn't yet figured out that he became a vampire through a nightmare, not an infection.

"They'll kill me when I wake up, won't they?" My voice is tired.

"Probably."

"And you can stop them?"

He just smiles, teeth sharp and wide. "I can do many things."

I find my hand going to my heart, even though I can't feel it hammering in my dream. It's just an instinct, a phantom sensation of something I do when I'm nervous and trying to make a hard decision.

Do I free a monster to save myself?

Or do I leave him trapped in nightmares to continue to ruin people's lives in their dreams?

I don't know what he'd do when out. I don't know if he'd still appear in nightmares, or if that's a condition of his imprisonment. I could ask him, but there's no reason for me to trust his answer.

I could also free him, and then he could abandon me to my death. I have no way to force him to keep his word.

Not that he ever even gave his word.

But I look down on the fuzzy dream vision of myself in the prison, and I know, if I do nothing, I'll die.

If I free him, I have a chance. A small one, but a chance.

Besides, if he's in the real world, maybe someone can shoot him. Or bomb him. He's certainly more vulnerable than in the nightmare realm.

Probably.

And if I'm wrong, and he lives to cause chaos, to change the people of Newham to monsters, to warp the world in his twisted image . . . so what?

Newham's already full of monsters.

What's one more?

"All right," I finally tell him, meeting his eyes. "What do I have to do to get us both out of here?"

33

I wake.

The world comes back to me slowly, slower than I want, my head still muzzy from whatever awful drug they put me to sleep with. Distantly, I hear someone calling, yelling that I'm waking up, they need to find Charlie—he wants to see what kind of Nightmare I've become.

Yes, please, call him.

I can't wait to show him exactly what he's unleashed.

My hair begins to melt into smoke, sliding away from my body. The Nightmare Phantom said that I needed to sacrifice a body part for him to twist into himself, and I asked if he could use my hair, because that grows back and nothing else does.

He just laughed and laughed, but he agreed.

My scalp tickles as hair after hair vanishes, and I hope I don't look too stupid bald, which really isn't what I should be thinking about right now, but here we are. The silvery smoke swirls around my head like a strange halo before sliding away from me, curling through the air, and coiling around a spot about a foot away. The tendrils twist and turn, forming into the vague outline of a human.

Or something human *like*, at any rate.

I roll over, giving me a view of the people outside my cage. Charlie Chambers is at the front of three soldiers, his eyes narrowed as he watches, clearly mystified by what I'm becoming. Or rather, what my hair is becoming.

The smoke swirls in its pattern, now clearly shaped, and it begins to thicken and harden, solidifying into a real form. First, the smoke hardens into black bones, ash colored and smooth, like a skeleton dipped in tar. Then the ligaments and tendons, connecting all the bones together, begin to resolve from the smoke, each of them dark gray and flat, like a charcoal drawing. The muscles form on top of those, slick and lighter gray, like something rotten.

I can't look away from the slowly forming body, so similar to a human but so entirely wrong.

Finally, the shell of thin white skin, pale as bleached bone, goes over the gray muscles, tinting the white a pale gray in multiple places. His nails are the dark gray of the veins beneath, and his lips a soft gray. Finally, a tendril of smoke wraps around him, solidifying into a long-sleeved smog-gray shirt and slacks.

The Nightmare Phantom opens his inky-black eyes, and he smiles, his teeth sharp as ever.

"What the fuck?" whispers Charlie, taking a step back.

I force my shaking body to sit up and rub my scalp. I'm surprised to find I still have some hair, though it's hard to say how much was taken. I might have to shave it all anyway if it's too patchy.

The Nightmare Phantom cracks his neck experimentally and takes a deep breath. "Ah. It's so nice to be back."

Charlie's expression is confused and irritated. "Why are there two of them? Have we ever had someone become twins before? Is that even possible?"

The Nightmare Phantom just smiles, wide and sharp, and places his hand on the smooth, clear glass door of our cell. He runs his fingers over the glass, his expression amused. Then he pulls his hand back.

He flicks the glass with one finger.

It shatters.

It breaks apart like it's ice turning to water, not glass turning into billions of tiny fragments. And within the span of a second, the whole door is gone, nothing left except the frame and a puddle of glittering sand on the ground.

I swallow.

I might have made a mistake.

I knew he could turn people into monsters. But I had no idea he could do . . . *that*. He melted that glass into nothing. Into dust. With just a finger flick.

What else can he do?

What have I loosed on the world?

Nightmare Defense is more than just their name, and the instant the glass door melts, they shift into action, weapons raised and aimed at the Nightmare Phantom. Charlie has stepped back, letting his soldiers take the lead, but he also has a gun out, and his eyes are flat and angry, ready to kill.

As a unit, they start firing.

Bullets whip through the air, but instead of sinking into the Nightmare Phantom, ripping through his flesh and shredding him into a bloody pulp, they ping on his skin, ricocheting off like he's a bank vault in the shape of a human.

Bullets fly through the air, I crouch low, covering my head, hoping nothing ricochets into me.

One of the men screams as a bullet bounces off the Nightmare Phantom and right into the soldier who shot it. He falls to the ground, screaming and clutching his chest as blood spreads across the floor, blooming like a flower in the sun.

It doesn't take long for him to stop struggling, but the blood keeps spreading.

Finally, the bullets trickle off, and the men scramble to reload. The Nightmare Phantom smiles, wide and toothy.

"My turn now!" He laughs.

Then he grabs one of the soldiers.

For a heartbeat, nothing happens. It's just the Nightmare Phantom, his long, thin white fingers wrapped like a skeletal claw around the soldier's arm.

Then the screaming begins.

The man's back arches, and a horrible cracking sound echoes through the room. Then again, and again. He twists and contorts, his bones crunching as they break and reform. Fur sprouts across his body, thick and black, tearing through his uniform like it's sharp as razors, shredding his clothes from his body. His face melts into a long, vicious snout, and his eyes change to red and slitted, his hands morphing into long paws with sharp claws. His gun clatters to the ground, his new form unable to hold it.

Where once was a man, now stands a massive wolf.

It howls, high and reedy. Charlie swears, swinging his gun from the Nightmare Phantom to the wolf that was once his companion.

He puts a dozen bullets in the wolf's head before it has a single chance to move.

The wolf sways for a moment before slowly keeling over, its thick, black fur matted with blood. It never got a chance to take a single step in its new form.

I can't stop staring at it. What would it be like to become the monster you feared most, and then, before you can do anything to indicate you're still there, still alive and aware in this terrible new body, your friend murders you?

I can't even wrap my mind around it.

The Nightmare Phantom is laughing, and the blood spreads across the floor from the bodies of the fallen soldiers.

Nightmare Defense is retreating, still firing at the Nightmare Phantom, though they have to know that's futile by now. He reaches his hand out, grasping a soldier's wrist and turning her into a cockroach, which he casually hurls into the air, where it flies away, into the rafters.

One by one, the soldiers fall to the Nightmare Phantom as he stalks them down the narrow halls of caged Nightmares, until finally there's only Charlie left, and he's grim and determined, still firing, right up to the end.

The Nightmare Phantom laughs as he reaches out and grabs Charlie Chambers, hero of Nightmare Defense, slayer of the Great Sea Dragon.

Charlie screams, body contorting and shifting, melting and pooling. His face morphs and mutates, becoming rounder and sort of chubby, his hair slowly falling out until there's nothing but fuzz. His body shrinks, growing soft and pudgy, pink like an overstuffed piglet.

A toddler sits where once a soldier fought.

Charlie looks to be maybe two years old at most, with small, chubby hands, far too weak to hold a weapon. He falls on his tiny little ass and begins to wail, the screeching, desperate wail of a terrified child who hasn't yet mastered the power of speech.

It's the only sound left.

Everyone else is dead or transformed.

The Nightmare Phantom turns back to me, smiling his sharp-toothed smile as though asking me to share in his delight.

"I forgot how much fun it was to be out here!" He laughs, arms spread wide as he spins around, delighting in the chaos he's caused.

Chaos I caused by letting him out.

But I'm free, and the people who wanted to kill me are out of my way—permanently. So even though there's a part of me that's horrified at what's happened here, there's a much stronger part of me that's relieved. That's reveling in the end of being afraid of these people, the end of this stupid boat-assassination-gone-wrong escapade.

These people were planning to kill me or sell me after

turning me into a Nightmare. Do I really care that they're dead?

No. I don't.

"See?" He smiles at me, slow and clever, like he can read my thoughts. "Aren't you glad you let me out?"

I blink and then rise slowly and step out of my broken cell. "Well, you've certainly held up your side."

"Glad you agree." He waves his hand as he walks away, heading down the hall and toward the stairs and the warehouse—and more soldiers. "This has been fun. Let's do it again sometime!"

"I'd really rather not, to be honest." Then I swallow and say, "But thanks. For, you know. Breaking me out."

He turns back and regards me with those inscrutable black eyes. Then he smiles, wide and bright. "I was just returning the favor."

Then he's around the corner and away. After a few moments, a new set of screams begins.

34

It doesn't take me long to figure out how to open Cy's cell and drag him out. The air in his cage is still hazy with drugs, so I hold my breath as I pull his limp form out into the hall. I try to avoid dragging him through the copious blood smears, most of which I'm trying really hard to pretend I'm not seeing. Ditto with the Nightmare bodies littering the ground like crumpled trash that missed the bin.

Cy stirs almost as soon as he's out of the cell and away from the drugs but doesn't fully wake. His brow furrows and his head lolls, as though he's trying to wake up but can't quite figure out how.

I'm sure his system will purge itself of the sleeping drug quickly, given his strain of vampirism's healing ability, so I turn my attention to the much less pleasant part of the escape.

Finding the keys to his cuffs.

I force myself to look at the dead Nightmares, at the first one who was turned, the massive black wolf covered in dry and flaking blood. I take a deep breath, steeling myself, before approaching the corpse, then kneeling to pick through the shredded remains of his clothing.

No key.

I go through the other piles of clothing too, one by one, until finally I'm forced to head to the one I least want to search.

Charlie Chambers remains where the Nightmare Phantom left him, a tiny toddler swaddled in a man's clothes. He's managed to crawl from the nest of clothes and, entirely nude, tucked himself in a corner, crying.

I'd feel bad, except he's a total shit and he deserves this.

Yes, I'm petty and vengeful. No, I don't care.

"I don't suppose you can still talk?" I ask him.

The child opens its mouth, but all that comes out is a keening wail.

I sigh. I guess I won't get an answer to what he meant about the Friends of the Restful Soul buying Nightmares. Unlike the Director, Charlie Chambers had seemed to like a good villain monologue, so I'd been hopeful he might even give me an answer.

But he won't be answering anyone anymore.

I fish through his clothes until I find the silver key to Cy's cuffs, then leave the wailing man-child behind to help my friend.

I kneel gently beside Cy, biting my lip in worry. His wrists are pink sludge, bone now clear as day as his flesh is slowly sluiced from it. I have to hold back my gag reflex as I try to unlock the cuffs with trembling hands. His cuffs are slippery with gore, and I keep cringing away from the feel of it, making the process even more awful.

Finally, I manage to wedge the key in and the cuffs come off with a click. I toss them across the room, far away from him. And me. Those things are absolutely revolting, just dyed with gore.

Cy's eyelids flutter slightly, before finally opening. He looks at me, his brow furrowed. For a moment, his expression cloudy and confused, as if unsure who I am and where he is, before recognition crosses his features. He groans softly, and closes his eyes again.

"What happened?" he croaks.

In the distance, people are still screaming, and beneath the screams is the constant thrum of the Nightmare boy's laughter. I don't really want to think about what I've unleashed or what he's doing to the rest of the facility, so all I say is, "I'll tell you later. We need to get out of here now."

He nods groggily but doesn't move. They probably pumped a lot more chemicals into his room than mine, knowing that he has a higher tolerance for that kind of thing.

Right. I guess it's my turn to rescue him from a sinking ship.

I drag his arm over my shoulders and put my arm around his waist as I haul him to his feet. His head lolls against my shoulder, and he groans pathetically, like even the effort of resting his head on me is too much work.

I half drag, half walk Cy past the cages of Nightmares, around the dead bodies. I get us lost in the mazelike hallways of the facility before I finally find the stairs out of the dark basement full of monsters.

It's a long stairwell up, and Cy is a dead weight for half of it, and I resolve after this to start working out, maybe do some arm training and leg training and any kind of training, because you really never know when you're going to have to haul your drugged and bleeding friend up the stairs and out of an evil murder basement.

We do make it to the top of the stairwell. Eventually.

I stop, peering down the empty hall, my ears straining as hard as my eyes.

It's silent.

We make our way down the hall and into the massive warehouse area full of vehicles, the place we'd originally disembarked. It's completely silent, save for the soft plop as beads of blood on the ceiling drip down onto the hood of one of the cars.

Bodies litter the ground, none of them discernibly human. The air reeks of the sickening metallic scent of blood, and I try to breathe through my mouth so I don't have to smell it, and I'm bizarrely grateful they starved me for a day because if they hadn't, I'd be throwing up everywhere.

I try to avoid looking too closely at the bodies and tell myself I should just be grateful that the Nightmare Phantom has cleared a path for me.

The main door of the facility is open, and I take it as a sign and head for it.

Outside, it's night, thankfully, though I don't know for how much longer. The air is thick and muggy and smells strongly of salt and rot. We're somewhere near the pier.

I gently lean Cy against the side of the building and then do a quick recon mission, where I run around squinting at things in the dark to see if I can figure out where we should go.

It's obvious we're in Newham, more so in the dark than it would be in the light. Simply because the city glows, a massive orange halo, a beacon in the darkness, neon lights paving the way for the lost. And the light surrounds us, a dim glow rising above the rows of massive warehouses, masking the stars and soothing my soul with its familiar aura.

It only takes a little more running around to figure out we must be in the northeast part of the city, one of the shipyard warehouse areas, where massive cargo ships unload their goods.

On the bad side, we're really far from Cy's place.

But on the positive side, there's a major road only a few blocks from here, and even in the middle of the night, there will be taxis on it. This area has a lot of poor artists who rent falling-apart, ruined warehouses because they're cheaper and there's room for them to spread out all their easels and canvases and painting materials.

Which means there are also a lot of cheap, sketchy speakeasies in this area, full of young, creative people who like to party late.

Which means taxis to take them home when they're too drunk to walk.

I return to Cy, who's looking a little more awake. It's easier this time, to sling his arm over my shoulders and start stumbling toward the main road. Less head lolling, more stable steps. His arms are still slicked with gore from his damaged wrists, but that's not going to change without a shower or ten.

I hail us a cab on the main road and load Cy into the auto. The cab driver is a grumpy man who clearly assumes Cy is drunk and can't see how covered with blood we are—or maybe he doesn't care. I don't even want to know what kind of madness taxi drivers see in Newham.

I give him the address and he speeds off.

"I know I just slept," I tell Cy, as I slump back in the vinyl seats, "but honestly, all I want to do when we get back is wash the grime off and sleep again."

He laughs, but it's an exhausted, pained sound.

"You okay?" I ask, my eyes flicking to his mangled wrists. They've started healing now that the silver is off, and I can't see the white shine of bone anymore, but they're still a mess.

He looks away. "Fine."

Well, that's a load of horse shit. But I'm not in the mood for anything except lying here in exhaustion, so that's what I do.

The cab drops us in front of the apartment building, and Cy sways a little as he gets out. But he does manage to get out on his own, without leaning on me for support, which I count as excellent progress.

Cy pays the cabby, who fingers the bloody money with a familiar sort of resignation before driving away.

I turn to the apartment building, but Cy catches my hand, pressing the key into it.

"I'll be back later." He tries to smile but fails. His eyes are shadowed and tired, and his skin is almost as gray and pallid as the Nightmare boy's.

"You don't even know what time it is. Dawn could be right around the corner," I tell him.

"I know."

"Cy . . ."

He winces. "Look, I'm just . . ." He takes a deep breath. "I'm going to see Estelle."

Oh.

"You're hungry," I realize.

"Why do you look so shocked?" he asks, rubbing his gory wrists.

"I don't know," I admit. I really shouldn't be, given how long it's been since either of us ate and how badly he was hurt. "I shouldn't be." I hesitate. "Is it as bad as the trek back after the boat?"

He hesitates, then nods. "Worse."

I grimace. "So you're saying if you don't go eat now, you're going to devour me in my sleep?"

He chokes. "What? No! Of course not. I'd never. I'm not—" He bows his head and swallows, choking back the final words.

"No," I agree. "You're not your father."

He flinches, then looks away. "How did you know I was thinking of him?"

"Come on, Cy, give me some credit." I give him a gentle smile. My mind turns to the conversation I had with the Nightmare Phantom. "And, Cy?"

"Yeah?"

I meet his gaze, my eyes steady on his. "No matter what happens, you'll never be him. No matter how monstrously your body's been twisted, no matter what someone else makes you into, your mind is *yours*. You control your actions, not your father, not your vampiric traits. You." I touch his cheek gently. "And you, Cyril, are not a monster."

We stay there, our eyes locked, his cold skin trembling beneath my hand, for several heartbeats.

He swallows slightly. "You pronounced my name right."

"Well, I worried it would ruin the moment if I called you Squirrel."

He smiles slightly and shakes his head. "How do you always do that?"

"Do what?"

"Manage to make me feel so . . . okay about my life?" He runs a hand through his hair. "Every time I mention something bad, like Beth or my father or any of it, you always manage to turn the conversation around and make me feel like a better person than I am."

"That's because you are a good person," I tell him gently. "And the only one who doesn't see it is you."

He flushes and looks away quickly.

"A-anyway." He clears his throat, still not looking at me. "I'm absolutely ravenous, and Estelle's shift ends right before dawn, so I'm going to go see her."

I'm about to wave him away when I remember. "Shit. I have to go with you."

He blinks rapidly. "What?"

"Remember the note she gave you? She won't see you if she hasn't seen me safe. And she doesn't work mornings. I went back there yesterday, but . . . ."

He groans, running a hand down his face. "Right. Okay. All right. This is fine. Do you mind just coming? It's only a few blocks away. Then you can head back."

Honestly, all I want to do is collapse. I don't want to go traipsing around town, and I don't want to brave the speakeasy Estelle works at. Especially not covered in gore from dead Nightmares and Cy's wrists.

I open my mouth to resignedly tell him I'll go with him to see Estelle, but what comes out instead is, "Why don't we just go upstairs?"

He stares at me, his expression falling. "Ness . . . Look, I know you're tired, but I really don't want to wait until dusk again to eat. Please." He gives me a shaky half smile. "I'm also miserable company when I'm hungry."

I lick my lips. The words slipped out before I caught them, but he didn't see anything in them. I can back out. I don't have to do this. We can just walk over to the bar, talk to Estelle, try to get her on break, see if she's up for an unscheduled appointment—

"That's not what I meant," I finally say, looking down, my own face flushing.

"I don't—" Understanding hits his expression like a cold glass of water. "Ness—are you—I mean." He swallows. "You don't need to offer anything. Seriously."

I feel a slight smile pulling at the corner of my mouth as I take his hand and tug him toward the door of the apartment complex. "Well, that's good, because this is a one-time-only offer, made because I'm tired and want to get into the shower as soon as possible."

He choke-laughs as I tug him through the lobby to the elevator. "That is a terrible reason to—"

"To what? Help a friend?"

He smiles slightly at that, but I can feel the nervous tension in his body. His eyes, when they flick to me are desperately hopeful, but they quickly skim away, as though ashamed of that hope.

He wants this. He wants this a lot—I can feel it.

"Ness," he says softly as the elevator rises. "Please. I—I don't want you to do something you'll regret."

"Who says I'll regret it?" I ask.

He swallows, eyes closed. "I don't want to lose you." He bites his lip so hard it draws blood, and he can't meet my eyes. "I—I've been so scared for so long that what I've become will be the end of my life. That I'll never make a real friend again. That no one will ever trust me again. I can't—" Finally, he raises his eyes to mine. "I can't mess this up. I can't lose you."

His eyes are sad and desperate, conflicted. He wants me to back out because he's scared he'll lose me.

But he also wants this more than he'll ever admit out loud. Because this is the ultimate expression of trust, physical proof that I completely trust him, something he never thought he'd have again.

And he wants it.

The elevator dings at his floor, and I reach out and touch

Cy's cheek gently. "I trust you, Cy. I know you won't hurt me. I know you'll stop if I get scared."

He steps forward shakily and cups my face gently in his hands. They're warm, and his palms are a little damp, from sweat and bloody wrist runoff.

"But are you sure?" he asks, his voice so soft it's barely there.

He's looking in my eyes, as though he's not sure he can trust my words and is instead peering right into my soul. As if he can divine my desires if he just looks deep enough.

The truth is, I want this too.

I'm not doing this just for him—I'm doing it for me.

I've spent years hiding in fear, hiding from ever taking risks, from everything that could hurt me. And that's the thing—you can't gain meaningful things in life without risking yourself. I've been afraid of failure, loss, betrayal. But you can't succeed without risking failure. You can't love without risking loss. You can't trust without risking betrayal.

And I want this. I want us to be the kind of people who can trust each other completely. I want to be the kind of person who isn't afraid of him, even in this small way. I want to kill the last tiny piece of fear in my heart, the one that trembles not just at the idea of the bite as something Nightmarish, but at the idea of that level of intimacy with another person.

I want to be brave so that I can kill that fear forever. Because I know now that if I let that little remnant of fear live, it could grow and fester and ruin everything.

I'm tired of letting my fears fester.

So I unbutton my collar with one hand and unlock the door with the other, my eyes never leaving Cy's, our gazes locked and steady.

"I'm sure," I tell him, and I lead him inside.

35

I wake up sometime midday, sleep slowly lifting its claws from my exhausted form. My throat is dry and my body aches from all the muscles I used yesterday carrying Cy out of Nightmare Defense.

But I slept well. Probably better than I've slept since I was a child. Because for the first time ever, I was truly safe. The Nightmare Phantom can't turn me into a monster when I sleep. I've faced my fears, and I've won.

Safe.

I blink my eyes open slowly. I'm curled in my tiny closet, just for me. Cy offered his bed again, but I like my closet. I like that it's mine, that it's small and dark and secure.

I suppose, even though I've faced my fears, some things will never change.

I slip out of the closet and take a peek in Cy's room. He's fast asleep, his chest rising and falling slowly. He's still wearing the grimy clothes from yesterday, but his wrists are smooth and mostly healed, nothing but an ugly, scarred red line where the cuffs cut into him. But his expression is relaxed and content, the worry lines smoothed from him until he looks at peace.

My hand itches to reach out and brush an errant thread of hair from his eyes, but I still it, not willing to risk waking him from a sleep he so desperately needs.

I creep past him, into the bathroom, where I strip and shower.

It feels so good to be clean again.

I get a little dizzy in the steam, probably from the blood loss. As I towel myself off afterward, I mourn the loss of my hair. I still have a bit, a thin layer of fuzz on my scalp and part of my bangs. I put on a tight knit hat to hide my mostly baldness from the world.

I wipe the steam from the mirror and tilt my head to look at the puncture marks on my throat. I raise a hand and touch them tentatively, running my fingers over the tender skin.

I spent a long time being afraid of having marks just like this. A lot of time being afraid of the idea of someone doing this to me. But the fear in my mind wasn't in the bite itself, but rather in the violence of being acted upon, the act of someone else claiming a part of my body I wasn't willing to give.

So much of the narrative around vampires has always been centered on *their* hunger, *their* desires, *their* agency, *their* choices. The stories, the films, they all focus on the vampire's hunger as though it's all-consuming, as though it's not a choice to attack people but an inevitability. As though the victims are unavoidable, a consequence of a monster's desire. They're nothing more than an unwilling participant in someone else's hunger, bitten by someone who believes their hungers are more important than other people's personhood.

But that's not what happened last night. I changed the narrative of my fears. I chose this. I wasn't a passive participant or a victim being acted upon. I was the initiator; I was the actor. We did this together.

That makes all the difference. The choice and the agency in my own body.

I put on clean clothes from my trunk, the feel of fresh, pressed shirt and trousers heavenly against my freshly bathed skin. I take my time buttoning up my waistcoat, and carefully arrange the collar of my shirt to hide my bite marks. I don't need the extra attention.

Then, quietly, I slip out of the apartment. Cy doesn't stir from the bed.

I have things to do.

It takes me a few hours to arrange everything, and the sun is starting to set by the time everything is ready.

It's time for me to end this.

I stand in front of the doorstep of a small apartment in an older building. The door has peeling white paint, with black spots in one corner that might be mold or might be rot, or might be some heretofore undiscovered disease. The numbers have faded off, and someone has redone them with a ballpoint pen, scratching the number into the paint of the door itself.

I got the address from bribing a bank clerk, and I'm hoping that he didn't give me the wrong place and take my money.

Especially since that took the last of the money I'd earned from talking to the *Post*.

I raise my fist and knock.

A moment passes, and I knock again. Then again. Finally, behind the door, someone swears, and the sound of heavy footsteps approach.

The door swings open, and an irritated face looks up at me. Elderly, with papery, thin skin and familiar, washed-out eyes. He's wearing a fluffy housecoat tied around his waist, faded blue slippers, and nothing else.

I smile, no teeth, with cold eyes, at my childhood math teacher.

"Mr. Columb. Hello again. It's Ness Near. You recall we met again recently at the Friends of the Restful Soul building."

He blinks rapidly, and then the genial smile comes out, smoothing over the irritation. "Oh, yes, yes, Ness. How nice to see you again! What brings you here?"

"Can I come in for a moment?"

He looks behind him and grimaces slightly, but he opens the door wider and says, "Certainly."

I step into a tiny apartment. It's one room, about the size of Mrs. Sanden's apartment. But unlike hers—and unlike what the exterior of the building would suggest—this apartment is lushly decorated, with soft rugs, pale-blue wallpaper, and a large window with curtains on the side. It's not a rich person's apartment—but it's certainly much nicer than what a normal teacher's salary should be able to afford.

"What a lovely place," I tell him.

"Thank you." He smiles indulgently. "It's better than the cages."

I shudder. "The cages" is what the locals call the older apartment buildings with bigger rooms that stack chicken wire cages on top of each other, each about the size of a coffin, three high. Twenty or so fit in a single room, and people only have the space in their small chicken wire cage for all their possessions.

And I wonder how I ended up in a cult. At least the living conditions were better than that.

"Yes, much better." I turn to him. "Though nice as it is, it's certainly much smaller than what you can get in the countryside. I can't imagine why you gave that up and came to Newham."

He blinks. "Oh. Well, I got a new job."

"Still a math teacher?" I ask.

"All my life."

"Not much changes for you, does it?" I look from an bottle of expensive wine to a stack of unmarked math tests on the table. "I feel like my life is constantly changing. Did you know someone tried to assassinate me at a funeral this week?"

"Oh." He shifts from foot to foot. "How terrible."

"Yes, it was," I agree. "I thought at first I was targeted because I survived the boat explosion, but I don't think so now. This assassin, she wasn't very competent or experienced. And the people who bombed the boat were professionals. So I got to thinking, well, maybe someone *else* hired an assassin."

Mr. Columb is sweating now, and his bony hands are clenched into tight fists.

"But who," I continue, "would want to kill me? Then I started wondering how you knew so much about Ruby that I didn't. And why you looked so nervous after mentioning it to me. How quickly you tried to backtrack."

"I—"

"I called the school you used to work for." I bulldoze over him. "You remember Miss Truong, don't you? She's the principal now. She said you were fired."

A bead of sweat drips down his brow. "Well, yes. Laid off."

"No, fired." I correct him. "Apparently you helped nearly a dozen kids get scholarships over the years." I hold his gaze. "And not a single one came back."

He flushes. "What are you implying?"

"Oh, I think you know." I smile at him insincerely. "I've been wondering though, really flipping back and forth on whether the parents really *knew* about the 'scholarship.'" I tip my head to one side, unconsciously mirroring the Nightmare Phantom. "I think they'd have had to, at least in some of the cases, to avoid them following up and discovering the lie. Or offering to take the kid to the school themselves. What do you think?"

All remaining veneer of friendliness has left him. "I'd like you to leave now."

"When I figured all this out," I continue blithely over him,

"I realized why you might want to get rid of me. After all, if I figured out what really happened with Ruby, I might blow the lid off your current scam." I pause, my eyes holding his. "At Newham Composite."

His face drains of color.

"Yes, I called them," I tell him. "They couldn't stop gushing about you. How you helped get two students this year into very prestigious institutions on the other side of the country." I smile toothily. "But they were even *more* interested when I told them about your last job and gave them Miss Truong's number."

Mr. Columb's hands are clenched into fists, and his face looks like the whole world is crumbling around him. Which it is. I've cost him his job and his scam.

And I haven't even gotten to the part where I called around to all the other schools in the city to explain the scam so that he'll never be hired as a teacher in this city again.

"Get out," he snarls, stepping toward me.

I don't move, just raise an eyebrow. "Don't you want to hear what else I did?"

"No," he snaps, stomping over and grabbing my wrist, dragging me toward the door.

His grip is hard and surprisingly strong for someone so old, but he's clearly used to dealing with kids who don't know how to fight back. I use a trick Priya taught me, twisting my wrist around, rather than pulling away, and his hand slides right off.

I love that trick.

He whirls on me, his body shaking with barely restrained violence. His jaw is clenched so hard I think he might pop a vein in his temple. He looks like he wants to beat me to death with his bare hands.

But he doesn't move.

He probably hasn't fought with someone older than thirteen in decades—he's used to being all powerful in all situations. He doesn't know how to handle the fact that I'm physically his match and that I came to this apartment holding all the cards.

"No need to get violent," I tell him with complete calm as I make my way to the door. "I only wanted to tell you one last thing." I pause at the doorway to look back at him with a pleasant smile. "Did you know that most assassin companies are in the phone book? Only in Newham, am I right?"

He stares at me, his expression murderous.

I smile back at him. "Well, they have confidentiality clauses, so they couldn't tell me who their clients were, but I warned them about a scammer by the name of Mr. Columb, who hires contractors but doesn't pay them."

Mr. Columb's eyes widen.

"I also"—my smile sharpens—"took the liberty of bribing someone at your bank to freeze your account for a week, so you'll be unable to access any money."

Mr. Columb's clutching his chest, and his eyes are bulging from his weathered face. "You—"

"Of course, if you didn't hire anyone to assassinate me, this shouldn't be a problem," I say breezily. "But say, if you did, those assassins are going to show up here soon wanting proof you can pay and probably payment up-front. And if you can't give them that, well." I smile insincerely. "I suppose what goes around comes around then, hmm?"

Finally he explodes, screaming at me. *"You bitch! I'll fucking kill you!"*

"I'm afraid you already lost that chance. Say hi to my father and Nick in Hell."

I smile, waggling my fingers goodbye as I close the door behind me.

36

I'm sitting in the Lantern Man's Restaurant later that evening at a small, secluded booth, trying their food for the first time.

It's actually not bad.

Priya is sitting across from me, devouring her spaghetti and meatballs as I slowly, in between bites of my chicken parmigiana, explain what happened over the last day since we got kicked out of the Friends of the Restful Soul. Her eyes are huge and rapt, and she keeps interrupting me with things like, "Ness, how could you have such a cool adventure without me?"

"You didn't answer the phone!" I insist. "And it wasn't an adventure!"

To which she just groans and blames her sister.

When I get to the part where I found out that Cindy was one of the targets of the boat explosion, Priya just shakes her head.

"Who the hell did she investigate to get on an assassin list?" Priya's eyes brighten. "And what did she find out?"

I sigh heavily. No sympathy on that front.

I'd go give Cindy a piece of my mind myself—and, you

know, warn her about the assassination attempt—but she's vanished. She's left the Friends, and even though she told us what newspaper she worked for, they claim they've never heard of her. I'm not sure if they're lying to protect her or she was lying about where she worked and who she was.

Again.

I finish telling Priya the rest of the story as I slowly polish off my dinner. Behind Priya, the television above the bar counter has the evening news, and the words **NIGHTMARES ESCAPE NIGHTMARE DEFENSE FACILITY, KILLING DOZENS, NOW LOOSE IN THE CITY.**

I look back down to my plate. I wonder what the Nightmare Phantom is doing now. Is he still in the city? Will he continue to turn people into their nightmares indiscriminately, bringing more chaos? I don't know. I haven't heard anything yet, but it hasn't even been a full day.

Maybe he won't stay. Maybe he'll leave to hunt down whoever or whatever trapped him in dreams in the first place. Maybe I'll never see him again.

Somehow I doubt that.

When I finally finish telling Priya everything that happened, she twirls her last bite of spaghetti on her fork pensively, her eyes unusually worried, her lips pursed.

"I'm sorry Nightmare Defense turned out to be evil," I say.

She shrugs, popping the last bite in her mouth. "It's fine."

I doubt that. Nightmare Defense has been her dream job forever, and she only *just* got accepted.

"But what will you do now?"

She blinks up at me, coming out of her thoughts. "Huh?"

"Well, now that you can't join them—"

"Wait, why can't I join them?" Now she's showing some real concern.

I stare at her. "Because they're evil?"

She snorts. "If I were fazed by a little assassination and corruption, I'd never get a job in this city."

"So . . . you're still going to join them?"

"Of course!" She grins, playful and wicked. "I want to fight sea dragons!"

I can't help but laugh. Some things change, but Priya isn't one of them.

Priya is smiling, and she opens her mouth to say something when her eyes lower to my neck, where my healing bite mark became visible when I threw my head back to laugh. Her expression darkens into something angry and protective.

Her voice is cold and hard. "Should I kill him?"

I cover my bite with one hand and readjust my shirt, flushing. "Please don't."

"Ness . . ."

"I offered."

She stares at me, stunned. "Who are you, and what have you done with Ness?"

I snort. "Stop being so dramatic."

She frowns, clearly not convinced that something fishy isn't going on here. "Are you sure he's not a strain eleven? I think they have mind control."

"I'm not being mind-controlled," I insist. "And no, he's not. And also, that's strain two, and the mind control only lasts a few hours."

"Hmm." Priya seems skeptical.

"I appreciate your concern," I tell her, and I do. I like seeing that she cares about me. It reassures me that she has my back when I need her. "But I'm all right. Seriously."

"I still think I should stab him just to be sure," Priya says, but she seems less murderous about it than before.

"No stabbing!" I laugh. "He's letting me crash with him until I'm on my feet again. I don't want him stabbed."

"But then you could just steal his apartment."

"That's not how this works!"

Priya is watching me carefully, and her expression is surprised and a little puzzled. "You really like him, don't you?"

I'm flushing even worse. "Of course I do. He's my friend."

"Mmmhmm. Sure." Priya puts her chin in her hand and smiles, something small and secret. "So when do I get to meet him?"

I smile. "Tonight, hopefully. He's coming over once the sun sets."

Priya grins toothily, her eyes full of mischief. "I can't wait."

Poor Cy. He has no idea what he's in for.

"Be nice," I warn her.

She strokes one of her knives she's pulled from her belt. "I'm always nice."

I roll my eyes, but I'm smiling. I can't help it—I'm a bit excited for them to meet. For all Priya's determination to find out if he's worthy of my trust, I think the two of them will get on famously. I really hope they do, anyway.

I go up to the bar to pay. A newspaper on the counter shows a picture of the Director, talking about the efficacy of therapy and how important it is for healing the people of the city of Newham. It's basically a giant ad for the Friends free therapy programs.

The therapy program is bait. I understand that now. Honey for a fly trap. Because the kind of people who need that type of help are often desperate and damaged—which means they're easier to manipulate, easier to control, and easier to make disappear.

There's no justice in this city, I know that. But it grates me to see someone who tried to shoot me and have me "transferred" living his life with no consequences, continuing to lure in more people to prey on. I still don't know what happened to the people transferred or why the Friends are buying Nightmares.

But I suppose it doesn't matter. I just hope the Director doesn't decide to come after me for bashing him on the head and letting Cindy steal all his files.

"Changed your mind about applying?" Estelle asks, coming over to me from behind the counter.

"Applying?"

She nods to the WE'RE HIRING sign beside me. I hadn't even spotted it, too busy worrying over the Director.

"Oh."

I spoke to Estelle briefly when I came in, to reassure her I was all right and that Cy and I were still friends. She seemed deeply relieved to see me and told me she was glad he hadn't been luring me back to his place with bad intentions because she was kind of fond of him. It would be a shame if he turned out to be awful.

I stare at the WE'RE HIRING sign a moment longer and then smile up at her. "You know what? I think I will apply. Do you have an application form?"

She grins. "I sure do!"

She slides me a form from under the counter, and I scribble out my contact details and check the box that says I'm willing to work nights in the speakeasy. It doesn't say precisely that, but we all know what's behind the wall in the back, and it's not a storage room.

Estelle takes the form when I'm done and smiles. "I can't promise anything, but I'll put in a good word with the boss."

I grin, wide and genuine. "Thanks. I appreciate it."

She winks. "Anytime."

I take a deep breath, relishing how loose my body is, how relaxed I am. It's going to be all right. I've lost everything, my home, my security blankets, my life as I knew it. But that only means that this time, I'm going to build my life again, and I'm going to do it right. A solid foundation, a better mindset. I'm not going to be afraid of everything. I'm going to stop hiding from life and start living it.

And I have the best friends in the world to help me get started.

The door opens, and Cy walks into the restaurant. He's dressed to the nines, black shirt and burgundy vest, eyeliner in place making his green eyes startlingly bright. His gaze lands on me, and he smiles, light and joyful, and I smile back as I go over to introduce my two best friends.

EPILOGUE

A young man sits on an outdoor patio at a café in the upscale part of Newham.

He looks like he could be nineteen or twenty, with smooth, blemishless white skin and hair so fine and silvery it could be made of cobwebs. A pair of black sunglasses covers his eyes, and he sips on his coffee slowly, careful to show no teeth.

The people around him chatter and buzz, completely unaware of what sits in their midst, smiling close-lipped at the waiter and watching them all with inky-black eyes.

He breathes in the fresh air, the smell of burnt coffee, car exhaust, and a hint of something rotting. There are no smells in dreams. He's missed them. Even the bad ones.

He breathes out, savoring the solidity of the cup in his hand, the smooth porcelain texture against the pads of his fingers. Anyone who looked too close might notice that he had no lines on his skin, no whorls of texture at all, no hint of fingerprints or palm prints or anything.

But no one looks that close.

He tips his head back to the sun and relishes his freedom.

He's out of his cage. After a hundred years, he's finally free again.

Now he's going to have some *fun*.

ACKNOWLEDGMENTS

This book should never have existed.

After the publication of *Only Ashes Remain*, I was in a bad place. It hadn't sold that well, and no one wanted another book from me. The rejections piled up, and book after book was cast into the grave. My career was trailing off, likely to be over after just one trilogy.

And then the Webtoon adaptation of *Not Even Bones* happened. It had been in the works for a while, but I hadn't thought it would have much impact—after all, much more famous books than mine were being adapted. I figured they'd get bigger while I'd fall into obscurity in yet another medium.

I was wrong.

Webtoon brought a fresh wave of readers and interest in my work. My sales, which had been struggling, shot up. By the time *When Villains Rise* came out, my publisher was changing their tune—they were willing to buy something new from me.

So, a huge thank-you to Webtoon for showcasing my work to a whole new audience, to my readers, who, through sheer buying power and enthusiasm, managed to get the publishing industry to give me another chance.

This book would not exist without any of you.

It also would not exist without the efforts of Suzie Townsend, Dani Seaglebaum, Alex Rice, Jim McCarthy, Samantha Ruth Brown, Michael D'Angelo, Molly Fehr, Joel Tippie, Erika West, Mary Magrisso, Trish McGinley, Gretchen Stelter, Marinda Valenti, Marisa Ware, Nicole Sclama, and the rest of the team at Clarion Books. Special thanks to my editor Elizabeth Agyemang, who adopted my book after my acquiring editor left, gave incredible advice on editing this book, and shepherded me through the publication process. You're amazing, and I'm so glad we're working together.

On the other side of the pond, huge thanks to Anissa, as well as everyone on my UK team at Hodderscape, especially Molly and Tash.

Also thanks to my emergency readers, who gave feedback on a tight turnaround because this book was crunched HARD: Natasha Razi, Julia Ember, Ella Dyson, and Xiran Jay Zhao.

Thanks to everyone who had to deal with my awful pandemic brain where my career was falling apart and I was trapped in a snowy hellhole in northern Canada. Especially to my mother, who had to put up with my nonsense after I ended up stranded with her for a big chunk of the pandemic.

And thank you, all of you who bought the book, for giving my books a chance, and letting my career have a second chance at life.